A Captain's Lady

The captain, this commander of so many men, looked down on Kate, bedraggled and thoroughly wretched, alone and seemingly friendless, and was at a loss. Finally, he knelt down and took her hands in his and raised her to her feet. She looked up into his eyes and between her sobs she said, 'I cannot walk, you know. I think I have twisted my ankle.'

'That being the case, Mistress Butler,' he replied, 'I must ask that you allow me to carry you.' And, without a further word, nor waiting for permission, he took her up into his arms and carried her, light as a child, through the press of men who clamoured around her, to his own quarters. She was already asleep when he laid her down on his own bed.

Jennifer Wray Bowie is married and lives in Yorkshire. *A Captain's Lady* is her first novel. She was educated at Airborough Grammar School in Leeds and read Comparative American Studies at Warwick University.

A Captain's Lady

Jennifer Wray Bowie

Woman's Weekly Fiction

A Woman's Weekly Paperback
A CAPTAIN'S LADY

First published in Great Britain 1994
by Robert Hale Ltd
This edition published 1995
by Woman's Weekly
in association with Mandarin Paperbacks
an imprint of Reed Consumer Books Ltd
Michelin House, 81 Fulham Road, London SW3 6RB
and Auckland, Melbourne, Singapore and Toronto

A CIP catalogue record for this title
is available from the British Library
ISBN 1 86056 065 2

Printed and bound in Great Britain by BPC Paperbacks Ltd
A member of The British Printing Company Ltd

One

Kate blanched in pain as the thorns bit deep into her shoulder. She ignored the ripping of her dress and forced her way through the thick hedgerow, egged on by the baying of the hounds behind her. In spite of the pain she smiled. The deeper she thrust herself the safer she felt. She did not fear the hounds, they merely followed her scent. Fitzmaurice's men would not risk their finery to pursue her through the bushes. They carried no muskets or crossbows, they did not want to kill her. Their sport would begin when they had run their quarry to ground.

At last she could see the light broadening as she worked her way through the barbed branches, cursing the weight and volume of her skirts which dragged behind, hindering her passage. Finally, she was through. She turned about and gazed, wild-eyed, at her pursuers. Sure enough the hounds were confounded by the dense corduroy of branches. Aimless now they circled about, waiting for their masters. Further back, the men had spotted the hounds' confusion. They were drawing across to the right, up the hill. Kate followed their course and spotted a gap in the hedgerow. It was a long way off, she reckoned, it would afford her time to put as much as a quarter-mile between herself and her hunters.

Turning about, she surveyed the landscape before her, so different from her native Ireland, so orderly and seemingly peaceful. Whilst she remained here, however, she was in mortal danger. On she plunged through a field of ripening wheat which crackled as she crushed it underfoot.

The sun beat down on her head, perspiration stung her eyes and dazzled her. Just beyond the field the first trees of the forest loomed before her. It would afford her shade and cover from her hunters' eyes, but there would be no protection from the dogs. She had to reach the Newbury road and hope that she could find assistance there. The road was still some three miles distant, though, and Kate had not been accustomed to running since childhood. She paid no heed to the pain in her side and the blood which streaked down her arm and forced herself on through the forest.

Behind her, the renewed baying of the hounds signalled that the chase was on again. Kate could practically feel the distance between them closing. She ran on. Suddenly she was down. The forest's carpet of leaves had concealed a pothole beneath a tree root. Immediately, she got up again and ran on. With every step her ankle pained her more and she could feel herself slowing; still she carried on. The hounds were louder now and she could hear Fitzmaurice's men shout as they sighted her.

Finally, the pain in her ankle grew too great for her. It gave way and she tumbled to the ground. Again she picked herself up and turned like an animal at bay to face her tormentors. In the distance she could hear them laughing and jeering as they realized that the chase was over and their sport was about to begin. They came on slowly now, relishing the moment of their triumph. The hounds were silent. They padded at their masters' sides, saliva dripping from their jowls. All was silent save the snapping of twigs under the hunters' boots.

The silence was broken by the sound of men's voices. Not the harsh cackle of those before her, but that of many voices uttering the single word 'Amen' from behind her. The huntsmen were checked by the sound and seemed confused as their hounds had been before. Kate seized on the moment and, summoning all her strength, turned and, half-hobbling, she ran toward the sound. Realizing that their quarry was eluding them, the men made one last attempt to run her down.

The voices could not have been more than a hundred yards distant, but the pursuit was gaining on her fast. There was an opening in the trees ahead. Kate made one last effort and ran again into the sunlight. She stopped suddenly. She stood on the edge of a steep bank, some fifty feet above a clearing. She looked down on the scene below: a company of soldiers were at prayer.

'Puritans – damn them!' She cursed under her breath. Still, even the protection of rebels was better than the alternatives available to her at the moment. They were almost on her now. So, gathering up her skirts, she launched herself slithering and tumbling down the wet clay of the slope.

'Ow!' she exclaimed, as she hit the bottom with a mighty bump and landed in a flurry of fern and shredded petticoats.

The prayer meeting ended abruptly. A hundred faces turned towards this creature of mud and bracken which had landed in their midst. A hundred mouths agape with amazement, yet not a sound was uttered.

Above, the hunters, cheated of their prey, leashed in their hounds and returned, unsated, to their master. They would have to concoct the story of their sport for Lord Fitzmaurice.

For a long moment not a word was said. Kate smiled weakly and felt the drying clay cracking on her face.

'I suppose I had better explain myself . . .' she ventured.

A tall man rose up from the congregation. The rest, still apparently in shock, remained kneeling. His hair was cropped short, even shorter than the Puritans were wont to wear it and though he was half-smiling, his grey-blue eyes surveyed her doubtfully.

'What are you, woman? Are you some wood-nymph of pagan tales, so affronted by the sound of good Christians at worship that you have come down to disrupt these worthy saints at prayer?'

The men around him laughed gently; though he was clearly speaking in jest, still his tone and bearing demanded an answer. Kate mustered what dignity she could in her current state. She thought it better to tell as much of the truth as was needful to explain her predicament.

'As to what I am, sir, I am as you can probably see . . . though' – Kate looked down at herself – 'though not clearly so . . . a woman of good birth and station.'

Again the soldiers laughed quietly. Undeterred, Kate continued, 'I was waylaid on the road this morning by the rough folk you saw above who sought to have some sport with me, though I believe that ultimately they sought my ruination. It seems that Providence has guided me to you for my salvation.' Kate smiled inwardly. Thus far she had told no lies. . . .

As she spoke, though, Kate noticed that some of the men had lost their smiles and were staring at her and whispering to one another. A younger man stood up and begged leave to ask a question.

'Captain Barnard, sir, it is clear from this woman's tone that she is not as she claims a good woman. She is an Irishwoman and is most likely to be a papist spy!' He sat down forcefully, amid murmurs of approbation from the crowd.

Captain Barnard turned back to her and raised his eyebrows quizzically. 'Well?' he asked.

Kate's tone became indignant. She had grown weary of this accusation which had dogged her since her arrival in England. This prejudice which was meted out to all her countrymen.

'It is true, your ears do not deceive you for I am indeed from Ireland, though I am of English stock.' (A half truth, she thought to herself.) 'My name is Katherine Butler. I am no papist – why should a Catholic cross the sea when they have the rule of their own country now that the English are fighting among themselves? My father sent me to the safety of his family as the rebels were closing in on Dublin. Though, as you can see, I have known little of safety, and less hospitality since I arrived here.'

At this point Kate thought it politic to reinforce her point by resorting to tears – a woman's weapon which she normally despised. Throughout the hardships she had suffered over the past six months – the bitter parting from her beloved father; her arrival in England only to discover that her aunt and protectress had died just the week before and that her husband, Thomas, Lord Fitzmaurice, worse than disdaining her, had sought to press his affections on her; the vile treatment she had suffered at his hand when she refused him; and, finally, these last few days after she had learned of the death of her own dear father, yet still she had denied Fitzmauricc and he had turned her over this very morning for the sport of his henchmen – all this time she had held her head high and maintained her dignity. Yet here she was now, caked in mud, in pain and bleeding and on the point of being denounced as a papist – when papists had killed her own father – it was too much to bear. Her tears were as sincere as they were uncontrollable.

The captain, this commander of so many men, looked down on Kate, bedraggled and thoroughly wretched, alone and seemingly friendless, and was at a loss. Finally, he knelt down and took her hands in his and raised her to her feet. She looked up into his eyes and between sobs she said, 'I cannot walk, you know. I think I have twisted my ankle.'

'That being the case, Mistress Butler,' he replied, 'I must ask that you allow me to carry you.' And, without a further word, nor waiting for permission, he took her up into his arms and carried her, light as a child, through the press of men who clamoured around her, to his own quarters. She was already asleep when he laid her down on his own bed.

She awoke with a start, thinking herself still at Fitzmaurice's. She looked up and instead of the grey stone ceiling of her chamber there was the light screen of a canvas roof. The memories of the day came flooding back to her. She looked down and was surprised to find that she was still dressed in the same mud-stained dress, her arm was still streaked with blood and, as she found to her cost when she tried to rise, her ankle would only support her weight with some discomfort.

'God in Heaven, what is happening to me?' she cried out in pain.

Straightaway, the head of a young boy popped around the flap of the tent.

'Ah, you're awake now, and none the worse for your rest, it seems.' He smiled and, just as quickly as he had appeared, he vanished. In a few moments he returned with a bowl and a jug of hot water and some towels. With that the boy made to leave.

Kate called after him, 'Stay a moment – where is everybody? It all seems uncommonly quiet.'

Without a word, the boy scampered out of the tent. When he was safely on the other side of the flap, he considered it safe to continue the conversation.

'The captain put the fear of the Devil into me that I should not tarry with you Mistress Katherine, nor should I be caught peeking in if you were cleansing yourself – which he considered needful, but none here would undertake. He has sent to the nearest village to seek out a good woman to attend you.'

Kate shuffled across to the bowl. The water felt good on her face and neck, but she found she could not wash.

'There is no soap,' she called out to the boy.

'There is little to be found these days and the captain says that we do well enough with clean water alone.'

'That's well enough for men, but I fear my needs require some.' Kate remembered her first question. 'I ask you again, young man, where is everybody?'

'Ah, well. The company are paying their respects, so to speak. The captain got report that some of Lord Goring's men were escorting a supply convoy to the assistance of Basing House. They intend that the Marquis of Winchester has no guests to dine with tonight – and that we shall dine on his intended victuals.' He laughed at his little jest. 'I will try and find you the soap you require.' Kate could hear him whistling as he went off.

While he was gone Kate took stock of herself. She

took off her dress and cast her eye over it. There were few rips in the fabric for it was made of coarse stuff, but it was difficult to tell its original colour. It had been blue, now it was stained grey-pink. At home she would have discarded it: now it was the only dress she had in the world. Her petticoats were in tatters; she would have to shorten them or discard them altogether. She rummaged about in the captain's belongings to find a looking-glass. When she could not find one she supposed that these Puritans must be careless of their appearances. There was a rustle behind her. She turned around to see the boy's arm thrust through the tent-flap. In his hand was a small cake of soap.

'It's all that I could find, Mistress Katherine, and even for this I will be in the debt of the sergeant-at-arms when he finds out.'

'It will well suffice, I thank you. All I need now is more hot water and a looking-glass and you will have rendered me perfect service.'

'The water I can bring right readily for there is always a cauldron in the camp in case of wounded. A looking-glass is another matter for they are all taken off to the battle. The men use their helms or their breastplates, brightly polished.'

The sun was westering when the captain and his company returned to the camp. Their eyes were greeted by an unusual sight, for strewn across numerous trees and bushes around the clearing were all the various garments which constituted a lady's dress, artfully placed to catch the last patches of sunlight. In the middle of the camp sat Kate, combing out her hair and chattering with the boy. Last into camp came the captain himself, supporting with one arm a wounded soldier who swayed in the saddle as if he were on the edge of sleep. Kate stood up as she saw them. She was dressed in the same fashion as the boy, save that she was barefoot and her breeches wallowed around her legs like two sacks; they would surely have fallen down had they not been secured by a stout belt. She looked up at the captain.

'I thank you, sir, for your many kindnesses. Your young man has furnished me with all that was needful for my restoration.'

'And, it seems, you have furnished yourself with all the rest,' he replied. 'I seem to recognize certain, if not all, the items of your raiment?'

Kate stepped back and made an elaborate bow, her hand describing the line of her clothes.

'For the maintenance of modesty in the company of such saintly fellows, I sought only such garments as would cover my poor body.' With the same hand she swept the damp hair from her face, and looked up at him smiling.

'With such stuff you could find amongst my own wardrobe, I see.'

'Even so, good Captain,' she replied, her smile broadening.

He turned momentarily and dispatched the wounded soldier to the care of another, older man and dismounted himself. The boy led the horse away.

'Our bivouac has taken on the appearance of a laundry, Mistress Butler. I am not sure that I approve.'

'Would you prefer it that I roam about, ragged and filthy like some wild woman of the woods?'

'On reflection I think we can suffer these feminine touches since they are in a good cause.' He seemed distracted for a moment, then added, 'You scrub up uncommonly well for a wild woman, Mistress Butler.'

'Katherine,' she interjected.

'I beg your pardon?'

'Please call me Katherine, or even Kate. At home my friends call me Kate.'

'Very well, Miss Katherine.' He was clearly unsure about this familiarity.

'And how should I address you, sir?'

He paused for a moment, as if considering the problem. 'Captain Barnard . . . for the time being – and always in the presence of my men.'

The smile dropped from Kate's face. He had spurned her offer of familiarity which, although she had seemed to offer it lightly, was meant sincerely. This man had shown her kindness and some measure of friendship. God only knew how few friends she had in this awful country – indeed, she mused, they could be counted on the single finger of a solitary hand. She made to turn away. The captain gently held her arm and spoke softly to her.

'For the moment it must be so, Katherine . . . Kate.' He smiled. 'Now I have other matters to attend to.' His manner became more businesslike. 'If you have need of anything, call the boy.' He was walking backwards as he spoke. 'As you can see from the carts and wagons, we have captured the Marquis of Winchester's supply train. We shall dine at his expense tonight.' He paused a moment. 'Oh, if your . . .' – he struggled for the right word – '*sous vêtements* are already dry, please take them down – they will drive my men to distraction.'

'Captain. One more thing. May I have loan of your looking-glass?'

He put his head to one side in incomprehension. Kate walked up to him and tapped his chest – it made a hollow, metallic ring.

Though her underclothes were dry and she was thus able to save the men of the camp from depravity, her dress was still far too damp to wear. Kate moved about in the ill-fitting garb she had misappropriated from the captain. The troopers were in high spirits after the rout of Goring's men, although they were never less than fastidiously polite when conversing with her. It became clear that they regarded her arrival in their midst as a lucky omen.

'We never took so rich a spoil with so little force of arms,' one of them remarked.

She sought out the sergeant-at-arms, and thanked him profusely for the use of his soap. He blushed.

'It is my great honour to be of service to you, Mistress Katherine – but you must keep it for yourself now. It is such a little kindness – and I could never bring myself to use it since it has been about your person. The men tease me so when they see me using it. Please keep it – you are saving me from my own vanity.'

A young man sought her out as she walked around. He gave a slight stiff bow.

'Mistress Katherine, my name is Praisegod Ferrer, I have come to seek your pardon. I meant not to move you to such unhappiness this morning – there is much ill will, and fear of your countrymen. We hear so many evil reports from that place. Still, it provides no excuse for my lack of Christian charity. Please forgive me.'

With that he gave the same slight bow and without waiting for her pardon, he turned on his heel and strode off. Now it was Kate's turn to be amazed. These Puritans, it seemed, were very strange people indeed. . . .

After the sun had set the men set to roasting great sides of meat on the camp-fire. Kate sat amongst the troopers, and though they were ravenously hungry – she could hear many stomachs grumbling, her own included – they knelt as Praisegod led them in prayer for a full half-hour. There was much to give thanks for: their victory of the day, the food they were about to receive and that their wounded companion, Denzil Ashley, was already up and about, having suffered no worse than a shattered elbow – and that in his rein arm. Finally, he gave thanks for Katherine's own safe delivery into their midst. With that the men said 'Amen'. For a moment Kate shuddered, remembering the first time she had heard that sound only this very morning. Being in the midst of it made her feel secure.

They served Kate first of all, on a pewter plate with a cup of wine.

'After all,' they said, 'you are our guest, and we have never entertained a lady in our camp before.'

The men dined off wooden platters and mostly drank their fill of the beer that had been destined for Basing. The sergeant came and sat beside her.

'I would have imagined your men would have refrained from beer and wine?' she asked.

'A common fallacy, Mistress Katherine.' He laughed

to himself. 'There are some of us who would prefer water when they can get it – but beer and wine are more reliable, so to speak – you get less of the camp sickness if you abstain from the water. Lord knows, we saw enough of that in the Low Countries. Hundreds died, many times more than in the fighting itself. Picked them off like flies it did.

'This is not your first taste of warfare then?' Kate asked, intrigued.

'Sadly not, Mistress. Most of the lads are from hereabouts; the best part of 'em from around Reading way, it seems. But the captain and me and a few others – Hal over there for instance – we go back over many campaigns. We met up 'bout six or seven years ago. Fighting for Prince Frederick Henry of Nassau at Breda we were. God, but that was a terrible do. As nasty a siege as you're likely to see and a very bloody storming at the end of it – begging your pardon, Mistress.'

'No, Sergeant – do go on.'

'Well, it was at Breda that we took John Barnard for our captain – though he was the youngest of us – but he's of gentle breeding so to speak, though he's bright in spite of that. Most of us spoke tolerable Dutch by the end of it; the captain spoke French and German – which came in very handy, many times. But there were so many different races there, godless folk some of 'em I can tell you, that many of the gentlefolk conversed in the Latin tongue, which was most useful of all. When we were out there he made sure we were well fed and quartered – which he still does. Most important of all, he's got a reputation as being lucky to follow into battle. It was on the walls at Breda he first showed that and he's never let us down since.'

Kate looked around her. 'Where is the captain now?' she asked. 'I do not see him here.'

'See, the light is still burning in his tent. He is probably still working away in there. He's been in an ill mood these past few months, brooding over his books. He takes things very seriously – though I would add that he has been in better spirits since this morning.'

'I could not presume to think that I have anything to do with that change,' she replied.

'As I have said, the captain is a gentleman. It sometimes does him good to be reminded of the meaning of the word.' The sergeant looked deep into his beer. Then he glanced up at her. 'You know that you are dining from his own plate . . . and drinking from his own cup. . . .'

He said no more, but stood up and wandered off to join his fellows. Kate was left alone. She looked across the roaring camp-fire to the tent where a single candle was burning. She rose and slowly walked across the clearing, pausing only to wipe the plate clean and to fill the cup with wine. She stopped at the entrance.

'Captain . . .' she called quietly.

His answer could barely be heard. 'Come in, Mistress Katherine. . . .'

John Barnard looked up. He had been crouched over his desk. As the sergeant had said, he had been reading. His eyes seemed tired, but glad to see her.

'Please . . . leave the entrance open.'

Kate did as he willed. 'I came to thank you for your plate, your cup . . . your many kindnesses.'

'They were little enough, though gladly given. . . . If you had not come soon I would have summoned you.'

Kate laid the wine cup down beside his book.

'Why is that, Captain?'

He rested his chin heavily on his linked fingers. 'Because I remain unconvinced by you.' He gestured for her to be seated on the bed. He turned to face her, his elbow resting on the back of the chair. The air was very still. He stared intently at her. His eyes bore no hint of a smile. 'We have taken you very much at face value. Thus far. . . . You landed amongst us and we watched the folk you claim waylaid you depart. You have charmed us this day and won the hearts of many honest men. . . .' He paused a moment, lost in thought. 'Yet there are many things you have not said, or deliberately left unsaid.'

Kate showed no sign of alarm at this sudden change in his attitude to her, though inside she felt crushed by his mistrust of her. She stared levelly back at him.

'There is much that I would prefer to leave unsaid,' she replied.

'I am sure there is. But I cannot allow it to remain so. You claim that you were waylaid on the road this morning, yet you have made no mention of your fellow travellers and I do not believe that a young lady of good character, such as you assuredly are, would be allowed to go abroad unaccompanied in these times. Furthermore, you have made no attempt to send word to your own people concerning your current situation. Will they not be driven to distraction to have news of you now that it is after dusk?'

Kate laughed silently and shrugged. There was nothing to be gained by lying to this man – outside this group of strange, godly men she would be alone and unprotected in this country at war with itself. She would tell the truth.

'The only news my own people – such as they are – will hear of me this night will be a detailed description of my ruination and my present death.'

Barnard's eyes widened slightly and his tone became more urgent. 'Explain yourself.'

She composed herself and began her story.

'I am, as I have told you, Katherine Butler. I am – or rather was – the only daughter of William Butler. I say "was" for I learned of his death at the hands of the rebels only last week. Before he died he sent me here for my . . . safekeeping.' She shook her head at the thought of the word. 'I was to be placed under the protection of my aunt, Lady Antonia Fitzmaurice – the late Lady Fitzmaurice. Late, but I would say not lamented . . . at least not by her husband. In the first few weeks his manner was gentle and consonant with his grief. He treated me courteously, though on reflection he was somewhat over-attentive. His mood soon changed.

'Captain Barnard, though you clearly have no trust in me, yet I must now have complete faith in you . . . you hold my life in your hands – now I must entrust you with my reputation.'

'Both are safe, Mistress Katherine, on the sole condition that you keep to the truth and do not attempt to deceive me. Continue.'

'My aunt had not been laid to rest even a month when I awoke in the night to find Fitzmaurice standing over me. He said he sought only solace and the warmth of another beside him. He made to climb into the bed with me. I pushed him away and we struggled. He still bears the marks, which are plain for all to see, on his face as a souvenir of that night. Because I would not submit to him, because I marked him and because he could not subdue me he had me beaten – I still bear my own souvenirs of that episode. They are still visible . . . mayhap they will be with me always. I will show you if you consider it needful – though I would think better of you if you did not consider it so. . . .'

Barbard said nothing. He shook his head. Still his manner seemed impassive.

'After that, life at Chalfcombe became very hard for me: I was no longer treated in the manner befitting a lady – I was hardly treated in that which befits a scullion. The meaner folk of the house took delight in my diminished circumstances. I was often struck for little reason and the other serving girls would pinch me as they passed. I would have been in despair but for the many good souls in the household who sustained me.

'This treatment continued until last week when I was summoned, alone, to his library. He told me of my father's death. His manner towards me became conciliatory. He proposed that we find comfort in each other's grief, that we should be married. His offer seemed honourable enough, if unappealing, until he placed the condition that he should know me before we were wed. I declined to give him an answer and he gave me a week to consider my position. I was restored to my former station, but I was not permitted to leave the house. Fitzmaurice came for his answer this morning. When I finally rejected him he turned me out of the house and set his huntsmen on to me . . . with very specific instructions. The rest of today's events you know already.'

All this time she held his gaze, unflinchingly. He took a deep breath.

'What of your family in Ireland?' he asked.

Kate was surprised by his question. She had thought at least that he would denounce Fitzmaurice for the scoundrel that he is. But no! He sat there and calmly asked about her family.

'I still have people in Ireland,' she replied, 'but since our family lands were overrun by the rebels I know not where they are.'

'And here in England?'

'Nobody – I think not that Fitzmaurice would welcome the sight of me still alive.'

Barnard's mood grew distant. He stared into the candle. He looked back at her. 'Then it seems that responsibility for your care devolves upon myself. At least for the time being. That is, of course, if you will permit me . . . Kate.'

'Then I may call you John?'

'Only when we are alone,' he replied. 'With my men I am still Captain Barnard.'

'Wake up, Mistress Katherine. Wake up!'

Kate sat up. It was difficult to focus her eyes. It was still dark. The boy was standing over her with a torch which cast fantastical shadows around the tent.

'What is happening, Peterkin? It is still night.'

'We've received orders to break camp with all haste. The captain is ordering the company. He bade me wake you and bring you these: Cornet Matthews' stuff, him being the only one of us about your size – me being too small. Your own dress is still too damp to wear. I've brought it in for you. The captain says that you be dressed and packed straightaway or he will bring the tent down around you.' On that note he left.

She was still half asleep as she dressed. She had been promised that they would sleep long and late into the next morning. After they had drained the cup of wine together, she and the captain had rejoined the company. They had talked long into the night. He had insisted that she sleep in his tent, for modesty's sake.

'You have endured enough to maintain your good name – I would not have it ruined in a single night by sleeping with common soldiery such as us.'

He had gathered together a few things and left her. Judging from the way she felt, Kate thought, that could not have been more than two hours ago.

'Are you ready in there Kate?' the captain called in.

'I'm not yet packed, but I am decent enough to receive visitors,' she replied.

The tent-flap opened and he entered.

'What is happening, John? You promised the men a day at leisure – and here we are, barely two hours later, busy as bees around a hive.'

'A rider came in not a quarter-hour since. There is a royalist army on the move. We are directly in its path. We have been ordered south to rendezvous with the other companies at Alresford. In all honesty, we've been abed for less than an hour, but since there is little love lost between ourselves and the regiments descending upon us, we prefer a shorter sleep now to an eternal one if we tarry.

'All right lads,' he called, 'this one is cleared. You can dismantle it.'

Kate scurried out just as the tent collapsed in on itself.

'Will you be able to ride with that ankle, Kate?' he enquired. 'I would feel easier if you did not have to lag behind with the baggage train.'

'It is well enough. I can bear my weight on it. I can ride if I am helped into the saddle.'

Barnard mounted up beside her. 'Our route will take us past Chalfcombe. Nothing would give me greater pleasure than to burn it down around Fitzmaurice's ears.'

Kate shook her head, laughing. 'Your offer is most attractive, believe me Captain. Were it merely Fitzmaurice who would suffer then I would gladly set the first torch to the house. But no. There are many good folk that depend on Chalfcombe for their livelihoods, so I could not warrant it.'

Barnard feigned disappointment. 'You are too forgiving, Kate Butler. On the continent we would have fired a man's house for less. . . .'

'But you are in England now,' she reproached him.

'Alas, you are right. Such an act might have proved difficult to justify before Parliament. Fitzmaurice is an important figure in these parts: he plays a clever game of shifting alliance and the gentry hereabouts follow his lead.'

Light was broadening in the sky as the mounted column approached Chalfcombe. As they neared the house they found that the gates were shut and barred against them. A scattering of armed men lined the walls. Kate recognized some of their faces from the previous morning. Thomas Fitzmaurice appeared at the parapet, armed with a hunting rifle.

Three weals still stood out, white and livid on his cheek, where she had marked him. She searched his face for the charming and sophisticated man who had wooed her when he had first come to the house, the man she had gone riding with in the early morning, whilst the mist still swirled about the Downs, the man who had almost captured her heart. . . . She looked up at his wild eyes, the fierce mane of grey hair, the arrogant jut of his jaw. There was no sign of the Thomas she had known. This was the man who had stolen into her room at night, the man she had fought with, the man who had tried to rape her. She looked up at his eyes and dreaded that they would fall upon her.

He looked down contemptuously at the captain and his company and, though they outnumbered his own following many times over, he showed no sign of fear.

'Good morrow, Captain Barnard. I see that you are leaving us. Has the climate in these parts proved too warm for your liking?'

'Not at all, Lord Fitzmaurice. If anything we have

found our reception here a trifle frosty. Nevertheless, we intend that things will be a good deal hotter in these parts ere long.'

'I shall be content to wait for that improvement – at least until you are off my property.' He turned to walk away. As he did so his eyes narrowed. He stared hard at the rider beside the captain. For a moment he was about to speak, then thought better of it and disappeared from sight. A chill ran down Kate's spine. He had recognized her.

The column rode on for a few minutes. The silence was shattered by a single crack of gunfire. The captain laughed grimly.

'Now I know that you are telling the truth, Kate.'

Barnard rode back to hurry along the baggage train which was lagging behind. Kate was left alone with her thoughts for a while. The captain, it seemed, was a more calculating man than she had imagined. Had he deliberately taken them past Chalfcombe to verify Kate's story? He had surely marked Fitzmaurice's expression as he looked upon her. She supposed his silence testified to his guilt. And, no doubt he inferred, as Kate did, that the gunshot signified Fitzmaurice's wrath falling on one of his unfortunate huntsmen. She was unsure how she felt about this turn of events: whether she should be insulted that, in spite of her sincere account of herself, he still required further proofs, or to be comforted that the man she had placed her trust in did not take reckless chances. . . .

As the morning wore on the column passed through the hamlet of Stratton. All the doors and shutters in the place were closed and the street was empty. The captain ordered his men to halt. He dismounted and went up to the door of the largest house and pounded his fist hard upon it. After a while it opened. A man of middle age brandishing a cudgel stood well back from the doorway. The captain seemed unconcerned by the weapon.

'Please bring your folk out of doors – we mean you no harm, but I need to talk to you altogether.'

The man seemed doubtful about this, but he had little choice when confronted by a hundred heavily armed troopers. He did as he was told. One by one the doors opened and the street slowly filled with villagers. Barnard remounted his horse so that he could get a better vantage point to talk to them all.

'I must speak briefly with you, for we have little time. Less than half a day's march behind us is a large force of royalists – many times our own number. We seek nothing from you for we are well supplied, but they will fall on you like a plague of locusts in Biblical tales. They will empty your storehouses and drive off your stock. Your menfolk will be pressed into service and I cannot vouch for the safety of the women here present. Those of you who remain are like to have a lean and hungry winter if you do not act now.'

The crowd murmured and nodded their heads in assent.

Barnard continued, 'You must take such things as you can carry and go with all your animals. Take them yonder – into the fastness of Micheldever Woods. You will be safe in hiding there until they have passed. Go now, and God be with you.'

The villagers needed no further encouragement, but set to preparing for their flight. Barnard's company rode on. The sergeant rode up to the head of the column. He congratulated the captain.

'A very pretty speech, John my lad. I was almost convinced myself.' He clapped the captain on the back. John glanced guiltily across at Kate.

'A parcel of half-truths, I'm afraid, Kate. Their village would almost certainly have been picked clean by their foraging parties, though their lives were in little danger. King Charles has decreed that his armies should not molest his subjects.'

'So why, prithee, the speech?' she replied

'Quite simple. When the King's men arrive at Stratton the place will have already been cleared of anything of use to them – by the village folk themselves. More humane and less hard work than razing the village and driving off the stock ourselves.'

'Aye,' the sergeant joined in, 'we saw enough of that when we were overseas. Whole countries devastated by years of warfare and pillage. Places where you didn't see village folk for weeks on end – save those hanging from gibbets. . . .'

'For our own part,' the captain continued, 'Parliament will not suffer us to forage for supplies, on pain of death. Everything we take we must provide restitution for. Though our own pay is infrequent, still we may not live off thè land.'

By midday they were approaching Alresford. Captain Barnard had been thoughtful for some time. At last he called up the sergeant again.

'Jack, I'm mindful that the colonel will not suffer us to have a woman in tow.'

'That's true enough,' he replied.

'Yet I have pledged my protection to Mistress Katherine. I cannot cast her off, she has no people hereabouts to go to.'

'I think I see your purpose,' the sergeant smiled.

'Take her back to the baggage-train and furnish her with such equipment as will be necessary. She will ride with Cornet Matthews.' He turned to Kate. 'You will have to put your hair up and give your face a stern expression – it is too pretty to pass for even a comely youth. Above all – if you find yourself in the company of any but our own fellows – talk as little as possible!'

She nodded. 'My lips are sealed.'

'Very good. Off you go. Sergeant, pass the word back that Mistress Katherine is to be referred to as "Cornet Butler" – at least for the time being.'

'We normally wear the visor up when we are not in battle, Cornet Butler.' Orlando Matthews laughed at her. 'My gear fits you well, Mist . . . forgive me . . . Cornet.' He thought for a moment. 'What shall I call you? I cannot address you as "Cornet Butler" all the time.'

It was Kate's turn to be thoughtful. 'Wait, I have it. If you are Orlando, then may I not be Ganymede?'

'Ganymede?' He looked at her quizzically.

'I swear, for all you English know about him, Will Shakespeare might as well have been an Irishman.'

'Will Shakespeare?' His look had not changed.

'You prove my point, Cornet. Still, I suppose Ganymede would almost certainly reveal me to those who know the play. I will take its author's name. Will – it was my father's name also – it should suffice for me.'

Cornet Matthews' expression brightened visibly. 'Very good – Will it is.' He seemed content that the matter was settled.

Kate felt uneasy in all this gear. The breastplate, which she had had to buckle up herself as none of the men would dress her, seemed to sit on her hips and remained in the same position while she lurched backwards and forwards inside it like the clapper of a bell. With the visor raised, her helmet had a propensity to fall forward over her face. Orlando showed her how to fasten the chin strap tightly to prevent this. The things that made her most uneasy though, were the pistols holstered in the saddle before her and the sword which hung at her side. The sergeant had insisted that the pistols be loaded.

'The cornet will show you how to prime and fire them – you never know when they might be needed,' he added, darkly.

Alresford was already full of soldiers when they arrived. She was surprised by the confusion which seemed to reign in the town after the orderliness of the captain's company. She was struck by the contrast in the infantrymen and the cavalry. The footsoldiers seemed little more than armed peasantry, rough-clad and poorly shod. Their mounted counterparts, however, seemed to come from different stock: the English gentry at war, she thought. As Praisegod led them through the town the captain came riding up. They talked quietly together for a few moments.

Praisegod seemed displeased by the captain's news. They turned off the main street and, as they made their way up a narrow cart track, the word passed back along the column: 'Making camp at Bishop's Sutton . . . with Greenslade's . . . pass it back.'

Orlando Matthews groaned and rolled his eyes at the news. When he had conveyed the message he turned to Kate.

'We'll have no happy memories of Bishop's Sutton, I'll warrant.'

'Why is that, Orlando?'

'Let us say that Greenslade's company have a reputation for . . . extremism. Anabaptists, Levellers – every sectarian in the army flocks to Greenslade's banner. Their motto: "Flesh is the vessel of the Devil" gives a fair summary of their inclination. Given the choice of close confinement with Greenslade's and the whole of the King's Army of the West . . . on my word, I should almost prefer the royalists.'

The captain came back down the line and joined them.

'Kate, how strongly do you feel about your hair?'

'What do you mean, John?' She was so surprised by his question that she forgot his instructions.

'Having started this charade we must carry it through. Martin Greenslade is a notorious hellfire preacher – and he bears little love for women. You would look out of place with your helmet on all the time we are encamped. Your hair will have to go – now. I am bitterly sorry, but. . .'

'Is this absolutely necessary?' she interrupted.

'If it were not I would never ask it of you.'

'Then so be it. Come on, let's be done with it.'

They rode back to the baggage train. After some searching they found some rough scissors. The company carried on as they rode off to a nearby copse.

Sunlight filtered through the leaves of the trees. Far off they could hear the column moving along the road, but in the wood the air was still and silent. Kate could see that John's hands were trembling.

'I think this is the hardest thing I have ever had to do,' he confessed.

'Surely there have been many worse than this?'

'I've done many bad things – things which I am ashamed of, things which wake me in the night, which I can see with my waking eyes as clearly as though they are still happening. But they were done in the name of duty, under the "rules of war", if you like. I have never willingly marred anything of such beauty, though.'

Kate took both his hands in hers and spoke softly to him. 'John, you are doing this to save my life. Without you I should be alone and friendless in this cruel place. If these tresses are the price I have to pay to be with you then I shall be grateful for every cut. My only sadness is in the knowledge of the pain it causes you.'

John Barnard took the first length of hair in his fingers. For a moment he seemed abstracted, lost in the way the light played on it as it fell over her back and shoulders. Then his expression changed as he became resigned to his task.

'Forgive me, Kate,' he said simply and made the first cut.

The woodland floor about them was strewn with long dark curls of hair which lay lifeness now, like a shed skin. Barnard looked dubiously at his handiwork.

'You look like an impish Joan of Arc.'

Kate looked into his breastplate as she moved her hair into some sort of shape with her fingers.

'I will be content with your comparison – as long as I do not suffer her fate.'

The thought of this moved John deeply. Involuntarily, almost, he took her in his massive hands. He stared hard at her.

'I would never suffer that to happen, nor any harm to come to you – I would die myself first.'

He drew her closer to him. There was the sound of metal ringing on metal as their breastplates came together. The noise seemed to bring John to his senses. He trembled slightly and relaxed his hold, though his hands were still about her shoulders. Again Kate took his hands in hers – so large and awkward for a man of such gentleness and subtlety, she thought.

'Then we must look after each other, John Barnard, for I could not bear for any harm to befall you.' She brushed his cheek with her hand. 'But now you must think of your present responsibilities. I can no longer hear your company – they must be far away by now.'

Barnard laughed quietly. 'Aye, that is a responsibility which is always with me – though for a few moments it did not rest so heavily on my shoulders, Kate.'

She reproached him. 'Remember, Captain, that I am Cornet Will Butler – at least for the time being.'

Greenslade's men were engaged in a fierce battle on the village green as Barnard's company rode into Bishop's Sutton. Orlando Matthews could barely disguise his disapproval.

'This is even as I would have expected them to be. Plotting. Planning their new Utopias – all of which seem to require the destruction of the society we live in.'

'That is a fine thing for you to say, Orlando. How can you claim to be so much better than they – when you wage war on your own King?' Kate replied.

'The King wages war on us, Cornet Butler. Remember that.'

'How so, Orlando? Do not mistake me, for I imply no criticism by my question. At home we had little time to debate events in England and since I have been here I have heard no one who would speak good of your cause.'

'How so indeed . . .' he said, bitterly. 'Do you know, many of my friends from Cambridge . . . fellows I studied with and enjoyed the best of times with, I see them now, armed and ranged against me – they would kill me and I them if needs be.

'I believe that we are right in this. The King claims that he rules by Divine Right – I cannot gainsay that, for I do not know the mind of God. And if he ruled wisely in God's name then all would be well enough.

Yet his rule is arbitrary and tyrannical. He ignores the rights granted to free Englishmen since Magna Carta. I do not doubt that he loves his subjects after his own fashion – but we are not children . . . and he is most assuredly not God. We petitioned him for the restoration of our rights – and when he wearied of our pleas he turned upon us.' He laughed ironically. 'We do not wage war on the King – in truth the King wages war on the country.'

Martin Greenslade was standing on an open wagon; he was coming to the climax of a passionate speech.

'. . . and we shall live as one people, under God, without popes, without princes . . . without Parliament.' His black eyes, black as coals, glowered at the newcomers, defying them to respond to his declamation.

Barnard rode up to him. He could barely conceal the anger in his voice. 'Master Greenslade, not more than ten miles hence is a royalist army, hell-bent on our destruction. This is no time to be preaching anarchy. I suggest your time would be more profitably spent ordering your company for battle.'

Greenslade seemed on the point of launching a crushing denunciation of the captain, then he obviously thought better of it, and bowed, mockingly.

'My men await your pleasure, Captain Barnard. We shall be ready in an instant.' He turned to his company. 'Brothers, the Lord's work is at hand. We must be ready for the idolaters when they come.' With that he dismissed them. He and the captain went off together into his bivouac.

'Greenslade may be a hothead, but he's no fool. He knows that the King's men are nigh as keen to capture him as they are to lay hands on Tom Fairfax or Oliver Cromwell.' Orlando shot a wry smile at her. 'Now then, Will my lad, I think it is time to see if these sectarians can cook as well as they talk.'

'I think it better, Orlando, if I remain with our own people – danger is so close, I would not bring it on myself by my own carelessness.'

'Perhaps you're right. I'll bring something over to you.' With that he left.

Praisegod noticed that Kate was alone and called across to her. 'Cornet Butler – this is no time to be idle. Come here at once!'

He took her aside and chided her. 'Mistress Katherine,' he whispered angrily, 'know now that I think the captain's scheme is damnably foolish . . . but whilst you are with us and under our protection you must act with circumspection. If you are found out you are like to be taken for a common whore – they will slit your nose. As an Irishwoman you may be considered to be a papist. And dressed thus . . .' – he waved his hand at her uniform – 'they would certainly take you for a witch and burn you alive.' He paused for a moment to allow her to consider this.

'I am sorry to be so blunt, but a knowledge of your present danger may help you to stay in your whole skin. Be wary, Cornet Butler – and do not make yourself obvious!'

Kate thanked him and looked around for a place to conceal herself. There seemed to be a large knot of men around the sergeant. That would be the safest place, she thought, and went to join him. She wondered if she would ever find peace, or even a moment when she would feel safe. In Ireland the Catholics were massacring her friends and family – for all she knew they might already be dead. Here in England it seemed whichever way she turned she was in danger. The whole continent was rent by warfare and bloodshed. She suddenly felt very small, very helpless and very alone, tossed about in the storm of conflict with little chance of survival. What little hope she had rested in the hands of a man she had known scarcely a single day. What if he failed her? It was a prospect she dared not even consider.

Kate was at work with a party of troopers, helping them to put up tents, when the captain called her over to him.

She was covered in dust from her exertions. He seemed pleased by this.

'In truth, Cornet Butler, even I would mistake you for one of my own now.' They smiled at each other. Then his mood became serious. 'We have received news that the royalists who were following us have carried on south and have met up with a force coming up from the south and west. We have been ordered to take up a position on the road to Winchester and report on their movements. You will stay here with the baggage-train. I have persuaded Greenslade to leave the camp in the care of Jack's troop. You will be safe with him.'

'Will there be a battle, do you think?'

'It is hard to tell. Neither force is very great – though they are greater than we. Both armies may well miss each other, as often happens. I think we should bring them to battle – they clearly have some grand design which we should thwart – if we can.'

'When do you leave?'

'We leave straightaway. With God's will we should be back by sunset on the morrow. If we are delayed . . .' – he raised his eyebrows as if in jest – 'then I will send word. When we return we shall be weary and hungry – tell Jack to find us some venison – we have seen many deer in these parts, and with the booty from Basing we shall have a feast.'

They said nothing for a moment but looked deep into each other's eyes. Kate broke the silence.

'I cannot send you off with the courtesies I would like to give you.'

'Dressed thus, I fear the men would talk.' He seemed to be maintaining a light-hearted face to her. Kate thought she understood his meaning.

'Take my hand, John,' she whispered.

To all the world they looked like a young cornet wishing his commanding officer luck. But all the world could not feel the tenderness of that touch.

'Keep your head on your shoulders, Captain Barnard.'

'God be with you, Cornet Butler.'

'And with you.'

With that he left.

The men of the company waved to her as they passed out of the village; she waved back at them. John Barnard was already out of sight.

As the last trooper filed out the sergeant came up to her.

'Things will be quiet here this evening, Mistress Katherine. Go and fetch your pistols – it would be well if you learned how to use them.'

Two

All through the evening, while the men were preparing the meal, the sergeant instructed Kate in the use of her pistols. Before he would allow her to fire one he demonstrated the loading and priming of the gun. He made her repeat these actions many times until she perfected them. Then he took her out on to the common. He carried a longbow and a quiver of arrows.

'Before we start making a noise and frightening off the game, I'll just shoot us a couple of those deer over there,' he remarked, cheerfully.

'You seem very confident, Jack,' she mocked.

'Hush . . . quiet . . .' he whispered. 'Look, over there.' He pointed to a smaller group of deer grazing by the forest fence. 'See, to escape they may only break one way. That will afford us a better chance.'

As he was talking, he placed six arrows down in the ground before him, taking the seventh and notching it onto his bowstring. Drawing it back, he paused a moment taking aim, then released it. While it was still in the air he fired the second and while that was in flight he loosed the third. On he went until the last arrow was spent. Three of the deer were down. 'Come mistress, and bring your pistols with you.' As they walked up he explained his actions. 'Three heartbeats between each shot, aiming to the right each time because I knew that they would break that way. Never take the leader for the rest will follow his line. If they saw him fall they would scatter – and then it would become more difficult. Three hits out of seven shots at a hundred paces – in less time than it would take a good musketeer to fire once then reload.' He patted his bow. 'With this simple weapon the English archers snuffed out the flower of France at Agincourt two hundred years ago, and still we cannot better it.'

The deer were still writhing and kicking when they reached them. The sergeant took Kate to the first stag.

'Point your pistol at its head, keep your arm braced and your elbow slightly bent. Pull the trigger gently. Remember – this is a mercy you are doing him.'

The stag's eyes rolled up and stared at her in resignation. Kate summoned herself and squeezed the trigger. The recoil forced her hand up sharply and she was knocked back a pace. The bullet had ripped a large hole in the stag's head. Kate closed her eyes and shuddered. The sergeant took her by the arm and led her to the second stag.

'Again,' he ordered.

This time it was worse. Her hand was shaking uncontrollably.

'Quickly, Mistress, you can see he's suffering!'

She fired again. The stag lay dead. She felt overcome by sadness, for he had in life been a majestic beast. The sergeant had dispatched the third, a beautiful young doe, by taking up her head and slitting her throat.

'You could have killed them just as easily yourself – why did you make me do it?' she said through clenched teeth, desperately trying to suppress the quaking which racked her whole body. The sergeant had ripped up a tuft of grass and was cleaning his knife with meticulous attention. He looked up. The sadness in his eyes reminded her of the deer she had just killed.

'When first I saw you, Mistress, when you came slithering down that bank, covered in mud, I thought what a funny little thing you looked. Permit me to say so, but I thought you the funniest thing I had seen in seven years of war. Then, when you had come up to me, limping all the way and in such pain, just to thank me for the use of a little piece of soap – well I can tell you, I was deeply touched. All my life, I've known little of kindness and courtesy and I'm accounted a hard man by all my lads – I call 'em my lads, but only to myself. . . .' He smiled for a moment, as if lost in a happy memory . . . then he came back to the present and resumed his account.

'When young John tells me that you would be staying with us and the manner of your staying, I was right glad – but I knew then and there the peril he was putting you in. I said to myself, "Jack – you're not going to be able to look after her all the time – there'll be times when she'll have to look to herself".' He shook his head sadly. 'I've seen so many lads as have taken up arms lightly, without a thought as to their proper function – they're made to kill with – and there's others there with the same weapons as would kill them, given half a chance. Well, they've joined the trained bands in peacetime and they've marched around after Christmas and harvest-time. But I've seen them in their first battle and they have to stab or cut another body – or shoot someone – close up, like you and me are. And I've watched them stay their hands, out of love and goodness, and be cut down for that.'

He paused again, then looked her straight in the eye. 'That choice you made today is the same choice as those young men made. And I will not suffer you to go the same way as they did. These pistols are for taking away life – and in so doing they will save our own.'

The sergeant was near to tears as he said this and Katherine embraced him for the love he so clearly bore her.

They walked back to the village. For the first part of the way they walked arm in arm, like father and daughter. As they neared the sight of the village, he took her hand and held it tight for a moment, then let it drop.

'I would not have the others sully your reputation by talking about any association with the likes of me, Mistress Katherine.'

The camp-fire was dying. Kate and the sergeant were sitting together. The watches had been posted and those men who were not on watch were fast asleep. He was staring deep into the flames. He spoke with slow deliberation. As Kate knew by now, though he said little in company, those things he said he meant with all his heart.

'John Barnard's mood has changed since he met you – I've told you that already.'

'Yes, Jack, that was one of the first things you said to me.'

'He's a good commander. He sleeps after us, he eats after us, he never takes chances with our lives. But still, I've a mind that he can be a difficult man.'

'What do you mean?'

'Well, we met him at Breda. He must have been, what, twenty-three then. Before that he was studying law at Cambridge.'

'Like Orlando Matthews?'

'Yes, yes. Though Orlando is only a boy. You'll find a great many Cambridge lawyers among the officers of our army.'

'What of it then?'

'What I mean to say is this: he's lived all his life in a man's world. He's not a stranger to women, but . . .' The sergeant was looking for the right words. 'He has a sister, but . . . well, what I mean to say is, he has lived a man's life.'

'Yes, Sergeant?' She would not let him stop at that.

'Well, in all honesty, he's never behaved with another woman in the same way as he has with you.' He seemed to be finished with what he wanted to say.

'That's all very well, Jack, but you cannot let it rest there. Speak your mind clearly.'

'Since you press me, then I will speak my mind. I love John Barnard dearly, and I hold you in great regard as well. Nothing would befit me better than to see you two together – and I think you would be well suited too – but first I would know your mind on this, and then I would tell you more of the man.'

It was Kate's turn to stare into the flames. 'What can I say, Jack? I've known him only a day. In that time he has doubted my word twice – twice, mark you – he has dressed me as a man and cut off my hair; he has brought me into the society of men who would maim or kill me if they knew my true identity. Yet he has also shown me such kindnesses as he has been able to and he has pledged his life for my protection. I have touched his hands and his face, yet when we came close together he withdrew himself from me. He is cold – not cold . . . distant. He will not allow me to approach him. . . . And now he is gone. Lord help me, Jack, I think I am falling in love with him.'

Kate surprised herself by her admission. She had not admitted it to herself until that moment. He was not the kind of man she had ever imagined being with: he was quiet, bookish, reserved – God, he was a Puritan! They had always seemed a strange people and she had avoided their company. How different they were from her idea of them. And now she had fallen in love with one. She shook her head in amazement.

Jack took a stick and turned a log over in the fire, sparks flew up into the sky.

'I thought as much,' he said, 'and I reckon the captain feels the same, if only he'd let himself believe it. These last few months he's started doubting himself; the war's going badly down here, nobody seems to want to take it to its conclusion. It was easier in the Low Countries. We were up against Catholics; Spaniards and the emperor's armies. Here it's different. We're fighting our own people, Protestants mostly, very much like ourselves. John looks around and he sees the people we are fighting with – folk like Greenslade, and he says to me, "What if we do win this war – what then? If we overthrow Charles what do we replace him with, a republic made up of Levellers and Radicals, Anabaptists and Atheists?" He wants to take the grandees of this army by the scruff of the neck and shake some sense into 'em, but he can't. Forgive me for going on so, but the point is this: he sees things a lot deeper than most and what he sees has left him sorely troubled, and that worries me.'

'In what way, Jack?'

'He's getting reckless in battle – as if he cares nothing about living any more. Anyway, that's why I'm so glad you happened along. I reckon you'll bring back the spark to his life.' He took her hand and squeezed it. 'It's getting late and I've got the early turn. I'll bid you goodnight. You've let me carry on some this evening, but I've right enjoyed our chat. Sleep well, and keep your pistols by the bed.'

The next day was hot and sultry. The still air was broken by the sound of far-off cannonfire, rumbling like a summer storm over the horizon. It seemed to go on forever. In her mind's eye Kate imagined the carnage and suffering that was going on over the hill. She prayed for it to end.

It was just after noon when one of the troopers came running in from the south.

'Cavaliers! About thirty of them – they're coming fast!'

'Take cover lads!' the sergeant cried.

As he spoke the cavaliers appeared, charging up the main street, their swords drawn. They let out a great cry as they saw the roundheads. Kate tried to run but her ankle gave way beneath her and she stumbled. One of them bore down on her, leaning out of the saddle, his sword swept wide to cut her down.

Kate struggled to raise her pistols. He was almost upon her. The ground trembled under his horse's hooves. She could smell it, feel its heat. The sword was coming down on her. She saw his bloodshot eyes, his strong teeth smiling as he sensed the kill. She pulled both triggers, the explosion knocked her back. His expression changed to one of horror as the impact of the bullets lifted him out of his saddle, two smoking holes pierced into his breastplate. Kate felt a ringing in her ears and a flash of blinding light before her eyes. She knew no more.

The light still dazzled her, but it was the sun. Then the light was blotted out. Someone was standing over her. She felt the splash of water on her face.

'Well, Mistress Katherine, this is a fine pickle and no mistake.' It was the sergeant. She felt many hands help her to her feet. One of the men handed her her helmet. It had a deep dent running along the crown.

'What happened?' she asked. Waves of nausea were passing over her and she felt as though she would faint.

'They rode straight through the village and out the other end,' one of them said.

'They had no interest in us – they just wanted to escape,' said another.

The sergeant steadied her. He spoke softly. 'It looks as though they were in flight. We picked off a few of 'em before they went, though.'

She looked around her. There were about half a dozen lying in the street. A wounded cavalier was being carried into one of the houses and some of the troopers were taking their horses to the picket lines. At her feet was the man she had shot herself, the same look of horror in his eyes.

'I killed him,' she said, aghast.

'He would have done the same to you,' the sergeant said, simply. He handed her back her pistols. They felt heavy and alien to her hands.

'I have reloaded them for you,' he said, grimly. 'Listen, the battle is still going on. We may have more work to do before the day is out.'

The cannon rumbled on through the afternoon as they buried the bodies of the fallen. The village minister was dragged out of his hiding place and read the funeral rites over the graves. Jack had been through their belongings and found the names of most of them. He had written them on planks of wood and set them at the head of each grave. Only one remained unmarked – even the wounded man could not identify him.

At four o'clock the cannon stopped. An unearthly silence fell around them. The sergeant peered into the distance. 'Now we wait,' he said.

Kate went across to the farmhouse where the cavalier

was taken. He had been stripped half naked and laid on a large kitchen table, which was streaked with blood. His head was lolling about from left to right. One of the troopers came up to her.

'Mistress Katherine, you shouldn't be in here. He has a musket ball in his thigh. It's not deep, so we have resolved to get it out ourselves.'

The cavalier looked up at her. 'Good God! A woman roundhead – we've lost the war, we might as well give up now if we have to fight your camp followers as well. . . .' His voice trailed off as he lost consciousness.

'Forgive him. We have been filling him with brandy-wine this last hour. He hasn't stopped cursing us all this time. We'd better start now while he's asleep – please go Mistress, the sick room is no place for a lady.'

She closed the door of the house quietly and went out into the street. The sun was still hot and her head was ringing. She took herself down to the stream which ran beside the village and bathed her head and neck. She felt the cold water trickle down her back under the breastplate, she shivered as it relaxed her. Slowly, her mind withdrew from the terrible events of the day and sleep overtook her.

Her rest was disturbed by something tickling her nose, which twitched, involuntarily. She moved her hand across her face and was woken with a start.

'A fine truant you are, Cornet Butler. . . .'

She looked up. It was the captain, laughing at her. He held his hand out to help her up. She took it and pulled him sharply down – too sharply – for he slipped and fell headlong into the stream, hitting the water with a mighty splash. Kate roared with laughter as he stood up, waist high in water, weed hanging from his head and shoulders.

'Why, pray, did you do that?'

'For the sheer devilment of it – and because I am so glad to see you alive, John Barnard.' She offered her hands to help him out. He grabbed them and pulled her in with him. Water swirled around her face, into her mouth and nose. She felt herself rising from the water as John Barnard lifted her out by the collar, and kept her hanging there. Kate lashed out at him with her fists and screamed at him.

'John Barnard! I cannot believe you just did that!' She swung out at him again and hit his breastplate with a clang. 'Ow!' she cried in pain, and he dropped her back in the water. After much struggling and splashing they dragged themselves back to shore.

'Come on Kate, I have to have some words with Jack.' He pulled her up the bank. Water pumped out of the top of her boots with each step she took.

She glowered up at him. 'John, I am wet and I have nothing to change into. And it is all your fault. . . .'

'My fault?' he protested his innocence. 'You pulled me in first.'

'At least you have something to change into. I will have to squelch around the camp looking like a half-drowned puppy.' She pouted, crossed her arms and stamped her foot in mock anger.

'But you are glad to see me?'

'I am not so sure anymore. . . .' Gradually, a smile came over her face, 'Of course I am. But what shall I do about these clothes?'

'You can give the whole lot back to Orlando and get out your dress. You need go about as a man no longer. I have been ordered by Sir William Waller to convey the news of our victory to Parliament itself. Tonight you will ride with me to London.'

Three

'We have about four hours of daylight left and the roads are dry, we should reach Farnham before dark.'

'How far is that, John?'

'About twenty miles. The battle should have drawn in all the royalists in the area and the last time I saw them they were retreating towards Winchester. With luck we should not encounter any on the way.'

'What of the party that passed through the village this afternoon?'

'I would expect them to make for Basing House. There are few other places friendly to them between here and London.'

They rode on in silence for a while. The day was so peaceful and the countryside so beautiful that it was hard to believe that this was the same day which had witnessed such scenes of brutality. Here she was again, in her blue dress, seemingly out riding with a gentleman companion. The pastoral theme ended there though: her gentleman companion was a fully armed and armoured roundhead officer and sitting in their holsters before her were two loaded pistols. She noticed that John was staring at them.

'Jack told me about the cavalier,' he said. 'I am very sorry you were brought to that.'

'If Jack had not taught me how to use these – then one of the graves in Bishop's Sutton would have been my own. I'll never forget that look in his eyes as he bore down on me – he would have been satisfied with nothing less than my death. I came so close to death this day that it frightens me to think of it.'

'Aye, and it was I who placed you in that peril by dressing you up in soldier's garb.'

'I think not that I would have been any safer had I been dressed as I am now.'

They fell silent again. Kate found herself thinking about the young man they had taken prisoner.

'What will become of the wounded cavalier?' she asked lightly, concealing her concern.

John shrugged, nonchalantly. 'If his wound heals cleanly, he will fare well enough.'

'And then?' she pressed him. He seemed surprised by her persistence. He looked coldly at her and raised a mocking eye-brow.

'Why should you show such compassion for a man who would have been happy to have left you butchered in the street?'

'Because he is a fellow human being,' she replied, 'just like you and I.'

John's mood changed. 'Yes, you're right Kate. And I tend to think the same. We do enough killing when it is needful to suffer further atrocity when it is needless. But a cavalry company cannot be encumbered by keeping prisoners in tow. I have left a few pence in the village for his upkeep until he recovers and I told Jack to ensure that when they decamp for Winchester on the morrow that Greenslade's company leaves Bishop's Sutton first. I would not trust any of his rabble – they would be perfectly capable of slitting his throat before they left.'

Then his mood changed and his eyes glittered, mischievously. 'Did you see Greenslade's face when he discovered that my young cornet was a lady? I swear to God it would have curdled fresh milk!'

They both laughed out loud, for Greenslade's face had indeed been sour as they rode out of the village. He had spluttered and ranted at the captain and used such language as she would not have expected from one who purported to be a man of the cloth. Kate had never been referred to as a 'Whore of Babylon' before.

'I fear I will have some explaining to do on my return,' John mused.

Kate looked keenly at him. 'And when will that be, John?' she asked.

He seemed to be calculating the time. 'Well, fifteen hours riding there . . . rest tonight, probably eight hours . . . report to Parliament . . . brief respite in London . . . fifteen hours to return . . . What does that make? he asked.

'Probably about two days at the outside,' she replied glumly.

'Perhaps that is a trifle optimistic. We sent out the fast rider immediately after the battle so that the news will have gone ahead of us. If we reach Westminster by late tomorrow afternoon, the Commons will still be in session awaiting my report. Then they will no doubt want to question me on the matter. There will be various committees to report to also – and I have quite a number of letters to distribute to the families of officers in the army. So, all in all, I would imagine two weeks might be a more realistic estimate. Does that suit you any better?'

'That will suit very well.' Kate beamed at him.

It was already dark when they reached Farnham. They made their way to an inn. The doors were closed, so John hammered on them with his fist. At once a man appeared at one of the upper windows.

'We've no room for quarter tonight!' he shouted, angrily.

'We seek no quarter,' John called up. 'We are a captain of horse and his lady. We seek accommodation – we are paying guests.'

The man's manner changed instantly. 'Give me a moment to get down and open up, Captain.' He disappeared within.

John turned to Kate. 'The army requires free quarter from the good citizens of the country – the good citizens, however, are seldom keen to offer it – as you can see. . . ..'

As the innkeeper admitted them, John's manner became distracted – almost arrogant. Kate would learn that this was the way he behaved with those he knew not or did not trust.

'We require food and wine – not merely board, mind you – but the best you have. We have had a hard day today and would be well rewarded for our efforts.'

'Most assuredly so, Captain. I will attend to it.' The innkeeper bowed as he spoke. 'Has the captain perhaps come from Alresford today?' he enquired.

The captain looked down on him with a disdainful expression. Kate had to look away as she tried to stifle her amusement.

'Innkeeper, the satisfaction of our present needs should be your prime concern. When they have been attended to then we have have some discourse. Have your man look to the welfare of our horses.'

'Immediately, Captain. Will you follow me?' He led them into a parlour-room and bade them sit down, and left. A few moments later, a boy came in and lit a needless fire in the grate. John and Kate said nothing, but she noticed the same glint of mischief in his eyes. Flames started licking up through the kindling and curling around the logs above. When the boy had gone, John's manner became stern.

'Kate Butler . . . if I ever hear you so much as snigger again when I am trying to be . . . well, I am sure you take my meaning, I swear, I will put you across my knee and. . .'

He was interrupted by a large, genial-looking woman who brought in a tray with the wine and also some bread, butter and cheese which she laid down on the table before them.

'Now then, dears, this should help to fill the gap while I get some proper vittles going – nothing fancy though, like you asked for, but just the sort of stuff as I can get together at this hour – and at such short notice.' She looked sternly down at the captain. Then they both smiled at one another, and she bustled out.

'That woman knows no fear, Kate. Why, if the Earl of Essex himself were to come here I expect she would behave in just the same way. I fear I have been found out.'

In spite of her warning, the innkeeper's wife made them an excellent meal. While they were dining, her husband brought in the panniers from their horses.

'I brought in these as well – it doesn't do to leave things like these lying about,' he said, holding up Kate's pistols.

When they had dined and the wine had relaxed them somewhat, they asked the innkeeper if he and his wife would care to join them, which they duly did. The captain started the conversation.

'You were right, sir, when you asked if we had come from Alresford. Have you had word of the battle already?'

'We heard yesterday that two armies were coming together about that place. We feared that you would come to blows there.'

'But you have not yet learned of its outcome?'

The innkeeper shook his head.

'Well, put briefly, we won the day – though it was in the balance for a while. Sir William allowed Sir Ralph Hopton's forces to clear the field in good order. I would imagine they will have fallen back on the City of Winchester. The citizens of that place will be alarmed when they wake up on the morrow to find the city under siege.'

'Were there many fallen?' the innkeeper's wife asked, clearly distressed.

'There are ever too many of them,' John replied.

'And what of your own company, John?' Kate asked.

'We fared none too badly. We took a muster after the battle; five men died – I have their names and the villages they came from, I will write to their families when I get the chance; a handful of wounded which I dispatched to the surgeon in Alresford; and two we could not account for – I hope to see their faces when I return.'

Since the captain was clearly ill-disposed to talk at any great length about the battle, the conversation turned to lighter things: they talked at length about the weather and the innkeeper grumbled about the extra taxes and duties he was having to pay under Parliament's rule. John argued that at least it was fairer now that the great landowners were having to contribute to the general good, which was a point the innkeeper had to accept grudgingly.

Since they had touched on a subject which he did not want to discuss, he sought to change the subject. 'Mistress Katherine, I notice from the holsters in your saddle – and the arms that you carry – that you are riding a trooper's horse. I am most intrigued to learn the meaning of this riddle?'

The conversation ceased abruptly.

'Well . . .' Kate began, then stopped.

'Well?' John added enquiringly. 'Since Mistress Katherine clearly finds the tale troublesome to relate – with your permission, Mistress Katherine?'

'Please, Captain, do go on.'

'Well, where should I begin? For the past few weeks we have been encamped about two miles south of Whitchurch, so that we could watch the comings and goings at the crossing of the north and west roads.' At this point his voice rose slightly as Kate kicked his shins – under the table. She smiled sweetly at him.

'A touch of the wind, Captain? I fear you might have eaten too eagerly on an empty stomach, the good lady's table being so amply provided. Pray, continue.'

The captain turned about, taking his legs away from further harm.

'Forgive me, the food was indeed the best I have tasted in many days. . . .' He bowed his head to the innkeeper's wife. 'Particularly as we have been camped so long at that crossroads, which is, I believe, where I left our tale.' He glanced across at Kate.

'Anyway, as I was about to say, we came upon a group of cavaliers – murderous fellows – who had ambushed this good lady on the road and slain all her companions. On seeing us, the cowards made off, leaving Mistress Katherine gagged and bound to a tree. Though we had saved her from molestation and possibly murder – the rogues made off with her horse and all her belongings. She had only the garments she was standing in.'

'The scoundrels!' the innkeeper exclaimed.

'Even so,' he replied. 'But such is the behaviour of royalists on the open road.'

'Mercy, saints preserve us! Walter – they are not wed!' the innkeeper's wife exclaimed.

'Good heavens wife – what are you creating about?'

'Walter – the room!' she whispered, none too quietly.

The innkeeper put his hand to his mouth. 'Oh, mercy, the room! Oh, Captain, forgive us! We thought you were man and wife. And we have prepared such a beautiful room for you, the one we keep for guests of some station. It has good air, and a light open aspect . . . and a fine, soft . . . commodious bed,' he added sheepishly.

'Ah,' the captain replied, 'I see your dilemma.'

'No, Captain, I don't think you do,' he replied. 'For when I said we had no room for quarter, I was speaking truly – we would not make over our best room for common soldiers – but it is the only free room we have in the house.'

The captain laughed, then sighed deeply. 'Well, in the name of this lady's virtue and the good reputation of your house, I would be obliged if you would permit me to sleep down here. That long form by the fire will suffice. Do you have any spare sheets and a pillow for my head?'

'Oh, surely Captain,' they replied in unison and went off to get them.

John pointed down to the panniers. 'I had a good woman in Bishop's Sutton make these up with such gear as you might find needful. Good night Kate – enjoy your fine, soft, commodious bed. . . .' He laughed quietly.

Though he had had a long hard day and there was the prospect of the same on the morrow, still John could not sleep. He had too many things running around in his mind; the battle, the letters he would have to write to the families of the fallen, the faces of the friends he had lost that day. He wondered how the company was faring in his absence; this was the first time he had been away from them in over a year and he felt a twinge of guilt at deserting them. He had actually asked Sir William for leave to make the report to Parliament. Sir William had granted permission readily enough, not realizing that the captain had an ulterior motive for making his request. He was surprised at himself, he had never done such a thing before. . . . He stared into the embers of the fire, engrossed by the way the deep red glow gradually consumed the dead wood, lending it a life more intense than it had possessed in its natural state – thus it was for him these last days. He thought of Kate upstairs asleep in bed, her head resting on a soft pillow. He tried to catch the image in his mind's eye and when he had it he smiled.

Kate, however, was far from asleep and she was not in bed. Even as the captain was smiling at the thought of her, the object of those thoughts was at that moment stealing barefoot down the staircase. She, too, had been unable to sleep. She placed her toe gingerly on the next step; feeling it begin to move she lifted her foot and placed it on the next. The creak from the next step seemed to echo all around the sleeping house. For a moment she stood, transfixed by the sound, then with all the speed she could muster, she flew down the stairs and scuttled along the hall. When she came to the parlour door she dashed straight in and closed it behind her, standing with her back against it and breathing hard.

'It is customary to knock, Kate,' came a voice in the darkness.

John was hidden from her by the high back of the form. She tiptoed across the room. He was leaning up on one elbow when she came into view. The blankets had fallen back from his shoulder. Kate was surprised to see that he did not wear a nightshirt. Though he did not seem angry, neither could Kate tell if he was particularly pleased to see her.

'Well, since you are here, you might as well sit down.'

He motioned to the chair on the other side of the fire. 'I take it that you could not sleep either.'

'I know that I should,' she replied, 'and the innkeeper is right about the bed, it is really very comfortable.'

'I am relieved to hear that.' He shifted uneasily on the form.

'But my mind is so full of things that I need to talk to someone or it will surely burst.'

While she was talking Kate had picked up the cushions from the chair John had bade her sit upon. She laid them down beside his makeshift bed, and sat down beside him, her elbow on the edge of the form. John tried to move back but there was nowhere for him to go – the seat he was on was too narrow.

'What do you need so badly to talk about, Kate?'

'Oh, nothing – and everything. I was thinking up there that this might be our last chance to be alone together for a while.'

'What do you mean?' he replied.

'Well, what with you being at Parliament and me – that's one thing I was thinking about – where are you taking me? Where will I lay my head tomorrow night?'

'Later tonight you mean, for it is already the small hours of the morning . . . I am taking you to my sister Gwen's house, she has a place beside Chelsea Fields. It is a largish house and she lives there with only her son and servants. Her husband, Michael, is a lieutenant of horse with the Eastern Association. I'm sure she will be grateful for your company.'

'And when will I see you?'

'Oh, I will be back every night, you can be sure of that . . . and some of the days too – depending on when the various committees I must report to are in session. You will have chance to weary of the sight of me, never fear.'

While he had been talking, John had been looking at her hair, the way the firelight brought out the red sheen. It was not so dark as it appeared in daylight. He lifted his hand and ran his fingers through it.

'I am so sorry about this,' he said, his voice no more than a whisper.

'Do not be, John. It will grow back. I am becoming quite accustomed to it; it's not so heavy and far easier to care for.' She tilted her head so that it rested in his hand. 'John, tell me about yourself. . . .'

'I thought it was you that was so eager to talk. Thus far you've said very little.'

'Most of my thoughts were about you. And besides, the sound of your voice might make me sleepy. . . .' John thought he caught an impish gleam in her eye. 'Your hair, for example, why do you keep it so short?' she asked.

He laughed gently. 'If you had seen me in April, you would not have said that, for it was as long as any cavalier's. If you really want to know, it is a habit I acquired from some Swedish officers in the Rhineland. They cut their hair once a year, at the beginning of the campaigning season. I can forget about it when I'm in the field, and by the time the winter comes I have enough to keep my head warm.' He shrugged. 'So there you have it – the story of my hair.'

'Tell me the story of yourself.'

He seemed surprised by this, but Kate was so insistent that he continued.

'If you insist, though there is little enough to tell. Let me see. . . . Well, I was born in 1614, my father is a lawyer in Ely. I remember little about my mother; she died when I was only four years old, when Gwen was born. My father tells me she was a gentle, saintly woman. He never remarried. I went to the grammar school, I was a good student and I was much influenced by the masters at that place. So much so that I wanted to enter the ministry. My father had other ideas, though. I was sent to Cambridge to read law. I found it interesting enough – but I was always in trouble for attending theology classes. I became passionately interested in the cause of the Protestants in Europe. I was, like so many others, incensed that the King was doing nothing to aid our brothers in the Empire and the Low Countries. So, when I finished my studies, my father sent me down to London to finish my education with a barrister there. I was given a sword to signify my status as a gentleman, a horse and quite a reasonable sum of money for my upkeep in London. As soon as I arrived I sold the horse, got a cutler to sharpen the sword and boarded the first ship that would take me to Amsterdam. I wrote to my father from the Low Countries. He was angry at the time, but since I came home, when this war broke out, he has accepted me again.

'The war in Europe was a series of long drawn-out sieges which drained the soul. I met Jack and the others at Breda; we were formed together as a single company from two which had been reduced to half strength by plague. For five years we went from siege to bloody siege across a countryside which had been destroyed by more than twenty years of war.

'When we got back to England, looking like scare-crows, our eyes sunken and faraway looking, the first battle at Edgehill had just been fought. The King was coming down to take London. We were sent off to raise a company in the Reading area. The last few years have been a series of skirmishes and small battles – like today.'

'Was today's battle so small a thing, John?'

'Compared to those on the continent – very small. And very gentlemanly fought, too. Waller and Hopton – the opposing generals – are the best of friends, fought together in the Rhineland at the start of the war there. Many good men died on that field today – and Sir Ralph was allowed to leave the field in good order. I swear, Kate, if we carry on in this fashion, this war will last forever. . . .'

'John . . .' she interrupted.

'I know, I am straying from the point. What else would you have me tell you?'

'Well, for one thing, I do not really know if I am in the company of a single or a married man.'

John laughed quietly. 'If you take me for any kind of gentleman, then I would not be lying here with your head in my hand – in a state of *déshabillé* – if I were married,

Kate. No, I am indeed a single man, I always have been. I've had little time for women in my life, though I was betrothed once, when I was very young.'

Kate's eyes lit up, she smiled gleefully and snuggled up to his arm. 'Go on, John. What was she like . . . your betrothed?'

'Well, this was another part of my reason for going abroad. She was a nice enough girl from a good family – needless to say her father was also a lawyer in Ely. We went to the same church. Our backgrounds were very similar. My father thought us an excellent match and we were to have been wed when I returned from London. I wrote to her from Amsterdam at the same time as I wrote to my father.'

'You scoundrel! And is this poor girl still waiting for you?'

'God, no. About a year later I got a letter from Gwen, my first news from home. She had married a slightly older, well-established lawyer in Ely. Very happy, I would imagine.' His eyes kindled in the firelight.

'What was her name?'

'Her name?'

'Yes.'

'Her name was . . . Bessie.'

'Pah! Bessie Barnard – the name has quite a ring to it!' She was quite beside herself with mirth. John laughed too, but quietly, all the time his gaze was fixed on the fire.

'No, I suppose it wouldn't have been so good a name – not like Katherine Barnard, for example. . . .'

Kate stopped laughing instantly. 'What did you say?'

'Oh, nothing,' he teased, though his eyes remained serious.

'I heard you – you said Katherine Barnard – admit it!' She pushed his bare chest.

'I was trying out the sound of it,' he replied. 'Besides there are many girls called Katherine – I might be talking about somebody else.'

'No you weren't, you were talking. . . .' Her voice trailed off as he turned his gaze to her.

'I was talking about you,' he said, simply.

For a long moment there was silence, the fire crackled. Kate could feel her heart beating, so very fast. She struggled to master her voice. 'What did you mean by it?'

'I meant that I would marry you and make you my wife. That is, if you were willing and you were free – and could stand to be a captain's lady.'

'It's not a very romantic proposal, is it?' she whispered.

'I'm not a very romantic person – though I think I'm the better man for that.'

Kate drew away from him and stood up. Her limbs, her whole body was shaking.

'I don't know what to say, John. Can you wait for my answer until morning?'

'Yes, if I must, then I will wait.'

'Then I will bid you goodnight, John.'

'Goodnight, Kate.'

It seemed to take an eternity to cross the room to the door. When she reached it, she laid her hand on the latch and stopped. Tears welled up in her eyes.

'John,' she whispered, 'do you love me?'

His soft voice came out of the darkness. 'Yes, Kate, I love you. More than anyone or anything I have ever known. . . .'

'Then God help us, John, for I love you too.'

He could hear her nightdress rustle as she returned across the room to him. She knelt down on the cushions and, taking his head in both her hands, she kissed him slowly and tenderly. At first she could feel his body tense, then slowly, gradually it relaxed as he returned her kiss. When they had stopped, she looked into his eyes, which were wide open and very blue: 'Like a little boy,' she thought. He blinked twice and smiled uncertainly.

'Kate?' he whispered hoarsely.

'Yes, John?'

'I take it that was your answer?'

'Yes, John.'

'And I do not have to wait until morning?'

She shook her head and smiled. 'If you will suffer an Irish wife then I will be happy to be a captain's lady.'

'What an unholy alliance we'll make.

'I don't really care, do you?'

'Not in the slightest.'

They kissed again and held each other tight for what seemed like a very long time. Then John held her out at arms' length and spoke in his mockingly serious tone. 'Though this is the happiest night of my life and the sweetest and the tenderest, still we have a long hard ride ahead of us, at the end of which I must make a report before the House of Commons and you must meet your future sister-in-law; and I would rather you were awake when you met her. It makes a better impression.'

'You are unfair, John. I was so warm and comfortable there. If this is a taste of what our life together will be like . . . then I want to reconsider.'

'Too late, much too late, my Katherine . . . I would never let you go back on your word, being a woman of good birth and station . . . though not clearly so – at the moment. . . .'

'What do you mean?'

'In a few hours the innkeeper and his wife will be about. And if they find you here then you'll be a ruined woman.' He considered this for a moment. 'I am not sure that I would like the idea of marrying a ruined woman, so off you go.'

'Ah, so the only way I can escape from your clutches is by the destruction of my reputation?'

He nodded.

'Then, it seems you give me little choice.'

Four

Kate swayed in the saddle as another wave of drowsiness swept over her. The afternoon was hot and sultry, mosquitos filled the air as they neared the river. John put out his hand to steady her.

'I've a mind that you hardly slept at all last night,' he commented.

She nodded meekly and attempted a half smile. 'I blame you though, filling a poor girl's mind with such wild ideas. How could I have slept after that?'

He poured out some water on to a white cotton cloth, which he handed over to her. 'Here, put this on the back of your neck, it will serve to revive you. We still have a long way to go and we cannot stop now. We tarried over-long at Kingston.'

Kate caught her breath as the water ran down her back. The shock of it brought her back to her senses.

'Tarried over-long? We were there barely a half-hour and that time we spent finding fresh horses. It was hardly what I would call restful. And on the subject of rest, which I must admit is very high on my list of priorities at the moment, you seem to be fresh as a daisy – indeed I would describe you as being positively cheerful, Master Barnard.'

He glanced across at her. 'I must admit, after you left me I slept like a baby. I was overcome by happiness and relief.'

'Relief?'

'Of course, what if you had refused me? If you had

made me wait for your answer then you would have seen a very different John Barnard. I would have been insufferable.'

'Even more insufferable than you are now? I don't think I can abide this merriment. In truth, I would have preferred it if you had kept your proposal to yourself. At least I might have slept last night.'

'You are a heartless woman, Kate. You would have made me suffer all through the night?'

'Better that you go sleepless last night than I endure misery this day.'

John's manner became solicitous, almost caring – Kate could tell he was mocking her. 'Katherine, my darling; I cannot believe that you resent my sincere and heartfelt expression of love?'

'John, the most sincere expression of love that you could show me at the moment would be a few moments respite from the back of this horse.'

'Very well. If we pick up the pace for a while – until we reach Clapham – we can put the horses out to field there for another half-hour. Half an hour, but no longer, understand?'

'So long as it is a half-hour of unmitigated rest?'

He nodded.

'Then I take back all I have just said and I will marry you.'

Kate was glad of the sleep she had taken at Clapham. She had to keep her wits about her as they forced their way through the press of people. They were approaching London Bridge and the crowds seemed to be milling about without any clear pattern or semblance of order. If she had thought the day was hot when they had been out in the open, it was naught compared to the still stifling air in the city. Her father had kept an engraving of the city on the wall of his study. It had looked so serene and majestic – it did not prepare one for the smell and the noise of the place.

The commander of the fort which guarded the gate

had provided them with an escort of four riders, two before them and two behind. One of them had a bugle which he blew frequently, every time the crowd ahead failed to allow them passage. Though they were moving fairly slowly, sometimes the people failed to get out of the way. Kate closed her eyes as it seemed they would be ridden down. Then at the last moment they would move aside and carry on about their business as though nothing had happened.

She called across to John. 'How can they live like this?'

'It's madness, isn't it? But this is London, quite unlike anywhere else in the country. It's worse since the war started; more folk stay within the walls nowadays.'

'If I have to stay here I shall go mad!'

'Fear not, Chelsea is outside the fortifications – you'll find some sanity there.'

After the bridge the crowds thinned and they were able to make better time. They rode along beside the river – what she could see of it through the wall of ships and warehouses which lined its banks. So many people, so much trade and commerce. There must be more wealth in this one city than in the rest of England put together, she thought.

The Palace of Westminster loomed large before them. To the right the twin towers of Westminster Abbey overshadowed them. They were admitted without question by the guards on the gates and they dismounted in the courtyard. John saluted the captain of the guard and briefly explained his business. He called Kate forward.

'Captain, this is Mistress Katherine Butler. I am escorting her to my sister's house in Chelsea Fields. I would be greatly in your debt if you would entertain her whilst I make my report. We have ridden hard and slept little since we were at Alresford.'

'It would be an honour and a pleasure to accommodate a lady of such fortitude,' he replied, graciously. 'What is my lady's pleasure?'

John took her hand and kissed it as he took his leave of her. She was amazed! He had actually kissed her hand –

such familiarity in public was entirely out of character. As she watched him disappear down the passageway, she was speechless. The captain of the guard cleared his throat.

'I await your pleasure, Mistress Katherine.' He was so tall and he was bowing slightly, Kate had the feeling his head was hanging over her.

'In all honesty, all I have need of is a place to lay my head, if you would be so kind.' Kate thought suddenly, this is the centre of all information in the realm and, unabashed by her accent, she asked him for news of events in Ireland.

'In Ireland, Mistress?' The captain was taken aback.

'Yes, my family, my friends are still over there. My father was lately killed by the rebels.'

'I see. . . .' His mood changed. 'Then I am afraid the news I have for you is not good. Your people are confined to a narrow strip of land around the City of Dublin. At last report there was no fighting, but it is said that the King has entered negotiation with the rebels to send a papist army to help his cause in England. Such is their confidence. I fear the cause of your people is closely tied to our own, for if we fail then Ireland will be lost.'

'Can Parliament do nothing?'

'While we fight for our own survival there is little we can do to aid them. I am deeply sorry, Mistress, to bear you such sad tidings.'

Kate allowed herself to be taken to a small room. The captain apologized for its spartan appearance.

'It is not a cell, but one of a number of places where members can come to sleep when the House has debated long into the night. You will not be disturbed.'

She lay down on the bed. For a while her happiness with John was overshadowed by the thought of the suffering her people at home must be enduring. She remembered how families she had known from childhood had taken up arms against them. How could they have done that? Had we been so bad? Her thoughts returned to the image of the whole continent at war with itself. John had dismissed the battle of Alresford as a small thing, yet it was great and terrible to her: and her homeland was so small compared to England. She was staggered by man's capacity to harm his fellow man. Sleep came upon her like a soothing balm, deep and dreamless sleep.

It was already dark when she awoke. Someone had set a candle beside her. For a brief moment she had thought again she was back at Chalfcombe. This was just such a room as she had slept in after she had been beaten and put to work. She tried to think how long it was since she had left there and was surprised to discover that this was only the fourth day since then. So much had changed, her whole life had turned around.

'Barnard is still talking,' the captain of the guard informed her when she found him. 'Would you like to see him?' he asked in hushed tones. Kate nodded.

'You must assure me that you carry no weapons and that you will not utter a sound.'

She nodded again and he led her along a twisting, turning passageway and up a narrow spiral staircase. At the top was a single trooper, peering through a tiny window. The captain whispered to her, 'See, we not only guard them from dangers without, we must be vigilant for peril from within. You must never tell anyone about this place – not even your captain.'

With that he ordered the trooper to stand back and Kate took his place at the window. She was looking down on a vaulted hall. She was struck by how small it was. It was lined on either side by tiers of benches; and though there were about 200 men seated there, the majority of seats were empty.

Their attention was focused on a single figure who stood alone in their midst. For the most part they listened in silence. From time to time there were murmurs of assent or disapproval, but still they listened. With a start Kate realized that the solitary figure was John. He had his back to her and she could not make out what he was saying, but she could hear the calm, measured tone he used to address the solemn heads which were nodding slowly at all he had to say. She was fascinated and flushed with pride for him. She could have stayed in that cramped and narrow place until the end, but the captain of the guard touched her gently on the arm and motioned for them to leave.

As they walked back to the guardroom, the captain spoke softly to her. 'He talks well, your captain. I was listening to him from behind the Speaker's chair. He has subtly turned his report on the battle into a case for a reform of the army. He is very brave; his appeal has met with considerable approval, but there will be many there who will not relish his words. . . .'

'Those who have reservations about the war?' she replied.

'Quite so, but I would advise you to keep your opinions to yourself. There are many plots and agendas which circulate in this place . . . undercurrents if you like. Be wary, Mistress Katherine. He has placed himself on the national stage with this speech. If he should fall – the landing will be very hard indeed.'

'Your words disturb me, Captain.' Kate shuddered at their hidden menace.

'That is their intention.'

'Then, why are you telling me this?'

'Because I admire what he is doing and I agree with what he says. He could do a great deal of good. I cannot approach him openly, but I sought to warn him of his peril. And if I am confronted I can deny this conversation ever happened.'

It was nearly ten o'clock and Kate was beginning to become anxious as the guard was changing; still there was no sign of John. Then, as if some flood gate was opened, a great crowd of men issued from the building. Most of them seemed not to notice her, though some inclined their heads gravely as they passed. Then they were gone and Kate was alone again. She peered down the passageway, but it was empty.

She was about to return to the guardroom when she finally saw him emerge from the gloom, walking slowly toward her. He looked very pale – and not too steady on his feet. He smiled as he saw her and motioned for her to come to him. He sat down heavily on a bench and massaged his face with his hands. When she reached him he held out his hand to her. He looked up; his eyes took a while to focus, then he smiled widely at her. His voice was very thin and hoarse.

'It must be nearly ten o'clock . . . what time did I go into the chamber?' he asked.

'About four o'clock,' she replied simply.

'God, I've been talking for nearly six hours. It is no wonder my voice is nearly broken.' He paused a moment. 'Well, the die is cast, Kate. My fate is in the hands of Parliament now.'

'The captain of the guard told me; he was listening; he admired what you said.'

'Did he? I think not that he was alone in his approval of the speech – but I am unsure how many approved of the speaker.'

Kate sat down beside him. They stared into the gloom together.

'Why did you do it?'

'Why did I not just give my report and go? In God's name, I know not. I suppose I realized that this would be the only chance I would ever have to force the people who matter to listen. I imagine I shall be a marked man henceforth. I am sorry, I do not make a very good protector. I trust you are not too disappointed in me?'

'I would have been more disappointed if you had let the opportunity pass and you said nothing for fear of my opinion. I watched you, you know, from a secret window – the captain told me not to tell you, but I did not give my word, so I can tell you. I was so proud. I could not hear what you were saying, but I could see that they were all listening.'

'Who knows? I might have done some good after all.' He stood up and helped Kate to her feet. 'We had better leave, we would not want to be locked in here and we had better get to Gwen's house before midnight as she knows not that we are coming. Besides, the sooner we get away from this place the better I shall feel.'

They were stopped by the guards at Chelsea Turnpike Gate, but they were allowed to pass with few words. Though there were still many houses beyond the city walls, they could see the countryside open up beyond. There was a harvest moon which hung low over the horizon, illuminating the landscape. Everything seemed very bright after the darkness of the city. John discarded his torch. His horse, which had been troubled by the smoke and flames, quickly settled. He heaved a sigh of relief.

'I think I am as glad as this nag to be out in the open again. I never feel happy in London, particularly at night,' he confessed.

Kate laughed quietly. 'I find it hard to believe that a big, bold soldier like you would be worried in London.'

'Not worried, more ill at ease. You see the countryside I grew up in was all open fenland; the air is different, the noises are different. You can breathe there. And Ely is such a small place, where one knows everybody. Yes, on the whole I suppose London does worry me. I cannot relax there. I am always on my guard.'

He stretched in the saddle and smiled across at her. Kate eyed him dubiously.

'I would have been more uneasy myself had I known your mind.'

'I would not have told you whilst we were still within the walls.'

The house was asleep when they arrived. It was, as John had described it, a largish place; it stood alone in its own grounds which ran down to the river. She could not make out much detail, but she thought it was almost certainly a new house. John noticed her admiring look.

'Gwen married well,' he said, simply.

As they dismounted a light appeared at one of the attic windows.

'That is a mercy, one of the servants must have heard our approach. I was concerned that we would rouse the whole house if I had needed to knock,' he whispered. His manner became confidential. 'Gwen is a good girl; she is kindly and cheerful, I know you and she will be friends. But if she is disturbed from her bed she becomes an entirely different creature.'

The door opened slightly and a man's face appeared.

'Who's there at this hour?' he demanded.

'Captain Barnard, and a lady. Open the door, Dodington, before your mistress hears us.'

With that, the door opened and Dodington ushered them in.

Kate was roused from her sleep by a flood of light.

'Good morning, Mistress. My name is Ruth, I am to attend to you. Lady Nevers has sent some fresh clothing from her own wardrobe as the captain says that you are about the same size. They await you in the garden.'

'Lady Nevers?'

'Yes,' Mistress, Lady Gwendoline Nevers, the lady of the house.'

Kate groaned and buried her head under the sheets. John had duped her again. 'My little sister, Gwen' he called her . . . 'she's a good girl' he had said. Her whole image crumbled with just two words: Lady Nevers.

'I must find an opportunity to be revenged on him,' she said to herself.

'I beg your pardon, Mistress?'

'Oh nothing. I shall be up in a moment.'

Lady Nevers and her brother were taking breakfast in the garden. They both stood as Kate approached. She curtsied awkwardly.

'Lady Nevers. . . .'

'Oh, I'll have none of that, Kate – may I call you Kate?' Before she could reply she had taken her by the hand and led her to the table. John bowed.

'Good morning, Kate. May I introduce you to my sister Gwen.' He waited for the ladies, then seated himself at the table. Kate noticed with disappointment that he was out of kicking range. . . . There was something different about him. It took her a while and then she realized.

'Why, John, you are out of uniform!'

'My fault, Kate,' Gwen replied. 'I will not suffer men in uniform in this house. Poor Michael has to change before I let him over the threshold.' She took Kate's hand in hers once more. 'Now, I'll have none of this "Lady Nevers" nonsense. It is a troublesome title, which I only use to impress people I dislike or if I want to put someone in their place. To my friends I am Gwen. You will find that John still calls me dumpling. . . .' – she shot an angry glance at him – '. . . I was very fat as a child, you see. Anyway, I dislike the term and only tolerate it from him because I love him – I only wish he would show me enough love to refrain from it.'

Kate sensed immediately that in Gwen she had an ally.

'Yes,' she replied, 'he can be most infuriating at times.'

'Oh, I am so glad we are of one mind.' She smiled gleefully. 'I am sure we can make things quite difficult for him whilst he is with us.'

John had gone off to play with his young nephew, Stephen, when Gwen's manner became more serious.

'I am glad you slept late this morning, Kate. It gave John and I a chance to talk. I am sure you would not be surprised to learn that most of our discourse concerned you.'

'How much did he tell you, I wonder?'

'We started with Fitzmaurice.'

'Then he has probably told you everything.' Kate said, sadly.

'I am glad that he did. After all, it is only right. We can have no secrets if we are to be sisters.'

'Then he has told you everything.' Kate's face brightened.

They smiled at one another, then Gwen's manner became grave. Kate thought how similar she was to her brother; they were both disposed to laughter, but beneath that they were both very serious people.

'I find Fitzmaurice a deeply sinister character. . . .'

'You know him?'

'Unfortunately, yes. He is a distant relative of Michael's – not distant enough, I would say. I was sorry when I heard about Antonia, I liked her. But she was surely not much older than me, and certainly no older than John. How did she die?'

'I have no idea. All the doctors could say was that she passed away quietly in her sleep.'

'I would not be surprised if he had killed her himself.'

'That is a terrible thing to say!'

'No more terrible than that which he would have done to you, Kate. We must be very wary of that man.'

'Does he come here?' Kate asked with alarm.

'Sometimes . . . not often. Michael knows how I feel about him. But he moves in many circles, both here and at the King's court at Oxford. It is conceivable that we might encounter him at some point.'

Though it was a warm morning, Kate shuddered. Gwen looked on with a sympathetic eye.

'In the meantime, we have more important things to discuss. John has offered you his hand and you have accepted him. Well, he is no fool and he has never offered himself to any other woman. He does not undertake anything lightly.'

'He told me about a girl called Bessic,' Kate interrupted.

'Bessie!' Gwen laughed. 'Oh, yes. Bessie.' She waved her hand, dismissively. 'Bessie was father's idea. In truth, Kate, you would have died laughing if you had seen him. Every Sunday, after church, father would drag him to her father's house. And he would go along dutifully and stand there as if he were made of wood, trying to make conversation – he was a very serious boy!'

When they had stopped laughing Gwen continued, 'Now, John is very good at asking leading questions, but I would wager that he has not mentioned such minor considerations as, for example, the naming of the day?' Her voice trailed off, inquisitively.

'Not a word,' Kate affirmed.

'Or seeking father's approval?'

Kate sighed. 'No. And that is, I must confess, something which I have been worried about. After all, though I am assuredly no scullion – I am equally not of the same stock as Mistress Bessie. . . .'

'Oh, you can rest assured on that matter, Kate. Father will bluster a bit, but he is a good man for all that. I remember he ranted at great length at the fate of the Irish colonists and how King Charles ignored their plight. He cannot object to having one of them in his family . . . and if he still demurs, then we will have to remind him that there is a little drop of Irish blood coursing in all our veins.'

'Is there really?'

'Oh, yes. It is a long way back – but it is there, nonetheless.'

John and Stephen were rowing a boat on the river and would be gone for some time, so Kate and Gwen were able to talk at great length on a myriad of subjects. Kate could not remember the last time she had talked so freely or so happily. The company of men was all very well for a time, but when their discourse was compared with that of a woman of a similar age and disposition, then men's talk seemed very dull and distant. Gwen noted, with some disapproval, that her own dress suited Kate better than it did herself. She asked her about her hair and was amazed to learn that John had been its architect. They talked about serious matters too, but somehow the perspective was more pragmatic than idealistic. It transpired that her husband was of a very similar disposition to her brother.

'I probably would not have married him if he was not, for John and I hold very similar opinions. But when those two come together – well, I often have to leave the room, they become so moribund about everything. But they seem to take delight in it, so I leave them to it.'

In very little time Kate became quite relaxed in Gwen's company. So much so, in fact, that she leant forward and her tone became conspiratorial. She told Gwen about how John had deceived her when he spoke about his sister and together they plotted their revenge on him. . . .

'Every time he comes here I contrive to make his life a misery. He knows that he will always be welcome here – but he also knows that there is always a price he has to pay.'

John had returned to Parliament at noon to report to the Army Commission. Many of the commissioners had heard his account the evening before, but they had returned to argue their own corners. Even those who had not been present seemed well appraised of what had passed. This was an entirely different assembly; matters which were debated in the Commons had already been decided on by the various committees and commissions of the House. It was in meetings such as this that the real struggle for power was conducted.

Ranged about him were about thirty men. Apart from the chairman, who sat directly opposite, there seemed to be no particular order of precedence, except that there seemed to be little discourse between those on the left and right. He recognized few faces there. Amongst those he did recognize was that of a man from his own area and background, but of an older generation: Oliver Cromwell, who sat in the middle of the group to John's right. After the chairman had called the meeting to order, it was he who spoke first. He apologized to all present that he had been unable to attend the previous evening's meeting, but that he had only arrived in London that morning. He begged leave to make a brief report on the recent Parliamentary victory at Long Marston in Yorkshire. John's eyes widened as the general's tale unfolded of tens of thousands of men ranged against each other and thousands of dead and wounded. He concluded that by God's grace, the north was now secured.

The commission now turned its attention to John's report. The battle at Alresford was a very small affair by comparison with events in the north, and John was surprised at the importance they accorded it. It was only when they came to question him afterwards that he realized this whole affair was being carefully managed. Practically all the questions came from the men to his right, those around Cromwell himself, although the general did not speak - instead, with every reply he glowered at those opposite him. The ensuing debate was centred on Sir William Waller's abilities as a general and the conduct of the Earl of Essex himself. As the debate became more heated, John stood up.

'Gentlemen, this discourse goes beyond that which I am qualified to hear. I must ask that you dismiss me.'

Though it was the chairman he addressed, it was Cromwell who replied.

'Captain . . . Barnard. You will be dismissed when we see fit to dismiss you.' He reflected a moment, but though he was silent no other man spoke. 'Yestereve,' he continued, 'you had the audacity to lecture the House on the conduct of war. Though,' he smiled, 'you had the subtlety not to make it appear so. I would suggest that you are of wit enough to remain in our company. In one respect, though, you are correct. We should not discuss the characters of your senior officers in your presence. In fact, such discourse is ultimately futile. The crux of the matter, gentlemen, is this: at Marston we outnumbered the royalists by more than three to two and yet Rupert nearly won the day; at Alresford we had our first taste of victory after many defeats in the south, yet Hopton is still allowed to leave the field with his army intact. How is this? Captain, you fought many years with our brothers on the continent, I believe. The Commission would welcome your . . . unreserved . . . opinion.'

So, this was it, John thought. Cromwell clearly knew that John's opinions would echo his own. He wondered how long Cromwell had actually been in London, if in fact Kate had been the only one who had secretly looked down on him the night before. He was cornered now – there was nothing he could do but to speak his mind.

'The King's armies are smaller than ours and, on the whole, of inferior equipment. Yet they range at will, particularly in the south, scoring victory after victory. Our own forces lumber about the country, paralysed by the indecision of our commanders. The royalists have no doubt as to the justification of their cause. We are rebels and traitors and as such we should be put to the sword. Our own case is more equivocal. As the Earl of Manchester tells us, though we may beat the King ninety-nine times yet still he is King – and we are still traitors.'

He paused to summon his thoughts. The silence was palpable.

'But we have started this thing. Thousands of Englishmen have died and our country is being laid to waste. In many counties the harvest will not be gathered in this year and there will be famine this winter. Many of you will have seen on the continent what years of prolonged war can do to a country. It need not happen here. Yet if we continue to dance about the countryside, hiding our lack of will beneath a cloak of mock chivalry – hoping that when peace comes the King's wrath will not fall too heavily upon us – then there will be no end to this war and our land will be devastated.'

Cromwell nodded. For a moment John thought he had finished and he could leave, but the general had not finished with him.

'Very well, Captain. But what hope do we have of achieving peace?'

'I do not believe the King will come to an accommodation while he still has a single army left in the field. All his armies must be utterly defeated so that he has no hope of victory by force of arms,' John replied.

'And then?' Cromwell looked up from a paper he had been surveying; he gazed keenly at the young officer before him.

'What happens thereafter is the preserve of politicians, but at least the bloodshed will stop and Englishmen may go about their rightful business once more.' John met his gaze and did not falter.

Cromwell smiled and then laughed grimly. 'And,

of course, you are a soldier not a politician, Captain Barnard.'

He turned to the man at his side and whispered something. The man stood, bowed to the chairman and left. The debate turned to general military matters and after a few minutes of this, Cromwell nodded to the chairman who called the meeting to order. John was thanked for his report and given permission to leave. He sighed with relief as he closed the chamber door behind him. Waiting for him, just out of sight of the doorway was an armed guard. Their commander approached him.

'Captain Barnard, would you please come with me.'

As he was escorted along the corridors and passageways, John was reminded of one of his sergeant's sayings, 'Moths which fly too close to the flame are apt to get burned.' Well, he had certainly flown close to the flame today. He had been used and now he was about to be discarded. He thought with a sigh, at least Kate is safe with Gwen – the thought of them together made him smile, in spite of his fate.

He was led, not to the cells, but to one of the private apartments, where he was left and ordered to wait.

The walls of the room were lined with books and after a while he took to perusing their titles. One whole wall was given over to works of a religious nature, mostly non-conformist tracts, the other to books on common law and natural law. It was a collection, he thought, he would like to own himself. He recognized some of the texts from his days at university and was on the point of removing one to read, when the door opened. This, it seemed, was Cromwell's own private apartment.

'Ah yes. You were a student of law, Master Barnard. For my own part I was unable to finish my studies,' he said as he placed a large pile of papers on his desk. 'I apologize for the escort, but I find an excess of force is usually more persuasive than a lack of it – a point which I thought you would appreciate. Besides, I have never trusted the messengers in this place, they are paid too little for the lifestyle they clearly enjoy.'

He indicated that John should be seated.

'Firstly, I would like to thank you for your words this afternoon. They were. . .'

'The form of words you would have liked to have said yourself. . . .'

'But I am unable to. Quite.'

'You manipulated me in there, sir.'

'It is the sort of treatment you must expect if you make bold speeches in Parliament.' He sat down heavily in a chair by the window. 'I thought you spoke well, Captain. You spoke your mind and you were not afraid. Though you say you are a soldier, I think you would make a good politician.' And here am I, a politician, though people say I make quite a passable soldier.' He took up a piece of paper from the top of the pile. 'It says here that you are a captain of horse in the so-called Southern Association.'

'So-called, sir?'

'Yes, they are a rabble. An ill-disciplined county militia which will not go beyond its own frontiers. We would certainly have lost the north if we had not gone to the aid of Fairfax and Leven. Anyway, my opinion of them is not important now. Since you spoke so openly this afternoon then I will be candid with you now. I have need of good officers in my own force and I want you to join us. The army is changing – for the better – and the Eastern Association will be the instrument of that change. What do you say to this?'

John laughed. Cromwell looked at him with surprise.

'Forgive me sir, but when we returned from Europe we were *en route* to join you when we were waylaid to join the southerners. For myself, I would be happy to take your commission if I may bring my companions with me. If you are agreeable then we shall come up at the end of the campaigning season.'

'How many companions will you bring?'

'We are only five. There were forty of us at the outset, all those years ago. We have grown very close.'

'Then it would be churlish to separate you. I will

issue the orders, you will join us in November. We shall be very busy over the winter.'

'I intend to be very busy over the winter, sir.'

As he was about to leave, Cromwell called him back. 'Captain Barnard. It says here that you have family in my cavalry.'

'Yes, sir. Michael, Lord Nevers.'

'Ah, yes. Young Michael. Then I would be obliged if you would convey this to Lady Gwendoline.'

He held out a letter. John hesitated, then took it. He was relieved to see it was written in Michael's own hand.

When John returned he felt tired, but elated. He was surprised to find that the house was a hive of activity. All the servants were rushing around cleaning and polishing. He found Gwen and Kate in the kitchens, in conference with the cook. They seemed not to notice his arrival. Finally, the cook coughed and pointed to him. They both looked up.

'Oh, hello John. Gwen and I are preparing the meal for this evening. How did you fare at Parliament today?' Kate asked, nonchalantly.

He was bemused. He hardly knew where to start. He remembered the letter, which he held out to Gwen. 'General Cromwell asked me to give this to you. It is from Michael.' He hoped that the mention of the general's name would spark some interest, but he was wrong.

'Oh, a letter from Michael,' cried Gwen. 'How splendid, two letters in one day!'

She snatched the packet from him, breaking the seal and reading the contents avidly.

'Good news. Michael has distinguished himself in a battle in Yorkshire and the general has promoted him to captain – he is just the same as you now, John. He asks after everybody and he hopes to be home in the autumn.'

She folded the letter away and placed it in her pocket. She and Kate returned their attention to their work, ignoring him. He felt very awkward. He wanted to tell them about the events of the afternoon, but he was unable to think of a way to gain their attention.

'Two letters?' he ventured.

'Pardon, John?' Gwen replied, innocently.

'You said two letters.'

'Oh, yes. So I did,' Gwen said without looking up.

'Who was the second one from?'

She rose. Kate's eyes remained firmly fixed on the lists in front of her.

'Yes, we had a letter from father. I would show it to you, but it has some things of a . . . personal nature in it. Anyway, it is a damnable thing, the post. It was written two weeks ago – two weeks!'

'Yes, but that is not unusual.'

'Not unusual, but it is most inconvenient. He says he is coming up to London. John – he says he will arrive tonight.'

'Tonight?' he echoed as he felt the blood drain from his face.

'Yes, tonight. Surely, you do not think I would have the house in uproar just for your homecoming?'

'Oh, my God. Oh, Kate.' John's face flushed as the blood returned to it.

She looked up. 'Yes, John?'

'I had not planned on seeing him for at least a couple of months. I was going to write to him. What can we do, we shall have to leave.'

'Do not be ridiculous, John. He will be bound to find out – what will he say then? You will just have to face him,' Gwen snapped.

'Surely he will be pleased at the news?' Kate added.

'But of course,' he stammered. 'My God. . . .'

Both women looked at him quizzically. 'You are in a very blasphemous mood, brother dear.'

'A ring. We do not have a ring . . . Gwen?' He looked at her imploringly.

'I am sorry, John, I have nothing that will suffice, save my own – and he knows that.'

'What shall I do?'

'Go and buy one, foolish boy. You are in London, the centre of the gem trade, there are hundreds of places. Kate, give John the ring you are wearing so he can take the size.'

Kate obeyed, and handed it to him. 'You know, you need not do this,' she said. 'I do not need any token – your love is enough.'

'It might be enough for you, Kate, but we have to convince our father that my brother is serious in his intentions – and that means a ring. Now off you go John.' She turned him around and pushed him out of the door. 'And mind you get a good one!' she called after him.

They heard him ride off at a great pace. Gwen turned to Kate.

'It never fails . . .' she said, smiling.

'I almost wish your father was coming,' Kate replied.

They laughed so much, even the cook joined in.

The next few days passed very much as John had predicted. Every evening he returned from Parliament exhausted, but elated. His proposals for reform were gaining support from many important parliamentarians. Still, he did not delude himself that the credit for this success was his alone. Behind the scenes Cromwell and his supporters were hard at work discrediting those commanders whose half-heartedness was prolonging the war.

For Kate, life at Chelsea seemed increasingly pleasurable. It was the height of summer and she spent most of her time in the garden with Gwen and little Stephen, who was the nicest of boys – though inclined to be a little too adventurous, particularly when he stole down to the river. The only thing which seemed to irritate her was the ring which John had given her. It was not its appearance, for it was assuredly a beautiful thing: a single diamond set on a simple band. It was the wearing of it which bothered her. All her life that finger had remained unadorned – waiting for just such a token of love as this to occupy it. Now her hand felt heavy and ill-balanced. She found herself playing with it and catching it on all manner of things. Often it would infuriate her so that she would make to remove it – then she would remember the moment when John placed it there. Before she had accused him of being unromantic and in truth she had been right. Romance was too light a sentiment to describe the depth and sincerity of feeling he had displayed at that moment. He had pledged her his life and his soul 'until death do us enjoin forever: for what is eternity if we cannot be together. If I cannot share it with you then I will have none of it.' Then he kissed her with such tenderness. . . .

Five

When the first week had passed Gwen came to her in her bedroom, before Ruth had even come to open the curtains. She threw herself down on the bed and lay on the covers with her head propped up in her hand.

'Now then, sister. I must confess to being frankly sickened to see you fill each of my dresses so much better than I do myself, so I have come to a decision.'

'And what might that be?' Kate asked, dragging herself up on to the pillows and rubbing the sleep from her eyes.

'Today we are going up to town. I have a dressmaker in Of Street. . . .'

'What Street?'

Gwen grimaced slightly. 'Yes, "Of Street" . . . bizarre name.' She waved her hand in her characteristically dismissive gesture. 'It was the caprice of the late King James. He desired to read the name of his favourite "George Villiers, Duke of Buckingham" when he surveyed the map of London. The rest are quite acceptable, but "Of Street" . . . anyway, that is where my dressmaker is and that is where we are going.'

Before Kate could object, Gwen was already up and walking out of the door.

'You will have to hurry, the coach is already waiting.'

They were greeted at the door and ushered into a reception room. Presently, they were joined by a slim, elegant woman in early middle age who took Gwen's offered hand as she entered.

'Now, Gwen. I did not expect to see you today. I thought you were coming next month. What brings you up to town today? I know you take little pleasure in your fittings. . . .'

'I have not come for myself, Grace. May I introduce Kate Butler, my brother's intended and my dearest companion.'

She extended the same greeting to Kate.

'Grace is the best dressmaker in London.'

'The only one you will come to, you mean.'

'Very well, that is true. All the others seem to fuss around and do nothing. Grace knows my preferences and my dimensions – and I trust her not to try to foist something inappropriate on me. Grace, Kate here is of the same proportions as myself and all her stuff is of the Dublin fashion. . . .'

Kate smiled at the white lie that neatly concealed the true reason for their coming.

'You must have some stuff you were preparing for me? We want her to look the part of an English lady.'

Grace nodded her head and looked up and down, as if appraising Kate's form. 'Yes, yes. We have some things – they were intended for you when you came next month. You will have to delay your next visit so that we can be ready for you – but I am sure that you will not object to that?'

'That would suit me admirably.' Gwen smiled sweetly.

The dressmaker disappeared into another room and returned with some assistants who bore about a dozen frocks and gowns. Most of them, though they were beautifully made, were clearly designed for daily wear. The last four though, were wrought of splendid silks and velvets and were meant for special occasions. They were masterpieces of the dressmaker's art.

'Gwen, I cannot accept these. The others I will gladly take for I can make restitution for them when I have contacted my family in Ireland. But these . . . I could not deny you the opportunity of being the first to be seen in them.'

'They are indeed beautiful . . .' Gwen agreed.

There was a long silence which was finally broken by the author of the gowns herself, who laughed at their predicament. 'The love you clearly bear one another will probably keep us here all day, and still you will have made no decision. So, if you will allow me to make this Judgment of Paris?'

The two younger women agreed at once, glad to have the decision taken from their hands.

'Good. I propose that you take two gowns each. I will decide on the first two for that choice is simple. This,' she said, as she lifted up a gown of powder-blue silk, 'would not have suited your colouring, Mistress Kate.' She handed it to Gwen.

'Oh, good,' Lady Nevers confessed, 'that was the one I was admiring most.'

'Whilst this deep-green velvet would suit you better.'

Kate took it and held it up to her. It was just the sort of thing she would have had made for herself.

'The other two I leave for you to choose between yourselves, for they will suit each of you equally well.'

Kate looked across at Gwen. 'You first.'

'No, you,' Gwen replied.

Again, there was silence. Grace shook her head. 'You are both insufferable. Very well, I will count to three and you will each point to a dress. If you choose the same one then I will have that copied in a different colour and you will each have one. Are you ready?'

On the count of three their arms crossed as they pointed at different gowns.

'You have excellent taste, sister,' Gwen laughed.

'And you . . . sister.' It was the first time Kate had allowed herself to use that term, but now it seemed quite natural.

John would return late that night and Stephen was already in bed. Kate and Gwen sat out in the garden and watched the last rays of the sun shimmering on the slow-moving waters of the Thames. Kate took Gwen's hand.

'You know, I was in earnest when I said that I would repay you for the things you bought today. I asked Grace to send me a record of their cost and when I have contacted my family in Ireland, I will be able to pay you back.'

'Please, Kate. There should be no talk of money between us, though I respect you for your offer – let us call it my betrothal gift to you. Soon you will be a Barnard proper and that will be repayment enough for me. Until now I have lived my life among men: father, John, Michael, Stephen and all their friends – God, even the dog is male . . . you cannot imagine how pleased I am that you are here.'

'Still, I must find out what is happening to my family. It is not merely a question of money and there is really no one close left since my father died; some aunts and uncles, cousins. But still they are my own kin and I would know how they are faring if only for my peace of mind.'

The sun was gone now, though the sky was still bright in the west and the air was warm. They walked down to the riverbank. Gwen had been quiet for a while, as if considering the problem.

'Very well. It pains me that you should be thus distressed and it is only right that you should know the fate of your people – and indeed your own standing under the law.'

'What do you mean by that, sister?' Kate asked.

'Simply this: since your father's passing and, as you say, having no close relatives, would you not stand to inherit his estate?'

'An estate which is in the hands of rebels. Kilerin is a substantial place, but it could be the whole of Ireland for all the good it would do me – it might as well be on the moon. . . .'

'An estate is not just land, Kate. Your father will have had investments and other property.'

'I would imagine so, for we were assuredly no paupers.'

'And you are his sole heir?'

'Yes, he always told me that I would inherit everything when he died. I used to laugh at him when he said that. I told him not to be so foolish . . . that he would live forever. I always thought that he would.'

She paused, lost in the memory of the life she had lost. 'I loved him so, Gwen. And now I know not even where he lies. . . .'

Gwen took her in her arms. Kate was racked by sobbing, but she could not cry. She felt too empty for tears. They stayed together for some time, then Gwen composed herself and dabbed her eyes.

'This will not do, sister. You must allow us to help you at least a little more. We shall go and see Mr Johnson. He takes care of all our family affairs. We will see what he can do.'

Two days later they received a message from the lawyer, indicating that he had some news for them and asking if they would attend his chambers that afternoon.

'The estate of William Butler, Master of Kilerin, you say?'

Mr Johnson took the spectacles from his nose and surveyed the two ladies before him. He smiled. In these troubled times he seldom found himself in such agreeable company. He was always pleased to see Lady Nevers, who was one of his favourite clients – so reassuringly familiar with the law.

But who was this other woman? Such a fair complexion and hair like a boy's? A most pleasing face, an honest face, he thought. He sighed: if only he were thirty years younger. He cleared his throat.

'I have had very little dealings with Irish estates in these last few years, although I have done much work on the transfer of assets between Dublin and London – especially since the beginning of the rebellion there.'

'But can you help us?' Gwen interjected.

He smiled again and nodded his head. 'I will always be

of service to you, Lady Nevers, and I have never failed you yet.'

'Your sense of humour is as poor as ever, Mr Johnson.'

He inclined his head, cleared his throat once more, and began. 'Since your message arrived the day before yesterday, I have been able to research into the matter. You are, I take it, Mistress Butler, daughter of the late Master of Kilerin?'

Kate nodded. 'I am.'

'Then I must compliment you, for your father was a very prudent man. He transferred many of his assets and holdings to England some three years past. Indeed, there is a letter of credit in your name with my colleague Edwin MacAulay – which, I note, you have not redeemed since your arrival.'

'I was not aware of it, sir. I was lodged with my uncle, Lord Fitzmaurice and he did not mention it.'

The lawyer's expression changed. 'Ah, yes, Lord Fitzmaurice . . . I was going to turn to him later, but since you have introduced him to the conversation . . .'

'What of him, Mr Johnson?' Kate interrupted. The very mention of his name was enough to put Kate on her guard.

'As I was about to say,' he resumed, 'Mr MacAulay has been the steward of your father's affairs for a number of years. It seems that two weeks past he received a message from Lord Fitzmaurice that you had absconded from his care, apparently in the company of a captain of horse. . . .'

'My brother, Mr Johnson.'

'Absconded! The effrontery of the man . . .' Kate fumed.

'Yes . . . indeed. It seems that his lordship is in London at the moment and has expressed a desire to see you, Mistress Butler. It seems that he has certain of your personal effects which you neglected to take with you when you left Chalfcombe. He appeared a most solicitous gentleman when I spoke with him this morning.'

'You spoke to him?' Kate's thoughts raced. 'What did he say?'

'He wanted you to know that he forgives you and that he rejoices in your safe delivery into the keeping of his beloved cousin, Lady Nevers.'

'Beloved cousin? The man knows no shame. Mr Johnson, what would you advise us to do?'

'Do? Well, firstly I would go to Mr MacAulay's, he lodges at the Temple. Redeem your letter of credit and make yourself known to him so that he can make over your father's assets to you. This might take quite a little time. In the interim, however, I would advise you to take up his lordship's kind offer of reconciliation. In all frankness, what harm can he do you?'

'What harm indeed?' Kate added grimly.

Outside, in the relative sanity of the street, Kate was white with rage.

'My God, Gwen. Is there no end to the villainy of the man?'

That evening, when John came home they related the tale of the day's events to him. At first he was as enraged as they were at Fitzmaurice's audacity.

'You should have let me burn his house to the ground when I first offered, Kate,' he commented wryly.

'It would have done no good, John. And I suppose I must meet him at some point – it might as well be when I am ready for him. The things he has in his keeping, though they are not valuable in themselves, are nonetheless dear to me.'

'Then shall I arrange with Mr Johnson for us to see him?' Gwen added.

'Nothing can be achieved by not seeing him,' Kate sighed.

'Then might I suggest this Saturday and that he should come here. We might as well meet him on our own ground. Besides, it will have to be soon – I will have to rejoin my company in the next few days. I would rather not leave you with this matter unresolved.'

Finally, it was agreed that they should see him on the Saturday, as John had suggested. Though they were no cowards, neither Kate nor Gwen relished the thought of meeting Fitzmaurice without him.

Gwen went up to bed early, leaving Kate and John alone together. John sat astride an armchair with his legs over the side and Kate on his lap. She put her hand up to his face, which was rough with early evening stubble, and gazed down into his eyes.

'Oh, John. You cannot imagine how much I fear this meeting. In all my worst dreams he has a leading role. I know it is unreasonable to be afraid. He cannot harm me now I am with you. But he will try to spin the truth, to make you and Gwen disbelieve me, and I could not bear to have you doubt me again.'

'Again? I have never doubted you. I merely required proofs of what my heart told me was true. You know, lying does not come easily to you – I could tell the first morning I met you that you were concealing the truth, but when you came to me that evening there was not a hint of falsehood in your tale.'

That night Kate teetered on the edge between sleeping and waking, where dreams become memories and memories return to life with a disturbing clarity. She was sitting before a mirror, combing the tangles from her hair. Over and under, again and again, repeating the motion. It was too long and thick to use a brush. Over and under, again and again, her scalp tingled and she stared at herself in the mirror, hypnotized by the rhythm. . . .

That morning she had been riding with Thomas. They had raced across the downs and the wind had swept his hat away. In the daylight his hair seemed more grey than usual – so strange that he should be that colour though he was not yet forty. In all other respects he was so vigorous and vital. He turned to her, smiling. His eyes so pale that they seemed to look through you. Not like John's. . . .

And now he was with her. He had taken her comb and the rhythm became more insistent. The comb disappeared and instead her hair moved to the command of his outstretched fingers, first of one hand then both. His hands were taut, his tendons stood out and his fingers bent back as they pulled away. Then they closed on her head. She was caught – unable to move – her body froze. She stared into the mirror. All she could see were her own eyes which filled the frame. She could feel his hands, closing ever tighter. She could hear his voice which held her mind.

'I shall have you, Katherine. I shall possess you and you will be mine . . . possess you and you will be mine . . . you will be mine. . . .'

'You will be mine . . .' she repeated. As she did so, the face in the mirror became his . . . the lips which spoke were his but the voice was her own. 'You will be mine. . . .'

'No!' she cried as she dragged herself from the world of dreams. But slowly, surely, the dark tendrils of sleep enfolded her. A woman's hand held the comb.

'He is such a fine man, the Lord Fitzmaurice . . . he would be a good catch for a girl like you. . . .'

She looked up and it was Antonia, her face grey, her eyes caked with earth. She screamed and ran away. The hunters were after her. She fell. This time she could not rise. The men loosened their belts as they came upon her. . . . They held her shoulders down. . . .

'Stop! Stop! No . . . oh no . . . oh John . . . John!'

'Wake up Kate. Wake up.'

Her shoulders were held, but the hands were his. He pulled her toward him. 'Kate, my darling Kate . . . I cannot keep the phantoms away, but while you are here with me you will always be safe.'

'Stay with me John, don't let me sleep alone.'

'I cannot, for whilst I may make light jests about keeping your reputation intact – still they are sincerely meant. But look, it is nearly morning. Get dressed and I will show you my favourite time of day.'

'Don't leave me John.'

'Then, with your permission, I will look out of the window whilst you dress.'

He led her down the stairs and into the garden. It was not yet quite first light. The sky was still grey and there were yet stars in the west. He took her down along the meads and watermeadows to a field where the mist still settled around the hollows.

'Wait a moment – stand still and listen. . . .'

She obeyed: at first there was nothing, she thought. Then, as her hearing became keener she heard the river in the distance behind her. Finally, she became aware of another sound.

'There is a sort of persistent rustling all around me, everywhere. . . .'

'Every blade of grass, every leaf. All of them opening, waking, preparing to greet the sun. It is the sound of the morning of the fourth day, before the creation of the birds and the beasts. This is the most magical time of all.' He put his arm around her and they walked together until the sun rose.

The clock on the mantelpiece began to chime the quarter-hour. Kate glanced nervously across at Gwen. Fitzmaurice was supposed to have arrived at two, it was now past five o'clock and still there was no sign of him. John had given up waiting in the parlour an hour ago and now he was playing out in the garden with Stephen. Kate fiddled with her ring.

'I think he arranged this meeting with no intention of coming just to torture me.'

'If he has not arrived by the half-hour, he will find the door locked in his. . . .' Her posture stiffened at the sound of a horse arriving at the canter. 'It seems that our visitor has finally arrived. Come, Kate. Let us receive him.'

Fitzmaurice was handing his riding gloves to Dodington as they came into the entrance hall. He glanced at them. In those first moments he was unable to disguise his disdain. Then, as he mastered himself, his face brightened. He smiled as he removed his hat, revealing a wolf's pelt of grey hair, and strode across the hall to meet them with outstretched arms.

'My dear Lady Nevers, my favourite cousin. I trust I find you in good health this afternoon?'

'Lord Fitzmaurice,' she replied, acidly, 'I am gratified by your sentiments, but the matter of my health this evening is not altogether pertinent to our business.'

Though his eyebrow flickered momentarily, the rest of his face betrayed no emotion. His pale eyes turned to the other woman.

'Dearest Katherine, it is the sun and the moon to me to see you thus safely delivered from your adventures.'

'No thanks to you, your lordship,' she replied, echoing her sister's tone.

His mouth tightened in a brief cypher of a smile. His eyes narrowed slightly as he encompassed the women opposite him.

'Do I detect the slightest chill in my welcome? Perhaps it is due to the lateness of my arrival, for which I must apologize profoundly, though I can offer adequate explanation.'

'Your reception would have been no warmer if you had arrived at noon,' Gwen replied, tersely.

'Very well, Gwendoline. . . .'

'I did not give you leave to be so familiar.'

'I rather think it is not a matter for you to be the judge.' He turned aside as though he were distracted. Kate recognized the gesture. It was the one which John had attempted at Farnham. Fitzmaurice was far more convincing.

'I am afraid that my earlier appointment has left me somewhat pressed for time. I must depart for Oxford very soon.'

'Can you cross the battle lines so easily?' Gwen taunted.

'I may go where I please in this kingdom.'

'In this Commonwealth, you mean.'

At this he smiled broadly, as if genuinely amused. 'I am grateful for your correction – it is a term to which I am only gradually becoming accustomed. Perhaps we should get on with the business at hand?'

The women parted to allow him access to the parlour,

though he insisted on their going before him. He waited for them to be seated, but remained standing. He did not wait for any further pleasantries.

'Katherine, I require you to return to Chalfcombe tomorrow.'

Kate was stunned by the statement. 'Are you insane? I would not go there though the Devil himself pursued me and it was the only safe haven left in the world.'

'You misunderstand me. I am not making a request. As your guardian I require your return.'

'My guardian? How dare you? You are no more my guardian than I am a child to be placed under your charge.'

'Katherine, I have in my possession a letter from your late father which places you under the protection of my house. It is a responsibility I will not lightly put aside.'

'You were happy to put it aside when you set your men on me. . . .'

'The huntsmen I sent to find you when you ran away. My sadness at your actions is matched only by my sadness at their loss. Whilst they were out vainly searching for you, they encountered a company of soldiers who mistook them for the enemy. I have ensured that their families are well provided for. If you had not run away, Kate, they would be alive today.'

Kate was stunned by this revelation. Surely, he could not have had them all killed? Yet he spoke now with such sincerity, such concern for their families; it was as though he had convinced himself that his story was true, and now he believed it implicitly. Here was a man unfettered by the rules of civilized society. He had enough power to behave exactly as he pleased and absolutely no conception of right and wrong. Both women were silent, aghast at the matter-of-fact way he had delivered this news.

The silence was broken by a noise behind them. John had entered through the french windows carrying Stephen on his shoulders. He lifted the child over his head and carried him to his mother, who held him close to her.

Stephen seemed confused by the tension in the room, he smiled uncertainly at Fitzmaurice, who returned his gesture with a look of such contempt that the child hid his face in his mother's bosom and started to cry. This seemed to irritate Fitzmaurice still further.

'Gwendoline, take your boy away. He does not know how to behave himself.'

'He knows better than you how to conduct himself,' she retorted as she comforted the boy.

'John, he wants to take me back to Chalfcombe – I will not go, I could never return to his house. . . .'

'I am afraid you have little choice in the matter,' Fitzmaurice replied, coldly, though his gaze was fixed on the other man. John came forward and placed his hand on Kate's shoulder. She placed her hand over his and held it tightly. John spoke in a quiet, restrained manner, though the underlying menace in his voice commanded everybody's attention. Kate had never heard him like this before.

'Lord Fitzmaurice, your presence here has disturbed the peace of this house. You have upset my sister, my nephew . . . and my betrothed.'

'Your betrothed! I had no idea . . . I will not allow it!' Fitzmaurice exclaimed.

John's tone remained quiet, unflustered by the outburst. 'I am afraid you have no choice in the matter,' he replied, stressing the word 'no'. He continued, 'I would have further discourse with you, but I believe you have vexed these gentlefolk enough. Let us go outside.'

'I will not fight you, Barnard. You are little more than a common soldier. A gentleman of quality would not sully his hands with the likes of you.'

John smiled at this. 'A gentleman of quality . . . it seems we have very different concepts of that term. To my mind a gentleman would never oppress those weaker than himself. So, you may be assured of your safety . . . here. Come, Lord Fitzmaurice, we have much to discuss.'

Though he seemed ill at ease, nevertheless Fitzmaurice followed him through the open windows and into the garden. John led him down toward the river, but Fitzmaurice would not go near the edge. Kate and Gwen watched from the parlour. John seemed to tower over the other man. His manner seemed calm and collected, whilst Fitzmaurice was animated – from time to time he shook his fist in rage. They could hear his raised voice though they could not distinctly hear his words. From this safe distance he seemed almost comical.

'It does not seem that your brother is having much success reasoning with him,' Kate observed.

Gwen smiled wickedly. 'I would not imagine for one moment that John is reasoning. If I know him at all, I might say he is issuing a series of threats. I wish I could hear what he is telling that vile man.'

They put their arms around each other in a comradely fashion. Presently, they felt themselves pushed apart as Stephen wriggled between them.

'Is Uncle John going to throw him into the river?' he asked innocently.

They seemed to be outside for ages. Gwen and Kate began to wonder if they would ever come in. Then, after nearly an hour, the men turned about and started walking back toward the house. The two women walked out to meet them. Fitzmaurice was the first to speak, though he did so with little grace.

'Katherine, it seems that I have underestimated the nature of your relationship with this . . . gentleman. After careful consideration I have decided to allow you to remain in the care of Lady Nevers – if she will give me her assurance of your safekeeping.'

Gwendoline curtsied deeply. 'You may be assured, your lordship, that it will be my great pleasure to be of such service to you.'

Fitzmaurice bowed stiffly and made to leave. He had not gone three paces when John called out to him, 'I believe you have forgotten something.'

He turned and addressed Kate, though he did not

look her directly in the eye. 'Your belongings will be delivered within the week. . . .'

John turned the screw a little further. 'There is another matter, Fitzmaurice.'

It seemed that Fitzmaurice's composure would break at any moment, but he managed to muster his self-control.

'The letter from your father to my late wife – I believe it is only . . . right and proper that I return it to you as I seem to have discharged my responsibility for you. It will be with your things.'

He bade them all good day and left. They all watched him go. When they heard his horse riding away they finally relaxed and went back to the parlour. John heaved a heavy sigh of relief. He bade Dodington bring a bottle of good wine even though the hour was yet early, and then slumped down into an armchair. When he did not volunteer the information the ladies so eagerly awaited, Kate and Gwen moved across and stood on either side of him.

'John,' Kate began, 'will you not tell us what passed between you?'

He smiled and indicated that they should be seated.

'It seems that your cousin keeps himself better informed than I had given him credit for. He was well appraised of all my comings and goings over the past couple of weeks. He knows, for example, about my commission to the Eastern Association even though it has not been issued yet. I wonder if he keeps spies at the Commons. . . .'

'Gwen said that you were probably threatening him.'

'Threaten Fitzmaurice, no . . . well, yes, I suppose I did really. I told him that, since we were going to return to patrol the Whitchurch area soon, my company would take advantage of his hospitality and winter at Chalfcombe. Soldiers are inclined to be a little careless – well, clumsy would be a better word – and a hundred of them lodged over a period of four, or even five months can be very clumsy indeed. The prospect did not seem to amuse his lordship. In fact, he practically blanched at the thought. . . .'

'More subtle than burning his house down . . .' Kate suggested.

'Yes, not quite so immediate, but the results would be just as satisfying in the end.' His manner became more serious. 'Fitzmaurice accepted all this because he knows that I am in the favour of General Cromwell. If he falls, or if the King returns to power, then things will not go so well for us. If we were not firmly bound to Cromwell before, make no mistake – we assuredly are now.'

A few days later, as he had promised, John returned to his company and so Kate and Gwen were left to their own devices. The next day Kate went to see Mr MacAulay to redeem her letter of credit. She was pleased to find that her father had amply provided for her and she was able to repay Gwen for the dresses, though she was only able to persuade her to accept payment for the two more elaborate gowns. Mr MacAulay was very helpful. It seemed that he and her father had been very close as younger men and already he knew a great deal about her. They talked at great length about her father, all his little foibles and eccentricities. Finally, their conversation became more businesslike. Mr MacAulay spoke about the provisions which her father had made in the last few years against just such an outcome. He had gone into meticulous detail, which was so like him, to ensure that Kate would be financially secure in the event of his death.

As the solicitor read out the careful instructions he had been given, Kate became more and more upset. These were her father's own words. He wrote in just the way he spoke and it was as though he was speaking now. It was as though he did not expect to survive the growing conflict at home, but that at all costs Kate should be safe.

'". . . you know as well as I, Edwin, how great was my loss when Ann left us. Little Kate is so much like her. Even now it catches me when she sometimes turns her head or says something in just the way that Ann would. She has her smile and the same way of mocking me when I have been foolish. Antonia says that if things go badly here, as I expect them to, then she will take her. I know that my life will be empty when she goes, but I cannot allow my own happiness to put her in peril. I will have to be content in the knowledge that she will be safe with my sister."'

MacAulay seemed unable to continue for a moment.

'There is so much sadness, Mistress Kate, and yet we carry on through adversities which we think would overcome us utterly. Even now a whole new life is opening up for you here in England – with people you would never have known, but for this unhappy turn of events. . . .'

'I must try to make the best I can with what I have been given. I should be grateful for the way things have transpired – but still I resent the loss. Who can say, I might have met John in the normal course of events . . . oh, I know, it is idle to speculate, but at the moment I cannot help it.'

'It is only natural, Mistress Kate. It will pass.'

'Mr MacAulay, it appears that I am, or soon will be, a woman of some means.'

The lawyer nodded sagaciously.

'Yet I am not at rest; I will not settle until I have found out how things are at home and more about my father. Will you help me, Mr MacAulay?'

'I would consider it my duty and my great privilege to do so. Of course, the vast majority of your wealth will be denied you whilst Kilerin is in the hands of the papists. But, as you say, you will be a woman of means at the very least. In the light of the love I bore your father it would be no less than my duty to do my best for you.'

Six

'How do I look?' Kate stood framed in the doorway. Gwen looked over her shoulder. Then, surprised by the transformation Kate had wrought, she turned around.

'Why, sister, you look beautiful.'

And indeed she did. The deep-green dress had many features which hearkened back to the last century. The high-winged collar ran neatly into the nape of her neck, then swept into a deep V which ended about her breast. At her throat, half hidden, Gwen noticed a silver choker, which briefly caught the light.

'What is that device you are wearing?' she asked.

Kate looked down and for a moment she smiled to herself. 'It is the Rose of Kilerin. The token of my house for many generations, and of the Masters of Kilerin for many centuries, before the Butlers ever came to Ireland.' She pulled her collar back. 'See, it is a Celtic rose. The forms of the petals are intertwined with the thorns of the stalk. My father always said that the man who tried to grasp this rose would suffer much pain.'

'It is a beautiful thing, nonetheless,' Gwen admitted.

They went downstairs together and Dodington placed their cloaks about them. The night air was cold and they hurried into the coach. Safely inside, they arranged themselves so that their gowns would not crease. Gwen tapped on the roof and the driver gently egged the horses on. They looked at each other and laughed.

'Jane will be so angry with us. We shall be famously late.'

Gwen was taking Kate to meet her closest friend, Lady Jane Winterton, who was having one of her 'small gatherings' at her London house. On the surface Gwen and Jane could not have been more different. Whilst Gwen had married above her station, Jane had married a man whom many described as being so far beneath her that it was impossible to imagine how they met. She had been one of the most famous heiresses of her day and young Colen – though he was an architect of great and growing repute in London, was considered to be a very poor match. Her family had insisted that, when they were married, he should take her name as his was so ignominious. Still, they lived blissfully together in their house in Suffolk, though the war had often taken him away to oversee the fortifications of many towns and cities friendly to the cause.

In spite of their circumstances, she and Gwen found that they had much in common. They had both married for love, and they shared a disdain for society, though she often pointed out that Gwen was the more fortunate.

'You are able to pick and choose whom you receive, whilst I must suffer the society I have been born into.'

Gwen knew that Jane would forgive her for being late, but not for making her suffer London society without a shoulder to laugh on.

They arrived so late that the other coachmen were dicing in their parties' carriages. Jane was not there to receive them, so they entered unannounced and made straight for the drinks. They were on their third glass of wine when their hostess finally tracked them down.

'Where in God's name have you been? I have had to suffer Heymann and his wretched wife for nearly an hour – can you imagine that? One day I shall make sure that you are cornered with them, then you will have some impression of how I suffered.' She closed her eyes tight and shook her head vigorously, as if to loosen the experience from her memory.

'An hour of livestock and bloodstock – do you know he compared me to a prize Hampshire saddleback? And not for a second did he realize the crassness of his remark. His wife – who would have borne the comparison – just nodded her head and applauded his wit. And not for an instant even bothered to close her flabby mouth whilst she was masticating away on a piece of pork which moved around her mouth as though it had a life of its own: it seemed like cannibalism to me. God, give me some wine before I am sick . . . I hold you responsible for this, Gwen. You could have been there to help me in my hour of need.'

The glass of wine had barely touched her lips before it was finished. She turned her attention from Gwen.

'You must be Kate. I have already heard a great deal about you. Gwen tells me that you had to dress as a trooper of her brother's company – that must have been very exciting. I must admit I envy women who have had adventures in their lives, my own seems so very dull by comparison. . . .'

Kate was not altogether sure how to take this woman. She seemed to talk without allowing herself time for breath, let alone time for thought.

'I suppose one might call my experiences of the past few weeks an adventure.' She looked very hard at this woman. The only thing which recommended her was that Gwen held her in great esteem. She looked again into her eyes and realized that Jane was testing her.

'Though when it comes to self-preservation, one does what one must – even if one finds it distasteful. I would surely not call it an adventure.'

Jane Winterton held her gaze for a moment, then smiled. 'It seems to me that many women would have made a great play of their experiences in such a situation.'

They nodded, in recognition of one another's privacy.

'You must excuse me, Kate. So often I am regaled by someone's embellishment of their own story, in an attempt to impress me. I grow very weary of it and thus I am always on my guard.' Jane sighed distractedly.

'Then you have probably missed out on the company of many good folk,' Kate replied, 'for if they are at all like me, then they would be affronted by your attitude.'

'I am sorry that you take it thus.' Jane's eyes narrowed.

'That you welcome me with mistrust? I find that uncommonly rude. . . .'

Gwen could see that the situation would soon get out of hand, so she moved between them. 'I think you are both being somewhat headstrong, and thus losing the possibility of making a good friendship. Come, it pains me to see my two best friends fall out at their first meeting. Please, for my sake, try to get on?'

The atmosphere was lightened as they both climbed down from their respective high horses, though neither of them could resist the opportunity gently to snipe at the other as the evening progressed.

Kate surveyed the people around her. There was something about the feel of this gathering which made her uneasy. It was difficult to place, but it was something about the people; they seemed to smile and laugh a great deal. It gradually dawned on her that they were smiling and laughing all the time. She noticed also that there were no men below fifty – and very few men at all. She decided to stay close to Gwen for the moment.

It was getting late and Kate was beginning to feel a little more relaxed. She found herself in the company of a group of half-a-dozen women, all of them about the same age as herself. They were talking about babies. One of the women turned to her and smiled.

'And do you have any of your own? I am so sorry, I do not believe we have been introduced?' She offered her hand. Kate took it, but there was little warmth in the greeting.

'Katherine, Katherine Butler. No, I am afraid I have no children, you see I am not yet married.'

As she spoke, she noticed the other women's expressions change. It seemed as though they each had a bad smell under their noses. Indeed, for a moment all faces turned to stare at her.

'I am so pleased to make your acquaintance,' the

woman said, without introducing herself. The other women nodded politely, then resumed their conversation. Kate noticed their ranks subtly closing and excluding her. She recognized their attitude and smiled grimly as she moved away.

People were beginning to leave. Kate was sat, alone, by the fountain in the conservatory. It was cold out here, but not as cold as it was inside, Kate thought. An elderly man was coming out to her. He seemed a little uncertain on his feet. Kate thought he was probably drunk. As he approached she realized she was right – he could barely speak without slurring his words. She winced as he tried to put his arm around her.

'Do you know . . . do you know what they say? They say there's an Irish here . . . Lady Wintert . . . Winterton actually invited an Irish – invited, mind you?'

He leaned over her. His breath was foul. Kate noticed with revulsion that his bottom teeth were reduced to blackened stumps.

'I'm lookin' for her . . . you know what I'll do when I find her?'

He started making thrusting motions with his pelvis. Kate noticed Gwen and Jane coming to her assistance. She could stand no more of this. She stood up and pushed him away. In so doing, he fell backwards and teetered on the edge of the fountain. Kate could not resist giving him the final gentle push which overbalanced him.

'It seems that you have found her,' she snapped.

The old man was wallowing about in the water, unable to control himself. Kate turned on her heel and stormed out of the conservatory. She hoped he would drown. The other two women helped him out and left him coughing and spluttering on the ground as they ran after Kate. She was in the process of putting on her cloak as they reached her. They closed the hallway doors behind them. They were alone. Kate's face was like thunder, but the other two were practically beside themselves with laughter.

'That was wonderful . . . simply wonderful – that was Heymann, you know, the pig-man I was telling you about.

Oh, Kate. I wish that could have been me – I would have loved to have done that.'

'It might seem funny to you, Lady Winterton, but it is certainly no laughing matter to me. God only knows what sort of people he thinks we are – and he thinks he is so civilized. Why, he's no better than an animal. . . .'

'Like a pig-man, perhaps?' Gwen ventured. She looked at Kate and shrugged her shoulders.

'What can we say, Kate? He is the worst of people – there will always be folk like that . . .' Jane ventured.

'Aye,' Kate replied, 'and most of them seem to be here tonight. Do you know I was snubbed by such a bevy of baggages – I would never have given them the time of day but for the fact that I was trying to be polite. I am surprised that you even invited them. I was led to believe that you were a woman of some discernment.'

Jane Winterton stopped laughing abruptly. 'In my position I seldom have the luxury of choosing my associates,' she replied, tersely.

'Then I would suggest that if you had the courage of your convictions, you might be able to make those choices.'

'In that case I shall. It is getting late and I think you should be leaving. Gwendoline, I hope I shall see you in the near future. Mistress Butler, I cannot say that it has been a pleasure meeting you, so I bid you goodnight.'

Without a further word, she left them and rejoined her guests.

The footman was ready with Gwen's cloak. She sighed as she put it on. 'I suppose we had better go home, Kate.'

As they were helped into their carriage, Gwen seemed in a reflective mood. 'I am sorry that you and Jane did not take to each other.'

'I suppose I expected her to be . . . well, more like you.'

'No. As you can see, we are very different. She knew you were right and that clearly irritated her – most people are keen to make a good impression on her.'

'Well I certainly made an impression, if nothing else.'

'Yes, you have given London society something to talk about, other than the war.'

Seven

Late in October John returned. He had handed command of the company over to Praisegod Ferrer and sent his companions up to Newmarket, where his new command was to be formed. In the meantime, however, he had a far more daunting task ahead of him, for in less than two days' time his father would be coming down from Ely to meet Kate. He had not seen the old man in nearly two years, indeed they had only met three times since he had gone to fight in the continental wars.

James Barnard was a most formidable man. Virtually self-made and self-taught, he had risen through the years to be one of the most respected figures in his city. An outspoken critic of both King and Parliament alike, he had a reputation as an upholder of public propriety and private morality. He had grown to manhood during the reign of the old Queen and often hearkened back to the days 'before the Scotch came pouring over the border'. He seldom came up to London and each time he did his talk was filled with denunciations of the depravity of life in the capital. He had been beside himself with wrath when his son had given up all the advantages he had never had to go to the Netherlands, but deep inside he felt a fierce pride that his son was doing what he believed was right. He rejoiced when John had returned safely, even if it was to fight in another war – though his son never really knew just how relieved he had been. He hoped that one day, when this business was over, the boy would settle down and take over his practice.

Even now, as John was once more back at Chelsea, warm and happy, his father was still on the open road. It was raining and his clothes were entirely sodden. It was hard to have a pleasant thought under the circumstances. He glowered at the muddy road ahead of him. He had received his son's letter more than a month ago, saying that he was going to marry an Irish girl called 'Kate' – no mention of a surname, probably Kate O' something or another. He was not entirely sure how to feel about the matter. John had told him that he would meet her when they came up to Ely in November – well, he was not having any of that: some half-wild Irish vixen coming into his own house without his even vetting her first – by that time it would be too late, she would already have her foot through the door and what then? The weather worsened. He consoled himself with the thought that at least he could get no wetter.

On Thursday morning he reached the City of London itself. He rather thought that London would benefit from a road around it so that decent folk would not have to enter its walls. At least the weather was fine – if only he was able to enjoy it. Though he was supposed to spend the night with a colleague here, he had more than half a mind to go straight to Chelsea and spend the afternoon in Gwendoline's garden. Yes, that was what he would do. He pictured himself playing with his grandson, a most agreeable prospect, he thought and spurred his horse on through the crowds.

It was only two o'clock when he reached the house. He hammered on the door. For a long while there was no reply, so he hammered again, just for good measure. It made him feel better. Finally, the manservant opened the door and looked at him sheepishly.

'Mr Barnard, Lady Nevers is not at home. You were not expected until . . .'

'Never mind that, Dodington, you ass. I am here now and I am going around to the garden, so make yourself useful and get my baggage.'

'But Mr Barnard. . . .'

It was too late, the old man was already on his way around the house. He stretched his back as he went, it was good to get off that damned nag, he thought, and even better to know that he would not have to get back on it for at least a week.

His train of thought was brought to an abrupt halt as he rounded the corner, for in the garden, quietly reading, was a young lady. From what he could see, an uncommonly attractive young lady – far too well dressed for a servant, he thought. Then it dawned on him: this was probably her – the Irish vixen.

He wondered whether or not to attempt some sort of deception, but thought better of it. No, he would confront the young hussy directly. She noticed him while he was still quite a long way off. She smiled brightly and, carefully closing her book, she rose gracefully and came across the garden to meet him. He noted that she carried herself uncommonly well and when she held out her hand to him, he surprised himself by taking it and kissing it in a very romantic fashion. He blushed.

'Good afternoon, Mr Barnard. I am afraid there is no one to introduce me to you, so I shall have to introduce myself. I am Katherine Butler, your son's fiancée. John is at the Palace of Westminster and Gwen has gone to see some friends in Kensington. For my own part, I thought a little peace and solitude would help me compose myself . . . before the inquisition.'

'I am sure I know not what you mean, Mistress Katherine,' the old man replied.

'I think we should be frank with each other. You have come all this way in such appalling weather so that you can take stock of me before it is too late to remedy the situation. Is that not right?'

He was impressed by her directness, it was a quality he admired and prided himself that he possessed. Well, she had done away with the need for beating around the bush, so they might as well set to.

'It is true. I am here to see if you will make a fit match for my son.'

'And how will you know that? Surely John would be the best judge of whom he would spend his life with?'

'Nevertheless, when you marry the man, you marry the family with him. You will have to live with us and we with you. I have not come to put a ban on your union, you seem like a sensible young woman and I approve of that. But I would know more about you before I give you my blessing.'

'Then let us walk in the garden together, that I might find out more about you as you learn more about me. In truth, I would also like to know what kind of family I am marrying into.'

And so for quite some hours they walked through the dense carpet of golden leaves. Even though the light was failing, still they remained outside, arm in arm now. And so it was that John found them when he returned after sunset, sitting together on the rough-hewn bench on the riverbank, in quiet conversation – as though they had known one another for years. His father rose and embraced John without speaking, then bade him sit down in this place.

'It is getting cold and my old bones are beginning to feel the chill in the air. I think I shall go in and wait for Gwendoline. You and Kate will have much to talk about.'

Again, Mr Barnard took Kate's hand and kissed it, this time with genuine affection rather than simple romance and this time he did not blush. He took his leave of them a much happier and more contented man than when he had arrived.

'You seemed to have charmed your way into my father's heart, and at a stroke relieved my greatest concern, Kate.'

'Charmed?' she mused. 'No, I did not charm him – if I had, I think he would have seen through me in an instant. He is a very perceptive gentleman, your father. We spoke very plainly, he and I.'

'I would imagine he would think the better of you for that.'

Kate sighed and looked up at the stars which were

appearing in the darkening sky. 'He loves you very deeply, you know, even though he is seldom able to show it. He made this long journey through terrible weather out of concern for your happiness. If I had been the sort of woman he had expected to find, I think he would have bitterly opposed our union. You would have been unhappy for a while and you would probably have resented him, but at least you would have been spared the misery of an unfortunate marriage.' She took his hand and held it tightly. 'I have been thinking, John. After the affair at Lady Winterton's . . . it will not be easy for you, having an Irish wife in tow. When this war is over you will have to take your place in society – and society is riddled with people whose minds are as narrow as theirs . . . having me at your side will be a barrier to your advancement.'

'What are you saying, Kate?'

'That I would not have you resent me in later years for holding you back and depriving you of the future you might have had . . . with a more appropriate wife.'

'Then you sadly misjudge me, Kate. If ever I progress, then it will be through my own ability – not because I have curried favour with those people whose company I would not suffer but for the advancement they might offer me. If folk turn their faces from us simply because you were born beyond the sea then they are fools and I will have none of them. Society can go to hell, for all I care, as long as I am with you.' He stood up and pulled her up to him, holding her very close. 'If this disquiets you, Kate, then the sooner we are married the better. We shall go inside and talk to father about the date of the wedding . . .' he smiled and he looked down into her eyes – 'but not at this precise moment. . . .' He took her face in his hands and kissed her.

Eight

All about them the land was covered in a white blanket of snow. As she left the house Kate shivered, in spite of the heavy ermine-trimmed cloak she had about her. A snowflake fluttered on to her eyelash and made her blink. She looked across to the coach, where the sergeant was waiting for her.

'Well, Jack, do I look like a bride? Tell me, how do I look?'

For a moment he seemed lost for words, then he smiled. 'Like the Winter Queen. I've never seen a woman look lovelier.'

'I suppose we had better go. I would not want to be late.'

'It's your prerogative today, they will expect you to be a little late. Still, there's no point in us freezing to death out here.'

He took her hand and led her into the coach, telling the driver to go slowly. Kate wiped a hole in the mist on the window. She looked out. The landscape seemed drained of all colour: the boughs and branches of the trees were grey and black, the figures in the fields were black against the dazzling snow. Only the sky showed a hint of blue as the sun burned away the morning clouds.

'How are you feeling?' Jack asked.

'Very nervous – and very hungry. I could not even eat a morsel this morning. I think not that I could eat anything now, but my stomach is so empty – I swear it will rumble all through the service. Listen, there it is again.'

Jack nodded at the grumbling noise. 'Well, there's nothing we can do now. You'll have to keep yourself under control and hope for the best when we get there.'

It was not a long drive from the Barnard house to the cathedral. In no time they were approaching the west door, where Gwen was waiting. The coach pulled up and suddenly it was very quiet.

'Oh well, here we go,' Kate mumbled to herself.

Gwen and Jack helped her down. Jack went inside for a moment, while Gwen took the cloak and arranged the folds of the bridal gown.

'I would imagine you are rather nervous at the moment,' she mused.

'You Barnards are masters of understatement,' Kate replied, with a tremble in her voice that was not from the cold.

'We Barnards?' Gwen looked up mischievously. 'I am no Barnard – though you will be in a few minutes' time. . . .'

It was a very long walk to the altar. Kate would have preferred to have been married in a church. This place was so imposing. John's father had insisted on the cathedral, though: he considered that he had paid enough towards its upkeep that he deserved some return on his investment. It was not as empty as it might have been, for many members of John's troop had come up from the south – they helped to swell Kate's side of the congregation which would have been empty but for them.

Jack whispered across as he walked beside her, 'With a bit of luck you'll only make this walk once in your life, so make the most of it.'

John and his father were standing ahead and to her right. He remained facing the altar, with his big square back to her. She noticed with amusement how long his hair had grown; it was nearly touching his collar. Then finally he did turn and face her. He seemed transfixed – he should have joined her and gone forward to the altar, but he seemed unable to move. She had passed him now.

'Come on, John!' she whispered.

Finally, his father nudged him in the back and he came forward. When he reached her he whispered, 'You look so beautiful – I was stunned.'

'Very well, I forgive you – but never do it again.'

'I was not planning to. . . .'

The vicar cleared his throat and the service began. They held each other's hands very tightly as they made their vows. Kate thought she had never seen him smile so much, he did not stop smiling from the beginning to the end. She could still feel him smiling as he kissed her, when they were pronounced man and wife.

There was a commotion behind them and Kate looked round to see all the troopers leaving.

'John, what is happening?' she asked anxiously.

'I rather think they have something planned for us outside.'

They came down from the altar and were immediately engulfed by their family and friends. Mr Barnard was the first to congratulate them and made sure he was first to kiss the bride. He smiled and whispered gruffly to her, 'Not only is John a very lucky man – I also feel very fortunate to have you as my daughter. Welcome.'

Gwen came up and hugged her tightly, creasing both their dresses, but neither of them minded in the least.

'Another woman in the family at last. I hope we both have lots of daughters, then we shall have these men on the run.'

John disappeared for a moment, then returned with the ermine-trimmed cloak. 'Come along, Mrs Barnard. The lads outside will be freezing to death.'

When they finally emerged, she was staggered to find the whole company formed up as a ceremonial guard, except that wherever they could be tied, the men had festooned themselves and their horses with white ribbons. They looked slightly comical, but it was a beautiful gesture, nonetheless. Praisegod called them to attention and Kate roared with laughter to see that they had tied ribbons to their sabres. They looked for all the world like morris dancers.

John swept her up into the waiting coach, which pulled away accompanied by its escort. It was then that Kate noticed the other additions to their uniforms, for they were all wearing jingle bells about them. John opened the window as Praisegod rode beside the coach.

'Very seasonal, my friend – though it seems that the code of dress has slipped somewhat since I left you.'

'Indeed, John. Dressed thus we might be mistaken for royalists.'

'Now that would be a pity.'

'A pity indeed. Enough of this – get back to your bride Captain Barnard.'

'Very well, Captain Ferrer.' He closed the window, for the air was very cold and the coach was going at quite a pace.

'Praisegod is in very high spirits today, John. Do you know, I believe I saw him smiling.'

Right at that moment the coach went over a pothole in the road and they were both thrown up into the air. Kate landed on the floor with a mighty bump and they both dissolved into a fit of laughter.

'Just as you were when I first saw you . . .' he laughed as he helped her up.

'Except without the mud,' she retorted.

'Even with the mud I still thought you were uncommonly attractive.'

'I would like to think I look somewhat more presentable now. . . .'

John took his time to answer, as if it were a hard choice to make.

'If you do not answer "yes" by the time I count to three, John Barnard, I swear I'll throw you bodily from this coach.'

He stayed her hand at three. 'I hope you will always look as beautiful as you look today. You have made me the happiest man in the world.'

They kissed and did not stop kissing until the coach drew up at the house once more. As John opened the door he was greeted by a single figure astride a big bay horse; they were both dappled with snowflakes, as though they had been waiting.

'When you said that you would be busy this winter, I did not realize just how busy you intended to be, Captain Barnard.'

'General. . . .'

'I noticed you have made certain unwarranted changes to the prescribed uniform. I trust you do not intend that the New Model Army should go into battle attired thus?' For a moment he glowered grimly at the company, then his expression changed. 'Perhaps the King's Army would be taken by such mirth that we could defeat them without firing a shot. . . .' He smiled. 'Come on then, John. Introduce me to your new bride. I have been here long enough.'

He dismounted and shook the snow from his cloak before helping them both down from the coach. 'Mrs Barnard. I watched you leave from the cover of those trees yonder – while you were yet a single woman. I must confess to an admiration which would now transgress the tenth Commandment.'

The wedding party was coming up the road. Cromwell seemed agitated. 'John, I cannot tarry, for this is your day. Enjoy your honeymoon. I am truly sorry that I can only spare you for a few days.'

'It is all that I would spare for myself.'

'Do not tell anyone that I have been here. If they ask, say that I was a messenger or something. Mistress Barnard,' he smiled, 'it has been a pleasure. I hope that we shall meet again.' He turned abruptly on his heel, mounted his horse and rode away. A brief flurry of snow swirled around him.

The wedding party was swollen by many folks from the city. They swept the couple into the house and the celebrations began. John's father had spared no expense; barrels of beer and casks of wine lined one wall of the large dining-room, which was already decked with holly boughs in preparation for Christmas. He had hired a small country band and soon the room was thronged with dancing merrymakers.

In their midst, Kate and John were bustled and jostled by the good-natured crowd. From the corner of her eye, Kate noticed that Praisegod and many of the other troopers were clustered in a far corner, still in their ribbons, but talking seriously together.

'John, they are not dancing – there are many girls about – shall I go and drag them into the dance?'

John shook his head and smiled. 'No, they will not dance, and we must not insult them by pressing them to do so. Theirs is a very rigid code which does not permit dancing. . . .'

'But. . . .'

'Look closely next time we come around – they are enjoying themselves even so.'

The dance spun them around again.

'They look very serious.'

'That is their way.'

Soon they grew thirsty and they went to take some wine. There was an excited buzz of conversation around them. A young man, his face flushed from dancing, came up to them.

'Is it true that the Master was here?'

'So word has got around, has it? Yes, it is true – he came to wish us well,' John replied.

Kate seemed perplexed. 'Who is the Master?'

'Master of the Fens, madam,' the young man said with pride.

'In these parts Cromwell is known as the Master of the Fens. This is his country and the people bear him great affection,' John explained.

'That's right enough, madam. They wanted to take the Fens away from us and give it all to the grandees – but he saw 'em off.' The young man's eyes were shining. He held his hands behind his back and stood up straight. 'Permit me, sir, but the talk is that you are mustering a company at Newmarket. Well, me and some of the lads – there's six of us in all – we're made men with our own horses and everything. We've come up here today to see if you'll take us on.'

Kate looked sadly at this young fellow, with his shock of fair hair and cornflower eyes. He could not have been twenty yet. She thought of the sergeant's words. He looked just the sort of boy who would stay his hand out of love. Surely, John would not take him? But already they were shaking hands, as though they were sealing a contract.

'I am instructed to recruit young men of honour. If you and your companions are resolved on this, then we will talk later. Have a drink, but not too much. I would have you clear headed when you commit yourselves to this.'

'Our minds are clear on this already, sir.'

He bowed and left them, making his way through the crowd to join a small knot of young fellows standing by the window. Presently, she heard them cheering.

'They are so very young . . .' Kate said sadly.

John sighed. 'Aye, and some of them will not grow old.'

They were interrupted by the insistent ringing of a bell, which indicated that it was time to eat. After the meal, those who had brought gifts for the couple presented them to the cheers of the crowd. James Barnard could not resist the opportunity of making a speech before he handed them his present – the deeds to a house just outside the town.

'You will likely find it a little large for you – so I suggest you start filling it straightaway.'

This was received by such a mighty cheer from the guests that the old man bowed before them. John and Kate blushed.

'We shall see what we can do, Father,' he replied.

After all the other gifts had been given, Orlando and Praisegod came forward bearing a long heavy bundle, swathed in muslin. 'With your permission, sir, this is for Mistress Kate – to remember us by.'

Kate unwrapped the bundle to reveal a mannequin

in the full uniform of a cornet, complete with sash, breastplate and helmet.

John laughed. 'How in heaven's name did you get this?'

For a moment there was silence, then the sergeant came forward. 'Well, John. You see it's like this: we put Cornet Butler's name on the muster-roll and requisitioned it from the quarter-master. So, Mistress Katherine this is yours by right. We just hope you never have to wear it. . . .'

After sunset the celebrations became more lively still. Some of the older guests had gone home to bed and the younger folk seemed set to dance the night away. John was talking to the young men, who had not moved from the window. Kate was talking to the sergeant. He reached inside his jacket.

'This is something to remember me by. I've had it for a number of years now, but it seemed . . . well you know – sort of fitting.'

He produced a small casket of dark wood, wrought with silver bands and a silver clasp. She opened it and inside was a cake of soap.

'It was my second greatest pleasure ever, giving you that soap.'

'The second greatest, Jack?' She inclined her head quizzically.

'Aye, my greatest pleasure was this morning, standing in your father's place beside you when you were wed.'

Finally, the time came for them to take their leave of the company. They all came out to see them off. John's horse was waiting outside for them. He mounted first, then lifted her up into the saddle before him.

'Hold on tight,' he whispered and he spurred the horse on. They left at a great pace, the horse's hooves throwing up the snow behind them. They had not gone more than a few yards when John cursed under his breath. 'Damn. The house is on the other side of town. . . .'

He turned the horse around and rode back past the cheering and laughing crowd.

There was a ligh. burning in the window already when

they arrived at the house. John dismounted and Kate slipped down from the horse's back and into his arms. He carried her to the threshold and bade her lift the latch, then carried her in.

'You can let me down now, John.'

He shook his head. 'Oh no, Mrs Barnard. I do not intend to let you out of my arms for a very long time. . . .'

Kate was wakened by the sunrise and a strange tickling sensation in her nose. At first she thought John was teasing her, but she could feel his slow, level breathing. She had fallen asleep using his chest as a pillow. The hair of his chest was brushing her nostrils. His heavy arm was over her shoulders; she liked the weight of it.

So that was love-making, she mused. It was a very strange thing, though she thought that on the whole she liked it. She had had an inkling of what it might be like – she had seen stallions at service in the fields at home. She was very relieved to find that John was not of quite the same proportions. That was something which had worried her since she was a girl. She gently lifted up the coverlet and peered down. It slept beside its master. Such a silly thing it looked now. She remembered with delight the shudder that had run down his spine when he had finished. It took him much longer to finish than the stallions ever had. It was a good thing, she thought, that he had taken so long. After the initial shock, she had settled down to enjoying the experience. She had liked the feel of his big hands caressing her naked body. . . .

She realized with a start that they had slept the whole night in a state of nakedness. She blushed right down to her shoulders. Never in her life had she lain thus. She did not know whether she was more embarrassed by the fact of it or because she enjoyed the feel of it. What would John think of her?

Her nightgown was laid out across a chair, at the far side of the bedchamber. If she could gently extricate herself from his arm. . . . Carefully, she lifted it up and eased herself out. Then, lowering his arm, she moved away from him. She slipped from the bed and stole across the room.

'Good morning, Kate Barnard.'

'John!' she exclaimed, scuttling to the chair. She grabbed the nightgown and held it before her.

He laughed and pointed behind her. 'I think you are forgetting something.'

She looked around and was dismayed to see herself on full show in the mirror on the wall.

'It is like to be safer if you come back to bed.'

She sidled across to the edge of the bed. 'Very well . . . but you must promise not to peek.'

John held both his hands up in the air. 'You are safe with me, I swear.'

With the nightgown still tightly gripped in front of her, she eased herself awkwardly back into bed. She disappeared under the covers and there was a great commotion, until finally she emerged, red-faced, wearing the nightgown. She smiled meekly and felt very foolish.

'Sorry,' was all that she could think of to say.

John shrugged. 'No matter. I did not realize that you were accustomed to sleeping as nature intended. . . .'

'How dare you? Why, I never . . .'

'I must admit this is quite a surprise to me. I shall think differently of you henceforth.'

'John Barnard, I'll have you know that I have never slept thus until. . . .'

She caught the wicked gleam in his eye and realized that he was leading her on again. She mustered her dignity and smoothed the sheets about her.

'This will be a fine marriage indeed. How will I ever know when you are speaking plainly to me?'

'When I put my arms around you, like this. And when I kiss you . . . like this. . . .'

Several long moments passed before he pulled himself away from her.

'And when I tell you that I love you. Then I will be speaking plainly, for that will always be the truth.'

They lay for a long time in each other's arms, watching

the light broaden in the sky. After a while, Kate broke the silence. 'The day is yet young Our first full day as man and wife – how shall we spend it?'

John yawned slowly and deeply, stretching his back. 'Well, I suppose I had better find my horse. I should not have let him go untethered last night. Still, I did have more pressing matters to attend to.'

'Is that what you call it?'

'Hmm. . . .' He smiled. 'I suppose you could. Anyway, he never strays very far, so that will not occupy me for long. We could spend the rest of the day getting accustomed to married life in our new home. Go on, Kate and get yourself dressed.'

'John, I cannot – I have not the slightest idea where my clothes are.'

'Then it would seem that our first task is to explore this new home of ours.'

They spent most of their first morning making a great bear out of snow. It had started out as a simple snowman and then grew as the fancy took them. In the afternoon they had a snowball fight. Kate had excelled at this since childhood and John was forced to surrender on many occasions, wearying at last of being caught behind the ear by a series of snowballs thrown with deadly accuracy. In the end he persuaded her to go for a walk with him in the fields outside the city. Things went well until Kate dropped back and reminded him of her prowess with a huge projectile which exploded on the back of his head.

'Not fair!' he cried as he turned on her and chased her back towards the house. He caught her just as she wallowed into a snowdrift and they landed, side by side, half buried in the snow. 'Wait a moment, Kate. Rise very carefully.' She obeyed, and they pulled each other up. There in the snow was their imprint, nearly two feet deep, side by side holding one another tightly.

They watched the sun go down, turning the winter landscape an ever deeper shade of pink. They went home and dried themselves in front of a roaring fire, then went to bed early.

The next morning Kate was woken by the sound of a horse riding away from the house. She felt beside her and discovered that John was not there. She dressed quickly and ran out of the house after him, but he was gone. Where had he gone and why had he not woken her? Why was he in such a hurry? The darkest thoughts loomed up in her mind. What if he had been recalled to the army? In her heart of hearts she knew that he would not leave without at least saying farewell. The thought kept nagging at her, though and it would not go away.

After nearly an hour, Kate heard the sound of a rider approaching and finally dismounting. John smiled widely as he saw her. 'Ah, you are abroad, I see. I hope I did not wake you. You looked so peaceful when you were asleep that I feared to . . .'

'Do not ever do that to me again,' she snapped.

John's expression changed to one of puzzlement. 'Do what to you?'

'Do not ever leave me without telling me where you are going. Do you realize I thought the most terrible things whilst you were gone?'

'But I only went to borrow some skates from father.' He held them up, sheepishly. 'I thought we could go skating.'

'Skating? All this time I've been wondering where in God's name you were while you were thinking about skating?'

'I thought I would surprise you.'

'Shock the life out of me, more like.'

'I am truly sorry, Kate. I will not do it again. What more can I say?'

Kate's anger abated slightly. 'You can promise me that the next time you have to leave me, that you will spare the time to let me know where you are going. Or, better still, never leave me at all.'

She held her arms out to him and hugged him. Then

she raised her head as if to kiss him. At the last moment she moved aside and bit him on the end of the nose.

'Ow!' he exclaimed. 'What was that for?'

Kate smiled sweetly. 'Just so that you'll remember – and to make me feel better.' She pushed him away and breezed past him. 'So, you've a mind to kill me on the ice today?'

'Have you ever been skating before?' he said with his hand to his face. 'That really hurt, you know.'

'No, I have never skated before and yes, I would imagine it would hurt – but not as much as you hurt me this morning. So, you can teach me how to skate now that I have taught you to be a little more considerate. Is that fair?'

When John finally managed to drag Kate out on to the ice, she began to suspect his motives. It seemed to her that, just as she had humiliated him the day before, she would be made a laughing-stock today. She just could not keep herself upright on the ice for more than a few moments. She would skitter along for a few frantic paces, then land flat on her bottom. Meanwhile, John was flying about with remarkable ease. Just to emphasize her ineptitude, he circled around her as she desperately attempted to get back on her feet.

'You know, I would appreciate some help with this, John,' she admitted, grudgingly.

He brought himself to an abrupt halt directly in front of her. The ice crunched under his skates. 'Come along, Kate. Give me your hands . . . do not lean too far forward. . . .' He caught her just as she was about to fall, then moved around behind her as she wobbled uncertainly. 'Very good. Now lean back slightly on me, then follow the way my body moves.'

He put his weight gently on to his left foot, then with a deft motion, pushed away with his right. Kate copied him and suddenly they were moving gracefully along the ice.

'Now we change foot and do the same.'

After a few strokes, Kate began to get the feel of the

motion. It seemed that she was an extension of his body, which was a feeling she liked. Just as she was beginning to thrill to this new sensation, she realized that the ice was coming to an end ahead. John felt the tension in her limbs and spoke softly in her ear. 'Relax . . . do not be afraid. More weight on your left, slightly change the line and push with your right . . . see, we're turning.'

The bank receded away to their right. Now they were describing a wide circle around the edge of the pond. Kate could feel that they were gradually getting faster. The wind grew sharper on her cheeks and her eyes began to smart with the cold. Her back was very warm, pressed closely against John. She felt that she could stay like this forever.

After a while, Kate realized that an essential part of her tuition was missing.

'John?'

'Mmm . . . forgive me, I was miles away there . . . yes?'

'John, how do we stop?'

'You do not want to stop, do you?'

'No, but if I did. . . .'

'Well, there are three ways. The first, which is my favourite, is to go hurtling into the bank and crash into the snow – shall we try that?'

'No! Please not that way.'

'Very well. The second way is the proper way. We can try it now. Get ready to lean down slightly to your right, then bring your skates sideways along until it bites into the ice. . . . Are you ready?'

She nodded.

'On the count of three then . . . one . . . two . . . three!'

For a moment all went well, then Kate lost confidence and went over, bringing them both down. They slithered across the ice together. Kate saw the bank looming up before them. They were unable to stop and they ploughed into the snow at the side. On terra firma once more, Kate picked herself up. John was still down in the snow, laughing.

'That was the third way – as you can see, it results

in much the same way as the first – though not quite so dignified.'

As the morning wore on Kate became more accustomed to this skating business. John was a good and patient teacher and soon she was able to make her way around the ice, unaided. She much preferred it though, when they skated together.

Nine

And so the honeymoon drew to a close. At sunrise on the Monday morning, Kate was woken by the sound of horses on the cobblestones outside. John was already up and in uniform, packing his gear into panniers.

'I was just about to wake you.' He came and sat beside her. She sat up and put her arms around him.

'Ow, your tin suit is so cold and hard.'

'Better the suit than the wearer. . . .'

'Never say that, John.'

'Forgive me. Still, this will not be so bad. In two weeks I shall return home for Christmas. Think yourself lucky: you can spend the next fortnight here in this nice warm house, whilst I shall be out in the miserable weather, drilling raw recruits into some semblance of a fighting company.' He shivered. 'Dismal work – I hate it.'

'And what shall I do?'

'I should think you would be very busy. You have your own recruiting to do. A house cannot run itself, you know. Ruth will not be able to do it all on her own.'

'Oh, my God. I had completely forgotten about her. She should be arriving today.'

'She will certainly arrive today. She has been waiting at father's house this past week.'

'Do you think that is her outside?'

'No, that is the young lads I recruited at the wedding. I had better get out to them soon or they will freeze to death.'

Kate sighed. 'Very well then. Kiss me and leave me – see if I care. So this is what it will mean to be a captain's wife.'

'Lady. Men have wives, officers have ladies. A strange distinction.'

'Wife, lady – it still means that I'm to be left on my own. Now kiss me and be gone. And next time you take your leave of me, wake me before you put your ironmongery on. In fact you can wake me while you are still in bed – then we may say farewell properly.'

When John closed the bedroom door behind him, leaving Kate all alone, she was able to stop play-acting. She hated to see him go, even for two weeks. She threw on her nightgown and ran to the window. She watched him ride away until he disappeared from view altogether and still she watched. The morning was cold and grey. She wandered around the room, at a loss for a moment. This is no use, she thought to herself. She went to the bowl and splashed some water on her face. She was surprised to find that it was hot. John must have warmed it for her whilst she slept. He was a very considerate fellow, she thought – though not considerate enough to stay with her and not go off soldiering.

Even as these thoughts were occupying Kate's mind, a lonely figure trudged through the snow, slowly making her way towards the house. It was Ruth. She saw the captain and his party leaving down the Newmarket Road, but she was too far away to call out to him, and she felt shy to be calling out to the likes of the captain.

She wondered at this, for how should she conduct herself? Mistress Katherine was to be her new mistress – but she was not to be a servant. Lady Nevers had told her she was to be a lady's companion. Ruth wondered what a 'companion' might do. She had asked her mother before she left London. 'Just be a friend to her,' her mother had supposed.

All the way up to Ely this had bothered her. She had finally resolved to take her mother's advice. What else was there for her to do? Mistress Katherine had taken to her because of her ability to make her laugh and was bringing her up to Ely as she had no friends in that place.

Well, it was too late to worry now she had reached the door of the house. She would be herself, she decided; if that was not good enough, then at least she had tried.

She knocked at the door. After a while she heard the latch opening and Kate looked out. She looked tired and her hair was dishevelled. She opened the door a little wider and ushered her in. Ruth looked at her with a twinkle in her eye.

'If you'll excuse me saying so, but you look like a woman who's discovered what a man is really for.'

Kate stared at her dumbfounded for a moment, then realized what she meant. She put her hand to her mouth . . . then burst out laughing. Ruth joined her and they laughed for ages.

'You know, that is the naughtiest thing anyone has ever said to me. Perhaps things may not be so dull here after all.'

Over the long months that followed, Kate had good cause to be grateful for Ruth's cheerfulness and her company. After Christmas John was often away, either with his own company or with the other officers of the 'New Model' forging it into a professional army, which would take the field for the first time that summer.

As winter wore on into spring, he came home less and less frequently, though he often wrote. He promised to be home 'when the bluebells come'. Yet the bluebells came and went and still Kate waited for him.

Old Mr Barnard was a frequent visitor during these times. He looked much older and more tired than he had before. He admitted that he had been working hard; he was on the Board of Commission for the city, raising funds and supervising the supply of horses and equipment for the army.

'It is no easy task,' he admitted, 'for though the worthies

of the city have given up their sons to the cause, still they are unwilling to dig into their purses.'

His visits stopped during early May. There was a great fear that the King's Army would march on the Eastern Association counties. Ely took on the appearance of a frontier town. There were soldiers everywhere. It was Mr Barnard's task to find billets for the troopers. Kate offered to take some in herself, but her father-in-law would have none of it.

'They are good souls, most of them, but I could not suffer to have troopers placed in the house of two young ladies living alone – especially when there are many households much better suited that have not yet opened their doors.'

Kate protested, but the old man was resolute.

The citizens of the city only realized the seriousness of their plight when, on a bright sunny afternoon, Cromwell himself arrived to take charge of the city's defences. He made his headquarters in a large house not far from Mr Barnard's own. The citizens held their breath and waited for the worst.

People's comings and goings were closely monitored and since Kate's house was outside the fortifications, it meant that Mr Barnard had to pass through the picket lines to visit his daughter-in-law.

He called these visits his 'afternoon constitutionals', a brisk walk into the country for the sake of his health. Kate did not delve any deeper into his motives for his visits. She suspected that John had asked him to keep a watchful eye on her. She was glad of his company, though. In the way he spoke and in many of his mannerisms he was so similar to his son. She wondered if John would be like him when he grew old.

It was on just such an afternoon that Kate and Ruth were in the garden. They were waiting for Mr Barnard to arrive. Kate had baked some buns – she was becoming quite proficient in the kitchen now – and made some malted milk which was in the pan ready to be warmed when he came. The two women were playing cards, with one eye on the road looking out for the old man's approach. He disapproved of such things and though they did not fear him, they did not want to disappoint him when it was so easy just to clear the cards away before he arrived.

The peace of the afternoon was broken by a commotion on the road in the opposite direction to the way they were looking. For a long time the source of the noise was hidden from them by the trees which lined the road. Then, finally, it became visible. A long military convoy of cavalry was coming up from the south. Kate's heart leapt as she saw a single rider break away from the others, galloping ahead. As he came closer his hand went up and waved at her. It was John.

She picked up her skirts and ran through the house to the front door. She opened it just as he was dismounting. She did not give him time to tether his horse. She threw herself into his arms and he held her tightly, crushing her against his breastplate. He lifted her up off the ground and she threw her arms about his neck, kissing him long and deeply, not caring that all the world could see them.

Kate could hear the column of riders approaching. John gently pulled away from her and let her back down. He looked over his shoulder at the men, then he turned back to her. 'We are heading up country, making for the Great North Road. I have sent some men ahead to Sutton and that is where we shall make camp for tonight.'

Kate's face dropped. 'You mean you are just leaving me like this . . .'

John stopped her by placing a finger on her lips and whispering close to her ear, 'When I have the men settled down, Jack has promised to take over. I shall be back before sunset.'

He smiled and made to remount his horse. Kate noticed a knot of blue flowers fastened to his shoulder-strap. John glanced at them and blushed.

'Cranesbill, I am afraid. I could not find any of the other. Will they suffice?'

The company was upon them now. Their private moment was interrupted by the noise and smell of a hundred horses stamping and snorting. She noticed the sergeant riding up the column to greet her. John was insistent.

'Well?' he smiled as he watched Kate's face redden with embarrassment. She looked up at him and smiled guiltily.

'They will do very well – now get off with you. The sooner you go the sooner you will be back.'

He laughed and spurred his horse on. The column followed on behind. Jack pulled his horse up beside beside her. 'Now, don't you go worrying, Kate my dear. I'll be keeping an eye out for him. He'll not come to any harm, mark my words.'

'Well, just you mind that you do, Jack. And while you are about it, you keep an eye on yourself as well.'

He took off his gauntlet and reached down to her. She gave him her hand and he kissed it. 'I can't tell you how happy I am to see you again. I was that worried about you, it's been that long since I've seen you.'

Kate nodded. 'It has been too long, Jack. But, as you can see, I am still the same as I ever was.'

'Just mind you keep that way. God be with you, Kate.'

'And with you, Jack.'

He wheeled his horse about and rejoined the column as it wound its way up the road toward the city. She watched them go until they disappeared from view. Even when they had gone, Kate stayed by the doorway; for, making his way down the road, at a good pace, was Mr Barnard on his afternoon constitutional. She went and met him half-way. He seemed in high spirits.

'Good afternoon, daughter. John tells me that he will be back this evening, so I hope you would not mind if I invite myself to dinner.'

Kate was beginning to think that Mr Barnard would never leave when, finally, he seemed to catch the mood of his son and daughter and picked himself slowly up from the armchair by the fireside.

'Well, it is a fine night for a stroll to walk off that fine dinner.'

At least he had been gracious enough to lie about the meal, which Kate and Ruth had thrown together from such things as were about the house. Looking back, she had been glad of the activity. It had occupied her mind while she waited for John to return.

They wished him a good night and sent him on his way. For a few moments they watched him waddle along the road, apparently not too sure on his feet – he had consumed nearly two bottles of their best wine. John closed the door and let out a great sigh of relief as he rested his head against it.

'I am sorry, Kate. But when I met him on the road I told him we were making camp at Sutton, he insisted on our dining at his house – what else could I do?'

Kate laughed. 'I know, John. After all he has as much right to you as I have. Normally I would have been happy in his company – but not tonight.'

'Still, we have the most part of it to ourselves.'

Kate slumped wearily into his arms. 'I am going up to bed. If you will snuff out the candles, Ruth and I will take care of this mess tomorrow. Just mind that you do not stay down here too long.'

As she pulled herself away from him, she let her fingertips play along his arm and down to his hand. They stayed linked together until she reached the stairs, then parted. Kate glanced over her shoulder at him as she went up. When she had gone, John set about the lights. He tarried a while over the last candle to give her a little more time. Then, finally, he licked his thumb and forefinger and pinched out the flame, making his way up the stairs in the darkness.

Their love-making that night was swift, but nonetheless sweet for that. There seemed to be an urgency in both of them, which could not be ascribed simply to their mutual desire, but to the uncertainty which lay ahead. When it was over, John was quaking in every muscle and sinew of his body. He held Kate so tightly that it seemed that he would never release her. After what seemed to be a very long time, the fit passed and his body relaxed, though they were still close-entwined. They lay there, without speaking for over an hour, until sleep finally enveloped them, still linked together.

The next morning brought another farewell in the grey light before sunrise. This time Kate was fully awake and about before John rose. For some reason which she could not explain, she did not want his last image of her to be of her supine and dishevelled in the bed – even though that was how he liked to visualize her. She wanted him to be left with the impression that she was able to look after herself. She dressed quickly but carefully, paying attention to the little details of her appearance. She woke him with a kiss and then another, on his face and lips. His eyes opened, bright blue in the light. He smiled, and yawned, stretching himself like a great bear. Kate resisted the urge to tickle him. She did not want to indulge in a bed-fight this morning of all mornings. She spoke softly to him, 'Hello John. The sun is almost abroad, my dear. The world awaits you.'

Kate was surprised at the almost mystical quality of her words and the mood which was upon her. She was a wife sending her husband off to war, as women had done for centuries before. In her mind's eye was the image of a stern Spartan woman, cold and unflinching as her own husband left her to fight the Persians. But this was an image from one of her father's books. She did not have it in her to be cold, but she wanted John to go away with the feeling that everything would be well at home while he was away.

In the end there were few words. Kate managed to hold back the tears which were behind her eyes until he was gone. In her heart of hearts she knew that he would be careful of himself and not risk his life needlessly. Yet, at the back of her mind was the nagging doubt that he might not return. What could she have done, though? The war was his life. She smiled at the irony of the thought. She could have tried to hold him back, to keep him for herself. If she had pleaded with him to stay, she knew that he would have gone in spite of her protestations. And what would he have thought of her then? The war had a hold on him, a prior claim. He was a soldier of conscience and he believed in the cause he fought for. That he would give it up for her was unthinkable.

It was still early and Ruth was yet abed. Kate went out into the garden. The air was cool and damp, mists still hung around the edge of the copse of oaks just beyond. She wandered down to the pond where John had taught her to skate. She listened to the babbling of the brook which fed it, and the ducks which it nourished. There were dozens of yellow ducklings, following their mothers about in uncertain lines, sometimes losing their way and crying out in panic at their loneliness. Kate longed to cry out herself, at the longing in her heart, at her own loneliness, but she knew it would do no good.

The mother-duck would come back and nudge the lost duckling along until it had caught up with the others, and they disappeared into the reed beds beyond.

Kate smiled at the little comedy she had been privy to and sat down on a grassy bank. The sun had begun to warm a small patch of the water's edge. She noticed some movement on the surface. She looked closer and saw that it was a mosquito, dragging itself from its winter shell. For a few moments it clung there, while the sun warmed its wings. Kate was fascinated at this moment of its birth. She looked on with delight as it took to the air, sunlight flickering on its wings. Delight turned to a mild revulsion as it immediately latched itself on to the back of her hand and began sucking at her blood. She brushed it aside and in so doing, crushed it, leaving a bright red smudge across her hand. From the moment of its birth it had been alone and self-sufficient, seeking out its quarry in the first few seconds of life. She considered the life which even now might be growing within her, and shuddered.

Ten

By the end of June, Kate's suspicions were confirmed. She had missed her time and each morning she was greeted by waves of nausea. Ruth regarded this morning sickness with little sympathy. Indeed, she treated the whole affair with unseemly hilarity, making fun of her mistress's condition. Kate began to weary of her attitude and, on her fifth day of suffering, she decided that enough was enough. She had assumed her ritual morning position with her head down in a basin. Ruth was rubbing her back, 'just to help things on their way', as she so delicately put it, when she launched forth with yet another spate of homespun wisdom.

'Ah, taking pleasure of men is all very well, but it leads us to this pass in the end.'

Kate wiped her mouth. 'That's a fine thing for you to say, my girl. I remember your saying that men were only good for one thing anyway,' she replied, grimly.

'Ah, so I did. But nature has a way of catching up with us. It is a gamble – the more you play, the more like you are to pay.'

'Speaking from your wide experience of men, I suppose,' Kate gibed.

Ruth became very coy. She had obviously hit a nerve.

'I know enough of men . . . but my mistress might think me loose if I were to dwell at length on my experiences.'

'Please dwell, Ruth. I will think none the worse of you for it.'

'I could not,' she replied anxiously.

'You cannot,' Kate taunted.

'It is not proper to talk about such things – and you should not make me. . . .'

Kate heard footsteps as her companion rushed out of the room. She would have gone after her, but she could feel another bout of sickness coming on. She would apologize later on, she mused. At least she might be more considerate from now on.

Her train of thought was interrupted by Ruth, who returned to the bedroom, very prim and proper, with a smug smile on her face.

'Mr Barnard is here to see you Mistress. He says it is a matter of some urgency. Shall I show him up?'

Kate spluttered at the news. 'You will show me up if you do. Tell him to wait, I shall be down in a moment. Keep him amused – he likes you. Go on!'

Ruth curtsied very properly, but as she rose, Kate noticed out of the corner of her eye that she poked her tongue out at her. Before Kate could say anything, though, she had disappeared. Kate groaned. She did not feel at all like seeing anyone, let alone her father-in-law. She splashed some water on her face and tried to arrange her hair into some sort of order. Peering into the mirror, she gave up the attempt – she looked like death itself and there was nothing she could do about it now. She threw on her robe and took herself gingerly downstairs.

Mr Barnard rose as she entered the parlour. Kate attempted a smile, then realized it would probably look more like a leer in the circumstances and gave up the effort.

'Ruth tells me you are a little under the weather this morning – I can see she is telling the truth,' he added unchivalrously.

'Good morning, father. Yes, it is true. I seem to be under the weather most mornings.' She noticed the old man's expression change. 'I think you have already guessed at my meaning. We might be greeting another Barnard in January.'

She watched his expression change from one of concern to one of delight. She was pleased that someone at least was happy at this turn of events. She knew that she too would be happy, if only she did not feel so sick. Mr Barnard came up to her and hugged her. Kate thought that if he held her any tighter, he might regret his actions.

'How splendid!' (Splendid for him, Kate thought.) 'Then I have received two pieces of good news this morning. I have a letter for you from John. He wrote to me also. He is in Leicester. The troubles of that poor city have been avenged, thank the Lord. But best of all, our forces have been victorious at Naseby. The King's Army is in full retreat and the threat to our Eastern Association is passed!' he exclaimed. He took a letter from his pocket and gave it to her. She scrabbled with it, John always sealed his letters so soundly; they were so difficult to open.

'Is he well? Has he been wounded?' she asked, still struggling.

'Oh, no. Better than well – he is in fine spirits – and a hero, by all accounts.'

Finally, the seal opened with a crack, she unfolded it and read avidly. Mr Barnard carried on talking, but she did not hear a word of it.

Leicester
19th June, 1645

Dearest Kate,

Let me first tell you that I am still in my whole skin and I have no punctures to speak of, though I feel so bruised and battered that I might have spent the last few days rolling around in a barrel and my ears are still ringing. Still, I would have fared no worse in a football scrummage, so I should be thankful for that. Jack sends his love and young Tomikin asks after Ruth – I think they have developed a high regard for each other – they met at Christmas, I believe. I hope all is well with you and that father is not making too much of a nuisance of himself. I hope you are not finding things too dull and that there are some sources of amusement.

So, what of my news? Well, unsurprisingly, we have spent the last three weeks in the saddle, and have crossed swords with the royalists twice, latterly only yesterday when we freed this fair city. I swear to you, Kate, the damage and mayhem the King's men wrought in the short time they spent here sickens the spirit. If we ever doubted the righteousness of our cause before, we have no doubts now. The place was strewn with bodies as yet unburied since the end of May.

I must confess, I was racked with doubt after the battle at Naseby, though I see that I am writing my story backwards. Forgive me, I would make no historian. My excuse is my weariness and of that there can be no doubt. I will start my tale from the beginning.

Firstly, you should know that we have been placed under the command of John Desborough – a good man and an able and courageous commander. I cannot tell you how happy I am that my charges are under his care.

We arrived at Naseby, a little village to the south and west of Market Harborough a little before midnight on the 13th. The rumour around the camp was that only the day before the King had been out hunting and his army were playing at dice – even though Fairfax was less than two miles distant. At first I thought this a token of their overriding confidence, I now realize that it was no more than another example of their folly. Though we were tired out from our march, I know that few of us slept at all that night; my men because it would be their first battle – Jack and I were kept awake for the same reason. To their credit, they spent most of their time in prayer, either together or, more often, alone.

After sunrise, we were treated to an uncommonly good breakfast and then we took up positions on the right, under Lieutenant-General Cromwell's banner. For near on two hours we waited for the King's pleasure and finally he came on. In the centre of his line were the 'Old Foot' – some of his best soldiers. I have never faced them myself, but I knew them by their reputation and I feared for our own infantry, many of whom were raw recruits and conscripts. At the same time Prince Rupert launched a charge on our cavalry to the left. I will speak plainly here, for I know the man who carries this letter well and he will deliver it faithfully.

Our left was commanded by one Henry Ireton, a favourite of Master Cromwell, but a man of little experience for all that. His line was shattered by the charge and his men were swept away. This would have been a grievous blow to our cause and I heard a groan come up from all around me. Then we all watched in stunned silence as the Prince led his men from the field to our rear. I had heard that he was prone to this but I did not believe it until then. We did not see him again until the battle was nearly over. At this, the general ordered us forward. We had to cut between a small copse and some thick undergrowth which would have fouled our horses' hooves. We took Langdale's cavalry at the full charge and we broke them as though they were not there. Cromwell led us about and we took their footsoldiers full in the flank. The King was to our right and we thought that he would come upon us so that we might be opposed on two sides. Instead he left the field. My men were that overjoyed that they laid on afresh. The infantry were left there, an island in our midst. Many of them laid their arms down straightway and were spared, but I am told that one regiment of Life Guards fought on and had to be cut down to a man. I say 'I am told' because we were dispatched to the pursuit of Langdale's cavalry. We chased them nearly all the way to Melton – we did not catch many of them and those that we did we offered quarter to, disarmed them and left them under guard.

What I must relate to you now is not so good and gave me the grounds for the doubt I alluded to before.

By the time we returned it was after dark. The army were in high spirits, as was seemly after so great a victory. There were many prisoners and they were being led off the field. It seemed that there were many hundreds of royalists dead, but our own casualties were light. All seemed well. Then I heard a great wailing and screaming of women. I looked in the direction of the noise and saw a party of women, maybe fifty in all, being driven like cattle. Their path crossed mine and, even by torchlight I could see that they were bleeding profusely from open wounds and gashes on their faces. Many had had their noses slit. My sensibilities affronted, I called to one of their captors and demanded to know the reason for this treatment of the ladies. The soldier spat. 'They're no ladies – they're Irish whores'. He spat again and returned to his task, which I could see provided him with great enjoyment.

I am sorry to have to recount this tale to you, but I cannot conceal my revulsion at this act. I had to unburden this tale on someone, and you are ever my closest confidante.

I cannot countenance this sort of action from anyone with an iota of goodness and honour in them. I have seen many foul things, but none touched me so deeply as this. It was only when we entered Leicester that I realized that we were as bad as the other. I shall be glad when this is all over and I can return to you. After such a battle and victory as this, I feel we are in sight of an end. I shall count the days until then.

Keep safe at all costs. I can only make sense of this madness when I think of you. I love you.

God Bless,

John

When she had finished reading, Kate was surprised to find that she was sitting down. Mr Barnard was staring at her intently.

'Not bad news, I hope?'

'Pardon?' For a moment she was lost in the image of the things John had written. 'Oh, no. No bad news . . . everybody is well enough.'

'May I read it?'

Kate seemed distracted. 'No, no. There are some things . . . yes, in fact you can,' she said with more urgency in her voice. She handed him the letter. He read it avidly. Slowly, his expression changed. He handed it back to her.

'I had no idea. When he writes to me, his letters are full of hope and excitement. Nothing like this.'

'I worry about him, father. How will he be when this is all over – how many things like this will he have to witness before the end? War has been his life for so many years, how will he settle down to the peace?'

He rubbed his forehead as if he was perplexed. 'In all honesty, I have no idea. You know him better than I. It grieves me to say it, but I hardly know my own son.' He shook his head and sat down beside her. 'Perhaps the news of the child will help him.'

Kate sighed and rested her head on his shoulder. 'Who knows? We can only hope.'

Even as their thoughts turned to him, John was again putting pen to paper. Now that he could see an end to the war, it seemed more important than ever that he should reassure Kate that he was well.

For the first time since he had left home he had actually slept in a bed last night. They were in Taunton, which they had reached in five days of forced march from Leicester. The march had been a sickening affair. Instead of taking on their usual role in the vanguard, going ahead of the army, they had been forced to take up a position behind one of the regiments of foot. Their task was one of guarding the infantry, not against attack from without – but from desertions within.

He was under orders to return any deserters to their commander to be shot. These were orders which he found he could not comply with. On the second night of the march his men had caught three of them. After many long hours of talk, he managed to persuade them to return to their regiment before they were missed. On other nights he had been less successful. Even now he had half-a-dozen men concealed in his baggage train and he had no idea of what to do with them. He thought he would probably try to pass them on to another regiment as new recruits, once they had come to their senses. If not, he would be forced to turn them loose to fend for themselves, though he knew that they would not last long. General Fairfax had roaming companies of dragoons, prowling the countryside with orders to kill deserters on sight.

He had nearly finished his letter when Jack came in. He took off his helmet and threw it on the table in disgust. The rag which was wound about his head was filthy and caked with blood.

'You ought to get some clean linen for that – you have been wearing that bandage since Naseby,' John commented.

'There's no time for that now. I've just heard that we're off to Bridgewater, moving out in an hour. Are there any vittles to be had? My belly's beginning to think my throat's been cut.'

John called out to the innkeeper. When he appeared he ordered him to bring them both some food and a bowl of water and some linen. He would dress Jack's wound himself, he said.

'Oh, no, you don't, John my lad. I know you, you're none too careful when it comes to this.'

'If you will not go to the surgeon and, as you affirm, we have only one hour, then you will have to suffer my tender mercies.'

When the food arrived, John would not let Jack tuck into it until he had had his wound dressed. Jack slumped in his chair, resigned to his fate. John soaked the bandage and began peeling it away. Before the wound had even been uncovered, Jack began yelping in pain. John was unimpressed.

'I swear, Sergeant, when it comes to this you are the greatest coward in the army. If you fear to have your wounds dressed then you should not go rushing around the field of battle like a man possessed.'

Jack mumbled some unintelligible protest and screwed up his face.

'It is no good complaining – I saw you. You should know better than to charge straight at a musketeer when he is about to fire. A hair's breadth nearer and you would have been killed.'

Jack laughed, then winced with pain. 'Aye, but it was funny, though. The damned musket ball rattled around in my helmet for ages, then it dropped down my back – it was hot as the fires of hell. Ow! Mind what you're doing there.'

'It is off now. Let me have a look at it.' John peered at the wound. It ran from his temple to just behind his ear. There were flecks of blue powder in it, but it was not deep. 'You are very lucky, as ever, it's clean. In faith, I know not how you manage it.'

'The Devil looks after his own, as they say,' he said with a crafty smile.

'I confess I am beginning to believe it. I have lost count of the times you have been cut up and yet every time you come away from it laughing. Come, let us eat. It can bleed for a while – let the air get to it. I shall dress it later.' John finished his letter while he ate. He sent it via the commissary rider. The fastest messages in the army were always those demanding more food.

By noon they were back on the road again. They were making for Bridgewater, but they had not gone very far when they received new orders to turn east. They were pursuing Lord Goring's army. With heavy hearts they realized that they were retracing their steps back east along the way they had come.

Over the next few days they were led a merry chase.

Goring was finally run to ground at Langport.

It was a hot, dusty morning. John felt himself slowly cooking inside his armour. Flies and midges buzzed around his face. They were close to the river and mosquitoes were dining on both himself and his horse. He felt it shift under him with each bite.

His company were waiting for orders to charge. The plan was quite simple. Goring was at the top of the hill and the only way up was across a narrow bridge and then up a similarly narrow lane. At the top of the hill Goring had two artillery pieces and there were musketeers on the other side of the river, waiting to pick them off as they crossed. John considered the plan. If it was successful it would be the most elegant and daring action he had ever seen. If, however, it failed – and it would only take a few fallen horses in the first wave to throw the whole thing into confusion, then they would be stranded on the other side of the river, unable to move and easy targets for Goring's musketeers. The only redeeming factor in this daring venture was that he and his men would be in the second wave.

Just at that moment Fairfax's artillery opened fire. The cannons roared behind and started their horses fidgeting. His own mount snorted as the first whiff of gunpowder reached his nostrils. He reared up, but John leaned forward and whispered quietly and soothingly into his ear, playing with his forelock. 'Gentle, boy, gentle. You know that smell – it means you are going for a little run in a while. We can go and play with our friends over the river. Wait a while. Be patient.' He patted the horse's flank reassuringly as he settled down. In the hedgerow on the other side small puffs of smoke were followed by cracks of musketfire. Fairfax had sent skirmishers across the river to keep Goring's men occupied.

This was it. They would get the order any minute now. John settled in the saddle and glanced back at Jack. They were stretched back in a long column, four abreast, ready to career across the bridge at full pelt.

The signal went out. Major Bethel's command up

ahead swung into action and thundered headlong at the bridge. There was a little scattered gunfire from the other bank, but within a few moments they were across and charging up the hill. Then Desborough's bugler sounded the charge and it was their turn.

'Keep low on your horses, men. I'll see you at the top!' John shouted as he spurred his horse on. They emerged from the woods into the bright sunlight.

John felt his horse rise and fall under him as it got into its stride. Every beat of its hooves juddered through his body. Again there were puffs of musket smoke, but now he could hear nothing but the horse's heavy breath which mingled with his own and the roar of blood in his ears.

On the bridge now, the beat of the horses' hooves changed to a clatter as earth gave way to stone. A musketeer rushed out from the undergrowth, swinging his musket like a club. John took out his pistol and fired at him. He did not see the outcome of the shot, but carried on heedless of his safety. There was no time to worry.

Ahead, Bethel had broken through at the top. He could hear fierce fighting, but he could see nothing. He urged his horse on. Along the road the hedgerow was lined with fallen horses and their riders. They had driven themselves into the bushes as they fell so that they might not hinder those who followed.

From the corner of his eye he spotted a knot of musketeers beating a poor trooper to death with their musket butts. Again and again the blows rained down on him. There was nothing John could do. He could not stop now.

He crested the ridge and was brought to an abrupt halt. Ranged before him an army of maybe 3000 men waited to be engaged. Bethel was already driving hard into them. There was nothing else for it but to carry on. He took his remaining pistol and held it aloft. They would make a 'thunderbolt' charge and hope to God that Fairfax would not be far behind. The men formed a wide block of charging cavalry and fired their pistols at the moment before they tore into the enemy. Men and horses were going down in earnest now, but still they charged on. If they paused, they would be engulfed.

Suddenly, the enemy infantry broke and John's company rode straight through them. He ordered the wheel and charge again, but already their adversaries were running across the field toward the companies that were yet unfought. John heard Desborough's bugler sound the pursuit. He nodded to his own, who took up the call. They chased the royalists across the field. Their fellows could not fire for fear of hitting their own. Neither could they set up a hedge of pikes, which would have impaled their comrades. They were unprotected as John's men swept down on them. Where was Fairfax?

They fought on for a full quarter-hour and still he did not come. Then, as it seemed that Goring's men were getting the upper hand, the rest of the army finally arrived. Bugles sounded all around the enemy position. With a sigh of relief he recognized the refrain of the royalist 'Withdraw!'

Fresh troops were coming through their own lines now and John called his own men off. They retired to lick their wounds.

He could not be sure how many of his men had heeded his call, but as he looked about him it seemed that their losses were grievously heavy. There could not have been more than sixty of them left in all. Jack was not amongst them.

'Did anyone see what happened to Jack Wyatt?' John shouted. A young soldier came forward.

'I saw him go down at the beginning of the lane, Captain.'

Suddenly, John was taken by panic. 'Was he shot? How did he fall?' He remembered the men with the musket butts.

The young soldier tried to allay his fears. 'No, sir. Two horses went down before him. He tried to vault over them and his mount stumbled. He fell, that is all.'

Another soldier continued the tale. 'He's right, sir. He would never have made the jump, but he essayed it anyway. I think I saw him get up but he was limping.'

John heaved a sigh of relief. He smiled sheepishly at his men. 'Thank God for that.' He looked around him. 'The battle has moved on. Go and gather up all our fallen comrades and take them with all haste back to the surgeon. I will go back and find Sergeant Wyatt.'

He turned his horse about and rode back up the hill. He had not gone very far when he encountered two riders coming the other way, toward the battle. It was Cromwell and Ireton. The general held up his hand in greeting.

'How now, Master Barnard. Surely the battle is the other way.'

John pulled up his horse and reined him in. He smiled as he saluted.

'Yes, sir. But the battle is nearly over and we have done our part. See over yonder?' He pointed to his company. 'They are the greatest band of heroes I have ever commanded, yet we are many fewer than when we crossed the bridge. I am returning to attend to my sergeant who fell on the road.'

The younger man sneered contemptuously at him. 'Then I take it that you and your men have no further stomach for the fight, Captain Barnard.' He turned to Cromwell. 'I thought this gentleman inveighed against those who fought half-heartedly, sir?'

John wiped his mouth with the back of his gauntlet. The sweat tasted bitter on his lips.

'And so I did, Master Ireton. But there was nothing half-hearted about the way my men conducted themselves today. They did the job that was set for them and more. We took heavy casualties and we were being relieved. I called them off, they had done their work. General, may I go and attend to my wounded?'

But Ireton would not give ground so easily. 'Then you received no orders to withdraw?' he demanded.

'My orders were to engage the enemy until the main

force arrived . . . sir.'

John glowered at this young popinjay. It was as clear as the nose on his face that he knew very little about conducting a battle and yet he had the command of hundreds of men. John was too tired to argue the toss, though, and besides he had more pressing demands on his time. He glanced at Cromwell.

'General, may I be excused?' he asked, wearily.

'Very well Captain Barnard.' He smiled. 'I will ride a way with you. Henry, will you go on ahead and pay my respects to Tom Fairfax, I will be with you shortly.'

Ireton could barely conceal the slight he felt at this. 'Very good, sir. I shall attend to it straightaway.' He spurred his horse on with needless violence. Cromwell laughed quietly as he went.

'You should pay him no heed, John. He is an impetuous boy, but he is brave enough for all that. He showed his mettle at Naseby.'

'You kept us too busy on the right flank for us to notice what was going on on the left, General,' he lied. It was better to lie than to speak his mind on this matter. The general clearly doted on Henry Ireton. The talk in the camp was that he was courting Cromwell's daughter. The general seemed pleased at this comment.

'Aye,' he sighed reflectively. 'God and all his mercies were with us on that day.' He laughed. 'And it seems that He was with us again today. I watched your charge. I must confess, my heart went out to you. Let us presently go and attend to your sergeant.'

Jack was sat with his back propped up against an oak tree. He had a pistol in one hand and a flask in the other. In front of him was a royalist musketeer, squirming on the ground, seemingly in great pain. When he saw John coming, Jack raised his flask.

'Ho, there, John. I thought my luck had run out there for a bit. I think I've broke my leg. My bloody horse rode off and left me and then this poor beggar comes along and takes me by surprise. I was that shocked I just let my pistol off – shot him in the cods, poor soul. But he had this on him,' he said, holding up his flask, 'which is keeping the pain at bay.' He laughed and took another long draught.

Cromwell laughed. 'It seems that your sergeant is in fine spirits. When he sobers up you may tell him that if I find him drunk again I will have him horsewhipped.' He clapped John on the back and rode off to rejoin Ireton.

When John mustered his men he discovered that things were not as bad as they had at first seemed. Though they had lost over twenty men, only three had been killed. Losses among the horses, though, were very grave, as often happened when cavalry charged full on a body of pike and musket. Many had been gored through the breast and had died a mercifully quick death, others hobbled about the field in pain. All about, single reports of pistolfire told the sorry tale of their fate.

John took his men back to camp. It was a long time before he could get a surgeon to look at Jack's leg. There were many more seriously wounded cases. It was well into the night before he was attended to. John went to find some food, but before he had gone far he heard the sergeant calling out his name.

'John! John Barnard – come here quick!'

He ran back to the surgeon's tent. Jack was wild-eyed and screaming. 'John! This damned sawbones wants to take my leg off – tell him he can't have it!'

John looked down at the leg. It was white and twisted, swollen and bruised around the break, but John could see that it was a clean break, down by the ankle. He looked up into the surgeon's eyes. They seemed dead, as though he was sleep-walking. He held a bloodstained knife in his hand, which he was getting ready to use. His arms were covered in blood up to the shoulder. The man was exhausted. He stayed the surgeon's hand, gently, and spoke quietly to him.

'You are tired, my friend. Too tired. You have seen too much suffering this day. This man needs a bone setting, not the knife. Look closely; the break is clean. Get some splints and bandages and set the leg.'

The surgeon seemed unmoved. 'The leg is damaged, it must come off,' he said, as if in a trance. John did not raise his voice, but his manner at once became more forceful and threatening.

'Whether you attend to his leg or not, it is not coming off. Either you set it, or I will take him away and attend to it myself. But if you persist, then I will kill you. Do you understand?'

The surgeon seemed so shocked by this threat that his manner suddenly changed. It was as though he was waking up. He stared at John, then he looked down at the leg. His expression changed to one of horror as he realized what he had been about to do.

'Oh, my God. Forgive me. I was beside myself. I have done so much cutting and sawing this day. I think I was losing my reason. Please, forgive me.'

He rushed off to get some splints and bandages. Setting the bone was a bitterly painful process and Jack lost consciousness twice before it was over. He was carried back to their camp on a litter. John walked beside him. He smiled up at his captain and took his hand.

'Thank God you were there. He would have done for me there and no mistake.'

'He was tired . . . we are all tired.'

'John. If he had ignored your warning – you wouldn't really have killed him, would you?'

John rubbed his eyes with his fingertips and stretched as he considered the question.

'After all the years we have been together and all that you have done for me, do you really think I would let a man like that turn you into a cripple through his own negligence? It's not the sort of thing I would jest about. If "push came to shove" then, yes – I would have killed him.'

Jack squeezed his hand. 'That's my boy.' He cackled with mirth.

Even though the bone was set, John had the immediate problem of what he was going to do with Jack. He could not just drag him around the countryside, from battle to battle. He decided at length to send him home to Ely. He would have peace and rest and would recover his strength. When he broached the idea to Jack, he was mildly surprised to find that he did not complain in the least – in fact he would, he said, rather enjoy the holiday.

Eleven

Jack had never liked the smell of mules and the mule-train driver next to him displayed all the sweetness of his charges. His conversation was little better and on the whole he thought the man could learn a lesson or two in manners from the animals he was driving. He turned his face away as he realized that the driver was about to spit again. It wasn't that he was squeamish, it was just that he had learned over the last three days that the muleteer's aim was not all it might be. He thanked the Lord that this was the last stage of the journey, for ahead of them the vast bulk of Ely Cathedral reared up from the otherwise unrelieved landscape.

The journey had taken him nearly two weeks. He reflected grimly that with a good horse, or maybe a change of horses, he could have done it in three days. The first few days hadn't been too bad. John had taken him with the company as far as Shaftesbury, where they had gone to sort out the Clubmen of Dorset – local farmers and labourers mostly, but they were helping themselves to the army's supply trains. He had had to watch as his own lads went off to fight. It was a strange feeling, watching them go. Suddenly he had felt very old. As they rode past him, he looked at their fresh young faces. There were very few of them who were more than half his age. Perhaps it was time for him to put up his sword. He thought he might open up an inn when he got his back pay – he'd always fancied himself as an innkeeper, he could grow himself a beer belly and a big red nose and spend all day propping up the bar, like he had done before he became a soldier. On the other hand, there was always the Widow Norris, a lady he had met in Ely, she would know how to help an old soldier through his twilight years.

The cart went over a rut in the road, which brought him back to the present. God, he was sick of mule trains, the smell, the snail's pace and the grinding boredom of the muleteers' talk, which was mostly about the minute details of their beasts' habits and the grinding boredom of their own lives.

When he had returned from dealing with the Clubmen, John had put him on a mule train bound for London. The journey had taken ten days in all. They had been obliged to take a wide berth around Winchester, which was still in hostile hands. Their route had taken them past Basing House, which still held out against Parliament, though its defenders were no longer the thorn in the side that they had been. Dragoons kept the road open during the day, but the route was still perilous at night and convoys that travelled after dark still needed heavy escort.

He had thought to spend a few days in London, looking up some old friends, but his money was running low. John had given him a purse of silver shillings to tide him over, but to his disgust he had squandered most of it dicing with the muleteers – they might be dull fellows, but when it came to money they were sharp as knives. So, he had taken the first transport he could find that was going to Ely – which, unsurprisingly, was yet another mule train. It had cost him half a crown, which was a princely sum for three days of unmitigated misery. Still, they were nearly there now, and their route would take them past Kate and John's house, so he had that to be grateful for. He wondered how Kate would receive him. He looked like a scarecrow that had spent too long in the field, he was caked in mud from head to toe and he imagined that he would smell quite ripe to a civilized nose.

At last it was all over. The cart pulled up outside the house. He managed to lower himself down, unaided – though the muleteer offered him no help anyway. He hobbled around to the back and got out his sack. The train rolled on with no word of farewell from the driver. Jack rested his shoulder heavily on the makeshift crutch he had fashioned and heaved a sigh of relief. He hobbled his way to the front door and knocked on it. For a long while there was no reply. Then a head appeared from the bedroom window above. It was Ruth, Kate's companion.

'Beggars to the back!' she cried and slammed the window shut before he could say anything. There was nothing else for it but to go around, he supposed.

Slowly, steadily, he made his way around the house with a step and a hop, then a pause as he dragged his sack behind him. It seemed to take an age. It was not altogether the greeting he had expected, but he knew that at least Kate would be pleased to see him.

When he got round to the back of the house he spotted Kate at the far end of the garden, cutting roses. He was about to call out to her when the companion attracted his attention:

'Over here, old man. I suppose you'll be wanting some dole,' she said, none too kindly.

Very well, Jack thought, if that was her attitude, he would play this out for a bit, just for a laugh. She set a platter of bread and cheese and a mug of water on the garden table and pointed to it. 'Now mind you don't take too long about eating it – and don't you go bothering my mistress neither,' she said sharply.

Jack bowed humbly, and touched his muddy forelock as he shuffled past her, hiding his face; though he looked so grizzled and grimy she probably would not have recognized him, anyway.

'Oi thank you kindly for your hospitality – there's not so many places be so welcomin' to a poor beggar fellow,' he said, putting on an accent.

Ruth was unimpressed. 'And you'd find none here if it weren't for my mistress's instructions, so mind your behaviour.'

He lowered himself gradually on to the stool and sighed contentedly; it was good to take the weight off his leg, even after so short a time. He looked across the garden.

'Is that your mistress over there?' he asked. 'She's a fine bonny lookin' lady if ever I did see one.' Ruth was behind him and she could not see him smiling. He took a long draught of water, which helped to wash some of the dust of the road from his mouth and throat.

'The cheek of you. A filthy beggar like you passing comments like that about a lady of quality – and in her condition too!'

The shock of this unexpected revelation sent the water up his nose. He almost choked on it.

'She's havin' a baby?' he spluttered.

'As if it's any of your business, you naughty man,' Ruth snapped at him.

She ran into the house and came out again, brandishing a broom – which she used to set about him. Jack had not expected this. He raised his arms to protect himself from the repeated blows. My God, he thought, she's worse than the cavaliers! It was all that he could do to keep her from breaking his skull.

Kate was disturbed by the commotion at the house. She turned around and was astounded to see Ruth beating some rough fellow with a broom. She ran across the garden to see what was happening. She heard him crying, 'Ow! Ow! Stop woman – you're killing me! Help! Kate help me!'

The mention of her name stopped Kate short, but Ruth kept on hitting the man. Suddenly Kate realized who he was. She called out to Ruth, 'Ruth, stop. Can you not see – it is Jack!'

The broom stopped in mid swoop. Ruth's jaw dropped. 'Oh, Sergeant Jack, oh no – oh dear.' She gently touched the lump which was growing on his crown. 'Forgive me . . . you should have said it was you,' she said awkwardly. She looked up at her mistress. 'He never said it was him – how was I to know?'

Jack lowered his arms and looked up, though he kept a wary eye on the broom which Ruth was still brandishing.

'And to think John was worried for your safety while he was away. For myself, I'd rather face the Whitecoats.'

Kate came rushing up to him, then stopped short as she got close. 'Jack, I am so happy to see you. But I hope you do not mind my saying this and I can think of no other way of saying it, but Jack – you stink.'

On the whole, Kate was glad to have Jack staying with her. He could be cantankerous and he was a terrible patient, always up and about, nosing into everything and making a general nuisance of himself. Still, his gentleness and kindness and his sense of humour lightened the days. Even though he was a bad patient, Kate found that caring for him provided a welcome distraction from her own condition. The morning sickness was beginning to abate and it was still too early for her to be showing. There were some days when, if it were not for her ravenous hunger, she could almost forget the life within her. Even so, there was one matter which weighed heavily on her. Finally, she decided to take the sergeant into her confidence and ask his advice on the matter.

He was sitting at the garden table, his favourite haunt – he took great delight in reminding Ruth about the first time he had sat there – when Kate came out and sat beside him. For a while they did not speak. He was poring over a book, an occupation which for him required great concentration. He followed the words with his finger. When he finished the passage he laid the book down and smiled at her.

'Did you know that it was John that taught me my letters?'

In fact, Kate did know, but he took such great pride in telling her, that every time he did, she pretended that it was the first time. He was on the point of relating the tale, when she interrupted him.

'Jack, it is John that I have come to talk to you about,' she confessed.

'Then you have my undivided attention,' he replied.

She knew that this would not be an easy subject to

broach, but Jack was to her a father-figure. If she could not talk to him then who could she talk to? He waited patiently for her to start.

'Well, Jack, it is about the baby,' she said awkwardly. She struggled for words. 'Not so much the baby itself, it is more about John.' She realized that this was not going the way she had intended. She took a deep breath. 'You see, Jack. I have not told him about it yet.'

Jack nodded as he considered this piece of news. 'How long have you known?' he asked.

'About six weeks, I suppose. Though I know for sure that it is nearly two and a half months now.'

Jack smiled. 'Then that will have been when we came riding through on our way north. I never thought he was such a romantic lad.' He laughed quietly. 'So why haven't you told him yet? If you'd written to him when you first knew, like as not he still wouldn't know now.'

'But his letters come so quickly, why should mine be so slow?'

'Because he can use the army dispatch riders, and because you're always in the same place. The mail is always following us around, sometimes it takes months. If you wrote him now, he might not find out 'til October. . . .'

'October!' she cried.

'Aye. So you might as well write him now – or he might get a bit of a shock when he gets home.'

It took a while for this to sink in. Whilst Kate considered this, Jack was looking at her with mild concern. He finally broke his silence. 'I hope you don't mind my asking, Kate, but why have you held off writing to him for so long?'

Kate sighed. 'That was why I wanted to talk to you. You see it is still not very long, two and a half months. I am told that, as this is my first, I still might miscarry. I did not want John to get his hopes up only to have them dashed when he gets home.'

'That's a woman's matter; you didn't want to talk to me about that, did you?'

'No,' she admitted. 'I need to know what effect the knowledge that he might be a father will have on him. The last thing I want is to have his judgement impaired by that.'

Jack laughed. 'My God, Kate – you do underestimate us fellows. We aren't so stupid as all that, you know.' He shook his head and suddenly he became very serious. 'No, I suppose you're right to be concerned, though we can take these things in our stride as well as you women. Still, do you not think he has a right to know if he is goin' to be a dad?'

'Yes, yes. I know you are right – but what if this makes him stay his hand, as you have told me yourself men do out of love, what then? I am so worried about him, Jack. When I read his letters – he sees and does such things – the way he describes them I can tell he is so sickened by the war.'

'Then your news will make him all the more eager to live and to get this whole thing over with. I'd say that the war is coming to an end now. At Naseby we captured thousands of the King's soldiers – seasoned veterans; some of 'em I knew myself. I was talkin' to them and they were saying that they had had a bellyful of it and all were glad to be out. It's only a matter of time now, Kate. Write to him; he'll be that happy, I swear.' He took her hand in his and squeezed it. 'And while we're on the subject of the end of the war, there's something I'd like you to do for me. I'd like you to invite the Widow Norris around one day. . . .'

Jack's pursuit of the widow gained pace as his leg improved. He managed to raise some money, under the pretext of recruiting a company of volunteers to defend the city. The worthies of the city, Mr Barnard included, were eager to grant him funds, for the remains of the King's Army were marching south and by the 20th they were in Huntingdon. Fairfax was still in the west and there was panic in the city. For a while it seemed inevitable that they would turn east and Jack's little band of boys and grey-hairs were all that stood between them and destruction.

Then, for some reason, the King's Army turned west and the city heaved a sigh of relief. Still, the citizens were grateful for Jack's service and they insisted on granting him a generous pension. Unbeknownst to Jack, it was Mr Barnard who had been instrumental in this, for he had a great deal more to thank the servant for, over all the years he had cared for his son. Little did he know that the sergeant would use his new-found wealth to woo his widow.

Every evening Jack would return with fresh tales of his courting. He looked very different now from when he had arrived. He had bought himself a fine black stallion and a new set of clothes. Though he would never admit to it, it was obvious to Kate and Ruth that he scented his beard with lavender. Though they often went into his room to search for it they never found the bottle. He must, they reasoned, carry it about with him. Though his leg was healed and he walked freely about the house, he had taken to using a silver-topped cane when he went on his visits, as he explained to Kate one night.

'Women take very kindly to a gentleman who has been wounded in their defence. A slight limp lends a certain dignity to a fellow's bearing. Of course, I refrain from telling her how I came about it, for fear of her sensibilities, you understand.'

'Why Jack,' Kate replied, 'you are nothing but an old fraud!'

'Ah, well. I wouldn't want her to know how I got injured, would I? And I'd be most grateful if you didn't let on – after all I have my pride,' he said trying to elicit some sympathy. Then he smiled. 'But I'll tell you something, you see this ring?' He held out his right hand. 'I've had to put this on the other hand so that I'll remember which hand to hold the cane in. I can hardly remember myself which leg I broke.'

Summer waned and gave way to autumn. Kate had done

as Jack had bade her and put her news in a letter to John, but each time he wrote to her, there was no reaction from him. Jack comforted her; he pointed out that from his letters it was clear that he was moving around a lot. In September he was in Bristol, but in October he was in Winchester. His last letter came from Basing which had finally fallen after Cromwell had called up some heavy artillery pieces. In the end the place still had to be taken by storm, but it was a sign that things were finally drawing to a close.

On a frosty morning, late in November, Kate was out getting a few logs for the fire from the pile at the back of the house. It was not a job she would normally have done, but Ruth was in town and Jack had not yet returned from paying a call on the widow last night – he was staying overnight more and more often these days. She had thought about taking him to task about it lately, but since neither of them were children, it was difficult to broach the subject. The only thing that stopped it from being the scandal of the city was that she lived in a big house in the country. If prying eyes had noticed his comings and goings then the game would have been up long ago.

She picked up the large basket which she had filled with logs and stretched her back as she slowly straightened herself. Everything seemed to be such an effort these days and this lump which went before her all the time did nothing to help the situation.

She heard a rider bring his horse to a stop out front. That will be Jack now, she thought, and decided to string this job out so that he would come and help her. As she heard the horse being led around to the stable, one of the logs fell out of the box.

'Damn,' she cursed under her breath as she began the long process of bending down to get it. 'Jack,' she called. 'You know you should be doing this. Come and lend me your hand, will you?'

'You are quite right, Kate. You should not be doing that. If I had known that you would be fetching and carrying in your condition, I would have come all the sooner.' It was not Jack's voice. . . .

John put his hands over hers and took them away from the handles of the box. He turned her around to face him.

'Now, let me have a look at you,' he said, holding her out at arm's length. 'You know, this is not quite how I pictured you, all these months. It comes as quite a surprise, I can tell you.' He looked her up and down. 'Are you sure that is not merely a cushion, or is it some new fashion women are wearing this year?' He laughed as he pulled her close to him. 'Oh, Kate. It is so good to see you again.' He kissed her and then held her tightly to him once more. The air was cold about them, but in John's arms it was so warm, she could have stayed there forever.

'John, thank God you are home, I have missed you so much.'

He gathered up the box handles in one hand and placed the other around her waist.

'Come, Kate. Let us go in. I am that tired, I have been riding all night.'

He sat sprawled out in front of the fire with his boots off, warming his toes. It seemed almost strange to have him home again after all this time. Kate stared at this great lump of a man. She had almost forgotten how tall he was. His chin lowered to his breast and then jerked up again. He glanced guiltily across at her.

'Forgive me, Kate. I was falling asleep. Did you say something?'

She smiled down at him. 'No, I was just looking at you, that is all.'

'I must make a sorry sight. Look at me,' he said, slapping his tunic and watching clouds of dust fly up. 'I look more like a scarecrow.'

Kate shook her head. 'You look good enough to me. Jack looked a lot worse when he arrived, but we cleaned him up well enough. You would hardly recognize him now – he looks quite like a cavalier in his finery.'

'So, he is still here?'

'Oh, yes. On and off. He spends much of his time with the Widow Norris nowadays.'

'My God. Does Father know?' He feigned a look of horror. 'Father had designs on that lady himself, you know.'

'No, I don't think so – or at least I hope not. It was largely thanks to your father that Jack has the wherewithal to court the widow.'

'What? Is Father subsidizing this suit?' he asked, genuinely surprised this time.

'Oh, no. He is being subsidized by the City of Ely. Jack is quite a hero hereabouts. I told you so in my letters.'

John reached down into the breast of his jacket. 'This is the only letter I received from you – or anybody, in all my time away. It is the sweetest letter I have ever read. It came two weeks ago and you wrote it in August.'

'Jack said the mail was slow, but that is scandalous. Where have you been?' Kate came and settled on his lap.

'Good heavens lady, you are a mite bit heavier than the last time you sat there. Sit up a moment.' He shifted his legs to accommodate her.

'You have become most unchivalrous these last few months, husband,' she said, settling herself down again. 'So, what have you been up to while you have been away?'

'Well, let me see . . . where did you get my last letter from?'

'Basing House. That arrived at the beginning of this month.'

'Basing, you say. Hmmm. . . .' He raised his eyebrows in surprise. 'Well, we can look forward to a few more letters yet. Since then we've been down in Devon.'

'Devon?'

'Yes, it is a beautiful county, but the people have been sorely oppressed by the King's men there. We have been harrying Sir Richard Grenville's army and trying to bring them to a fight, but to no avail. Yet still he strips the country bare, stealing and burning as he goes. There are few royalists for whom I bear any malice – but Grenville, he is a criminal and should be brought to justice. Anyway, much of the army is wintering with Fairfax in Exeter. My own lads have been sent back to Newmarket as there is not enough fodder for our horses there, and when I got your letter I presented the company with the option of a quick ride home – which they jumped at. We arrived in the small hours of this morning and I gave them a fortnight's leave. I left young Tomikin at Father's as he has nowhere else to go – I expect Ruth will be pleased to see him.'

Kate snuggled into his arms. 'Nearly as happy, I would expect, as I am to see you.'

Jack returned at noon. Kate was still in John's arms, but he was asleep. She put her finger to her lips for him to be quiet and Jack obeyed. Tiptoeing through to the kitchen he whispered to Kate, 'I've just seen Ruth in town with your Tomikin – they don't waste much time these young 'uns, do they?'

'About as much time as you old 'uns, Jack Wyatt,' John replied, opening one eye. 'What's all this I hear about you chasing my father's widow?' He held out his hand to the sergeant, who grasped it warmly.

Kate giggled. 'I thought you were asleep!' she cried and set about tickling his ribs. He fought her off and, still laughing, he replied, 'And so I was until my nose was offended by the pungency of lavender which suddenly pervaded the room – my God, Jack, you smell like a Scottish dandy.'

Jack did not take offence, he simply winked at him. 'Tools of the trade, my boy. Only tools of the trade.' He pulled his friend up. 'I came home as soon as the lad told me you were here. It's good to see you.' He jerked his thumb at the kitchen. 'Kate's been letting me brew some beer while I've been stayin' here. I figured you'd be home soon and it's just ready. Mind, if you'd have stayed away any longer I'd have drunk the lot.'

'And when are you here long enough to drink it?' Kate demanded.

He smiled and bowed, very courteously. 'Well, Mistress Katherine. I'm here now. And so is my best drinking partner – or, I should say, drinking partners, for I hope you will join us?'

Kate patted her bulge. 'I will join you for a small beer. But I would not want to start this little one into bad habits, would I?'

Ruth returned with Tomikin in tow about an hour later. Already, the others were in fine spirits. Jack had started cooking the dinner. It was the only meal he knew how to cook – beef in beer. For the rest of the afternoon and into the evening, it was one long-running party. That night, for the first time in months, Kate happily snuggled into her husband's arms and slept as peacefully as a babe.

That Christmas, Mr Barnard – slightly greyer and wider about the girth than last year, stood up and announced that his prayer had come true, for his family were all safely gathered around the table. Stephen was a good deal taller than Kate remembered him, though he still needed a cushion under him to eat at the table. Kate had to eat at arm's length – she was carrying an enormous bulge even though she still had two months to go. Jack and the Widow Norris kept their mutual secret well hidden. John and Michael seemed in excellent fettle – they talked about setting up in partnership after the war. Only Gwen seemed unchanged, she was just as merry as she had ever been. The celebrations were crowned by Ruth and Tomikin, who announced that they were to be wed before he returned to the company after New Year and they asked if John and Kate would stand as their witnesses. The war was nearly over and everyone looked forward to an even happier New Year in 1646.

Twelve

'God! Oh God! Where is John? I want John!' Kate writhed in pain as she felt her body being forced apart. The pressure seemed to crush her lungs. She fought for air. Another rush of blood roared in her ears. Her throat was hoarse from the bitter bile which rose up with each convulsion of her body. The fit passed for a brief moment, then with a sense of panic, she felt the next one rise within her. She stared up, eyes wild and bloodshot.

'Oh, Gwen . . . here comes another one . . . oh God. Oh no.' The agony grew worse as the pressure mounted.

Gwen glanced down at the midwife. She tried to remain calm, to control her revulsion. There was so much blood – too much blood. The midwife's face was tight-lipped and anxious as she pushed and pulled at Kate's thighs. She looked up momentarily, her expression unchanged. It was taking too long, far too long. . . .

'Push again, Kate. Force yourself. Come on . . .' Gwen urged.

'I am pushing, damn it!' Her sister shouted, heedless of anything but the pain.

'You must try harder. Now!' the midwife snapped.

Kate rose up on her shoulders and gripped the bedstead above her, she drove down with all her might. The pain grew to an unbearable height, then suddenly abated. Gwen looked down in awed revulsion as the tiny head appeared, blue and purple, limp and lifeless. The midwife's expression became more anxious.

'Push again woman. Quickly!' Her hands worked feverishly as she tried to free its shoulders.

Kate obeyed and drove down again. Gwen could see the tension build in her sister's body. The muscles in her arms and legs quivered with exertion. The sinews in her swollen throat stood out like taut cords. Sweat poured from her brow and ran down the tracks of her bloated veins. She could not stop now. She knew Kate was nearly exhausted, but Dear God, don't let her stop now. . . .

The shoulders were out. The midwife ran her hands up its body and quickly pulled it out. The mother was forgotten now. All her attention was focused on saving the baby's life. They were still joined, then Kate felt an involuntary rush within her as the afterbirth issued forth. The midwife paid it no heed. She cleared the baby's nose and mouth and blew up its nostrils, then into its mouth. Kate's sense of foreboding grew as, second after second, there was no reassuring cry. The midwife took it to one side, the cord still hanging, and held it to her breast with its head down. She placed her hand on its back and pushed sharply, then again. The third time there was a tiny choking noise and a dark gout fell from its mouth. She held it up by the heels and smacked it. Kate was overcome with relief as it started to cry. The midwife glanced across at her and wearily smiled.

'Mistress Barnard, you have a daughter.'

Gwen heaved a great sigh of relief. 'In God's name, that seemed to last forever. It must have been one of your most difficult births, surely?'

The midwife smiled and shook her head. 'Not really, your ladyship. There were a few awkward moments. Something must have ruptured, that was why there was so much blood. The child's cover was torn and so I more than half expected her mouth to be blocked. Otherwise, it was a very straightforward confinement – if somewhat longer than usual.' She handed the child to her mother.

'Do not be distressed by her swollen head, she has spent the last four hours pushing with it. It will soon go down.' And with that, she started about the business of cleaning up around her.

Kate looked down at her daughter. She had thought that she would be overcome by the magic and wonder of it all. But in truth, all she could feel was relief that it was all over. And now she had this little baby – she was a curious little thing, all purple and slimy. She thought she had better get some of it off. She wiped her head with the edge of her wrap, getting the stuff from around her eyes.

'Good morning, Elanor – that is your name, you know.' Kate nuzzled up to her. Straightaway, the child started to cry again. Kate looked up to the midwife.

'What do I do now?' she asked.

'You're a mother now,' the midwife replied, 'you'll know.'

In many respects, the midwife had been right: Kate recovered quickly from her confinement and within a couple of days she was able to fully take up her motherly duties. She delighted in her little girl and longed for John to return, so that he could share her happiness. But he was away, God only knew where, at the war.

Gwen and Ruth's reaction to her changing the baby often made her laugh. On one occasion she actually saw Ruth's face turn green; she had thought before that it had only been a figure of speech, but Ruth had definitely been a pronounced green as she had been obliged to leave the room. Her time will come, Kate thought. After all, she was a married woman now.

As the first week of Elanor's life progressed, Kate noticed that the child did not seem to settle well. She always seemed to be crying. At first, Kate thought little of it, she had been warned that this was quite natural: she had been warned that at least for the first year, she would be a stranger to sleep and that moments of peace would come as a blessed relief. Those moments, however, were becoming more and more infrequent as the week went on.

Things came to a head one bitterly cold February

morning. Kate and Gwen were sitting in front of a great roaring fire. In spite of the inclement weather outside, the room was pleasantly warm. They had been talking for about half an hour, when their peace was broken by Elanor starting to cry in her crib beside them. Kate picked her up.

'I knew it would not last,' she muttered, philosophically. She checked Elanor's nether regions and when she found that this was not the problem, she started to unbutton her dress. 'Feeding time again, I fear. I swear, this child's appetite is insatiable.'

She shook her head and laughed resignedly, placing the baby to her breast.

Gwen looked on as Kate was nursing her daughter. She noticed a look of anguish on her sister's face. She shifted uneasily in her chair as the baby was suckling at her.

'Is there something amiss?' she asked.

Kate looked up. 'I know not. She seems to know what to do, but she is always hungry. I do not think I have enough milk for her. There is barely a trickle, Gwen. It is not something I want to do, but I think I am going to have to get in a wet-nurse.' She shook her head ruefully. 'What else can I do?'

Gwen nodded. She remembered the sense of failure she had felt when she had had to resort to another woman's milk. Her heart went out to her sister, but it seemed that there was nothing else for it.

'I will go into town and find a woman. There is nothing unusual about it,' she added cheerfully. 'I had to do the same for Stephen, and he is none the worse for it.' She stood up and went for her cloak. As she opened the front door she heard little Elanor crying and her mother trying to quieten her.

'Oh, God. I'm so sorry. Don't worry – all will be well soon. . . .' The mother's weeping mingled with her child's as Gwen quietly closed the door.

As the afternoon wore on, Gwen became more anxious. She had called at the doctor's and the midwife's, but neither of them could recommend a reputable nurse. Her search took her finally to a small dismal house behind the market place. The door was open, but she knocked on it anyway. She could hear movement within, but for a long time no one answered. Finally, a sullen looking child came to the door and ushered her in.

Inside, the house was badly lit and damp. The child ran back across the room to join some others who were clustered around a small fireplace. In the far corner of the room a woman sat in a rocking-chair, nursing her own baby. Gwen could see that at one time she had been beautiful indeed; but, though she was probably no older than herself, the ravages of time and children and poverty had wrought their toll.

She looked defiantly at this unbidden visitor. 'I know why you've come,' she said. 'There's some fine lady in a big warm house, but for all her riches, she can't do this.' She glanced down at the baby clinging to her breast. She shrugged ironically and a dribble of milk spilled on to the baby's cheek. She looked down at the children huddled around the fire. 'God knows, I've had to do it before – all this lot have shared their feeds with some other who's warm and well fed now, who would have died but for my own going hungry.' Her gaze returned to her baby. 'And now it's his turn.'

Gwen looked down pityingly at the woman. 'I will ensure they do not go hungry any more.'

'That's what they all say – and they keep to their word while they have need of me. But afterwards? They all cross the street to get away from me, with their fat, rosy-cheeked brats who laugh and point at our rags.'

'I will pay you well, I assure you.'

'Well, I need the money – there's no mistaking that.' She looked around her. 'They pay me by the feed. Usually they have their tuppences ready for when I've finished.' She laughed to herself. 'Sometimes I even have to remind them for that.'

Gwen was curious. She had seen poor people in the streets before, but never at such close proximity. She had never ever been to a place like this before. And there was something familiar about this woman. It was nagging her.

'Do I know you?' she asked.

'No, but I know you. My dad used to work for your dad, afore he died. Up to then I used to get all your cast-off clothes – there wasn't a thing I wore that you hadn't worn first. 'Course, I never got to wear the nicer ones – we had to sell them on for money. Your dad didn't pay that badly, but there was never enough to go round. Then, when he died . . . well, you know. . . .'

'Then you must be Harry Poynter's daughter. You used to stand outside our house waiting for him.'

'Yes, that was me,' the woman replied. 'But I wasn't waiting for my dad, I was waiting to see you. Waiting to see what you were wearing, wondering if I might get to wear it one day.' She turned to the children by the fire. 'Angel, stand up a minute, dear.'

The girl stood up, reluctantly. She was wearing a deep-blue velvet dress. It was worn at the elbow and the shoulder and a little too small for her, but for all that it was clean. She smiled awkwardly, then turned and went back to the fire. Her hair was tied with a ribbon of the same material. 'My mum took that from the hem to tie my hair with. She loves that dress dearly, don't you Angel?' The girl looked up and smiled. 'Almost as dearly as I loved it when I was a girl.'

'Was that one of mine? I don't remember,' Gwen confessed.

The woman sighed. 'It's the last one. I wouldn't part with it, even when times were bad. One day, I thought, my own little girl will get to wear it for her Sunday best. I never dreamed it would be her only dress.' She fell silent.

'Where is your husband?' Gwen asked quietly.

'Rob? Oh, he's in the army. There wasn't no work for him in the town or in the fields, so he signed up when it all started. He used to get paid regular. Times were good then, but he hasn't had a whiff of pay for nigh on a year now. He's off fighting the grandees' war and I haven't seen him since . . . well, since he gave me this little leaving present.' She bounced the little boy on her lap. 'We have to rely on the parish now. They let us have this house and we get a bit every week on account. I go and wait in line for it and they dole it out as though it was charity – even though they owe him a year's wages. I hate them.'

Gwen's manner became businesslike. 'Now, you say you charge twopence a feed. Well I think we can better that. I will give you a shilling a day. Here is a crown on account.'

She pulled a large silver coin from her purse, but the woman stopped her.

'Oh, no. You can't go giving me that,' she said.

'Why not?' Gwen replied. 'It is not as though it was charity.'

The woman laughed. 'Oh, I'll take your money and right gladly. But I couldn't take a crown from you. If I tried to spend it people would think I had stolen it.'

'Very well, I have nothing smaller, though. We will have to go back through town to get to my sister's house. We can change it there. By the way, I do remember you; your name's Gwen, like mine.'

The woman did not look up as she laced her bodice.

'Aye. It was yourself I was named after when I was born.'

By the time they returned to the house, Kate was in a fury.

'My God! Where have you been? You have been gone for hours!' She pointed angrily at the baby, which was screaming in its cot. 'Look at the poor thing, it's starving.' She took one look at the stranger. 'Who the hell is this?' She waved her hand at the woman. 'If you think I would let this dirty trollop anywhere near my baby – then you're a bigger fool than I took you for,' Kate stormed.

'Kate, this is Mrs Hollins – she has come to help us.' Gwen turned to the other woman. 'I am deeply sorry for this.'

'Don't worry,' she reassured her, 'this is common

enough. It's like water off a duck's back to me.' She folded her arms and stared Kate straight in the eye.

'Now then, Mrs Barnard, you don't need to worry about the way I look, just as long as I keep my tits clean – and you can be sure of that. So. Do I have your permission to feed the little mite before it screams its little heart out?'

Kate's anger became icy cold. 'You can do what you like for all I care.' And she stormed out of the room.

Mrs Hollins took the baby from her cot and put her to her open breast. The crying stopped immediately as little Elanor started to feed. She bade Gwen sit down.

'Now look. Since your sister's gone off, I'll have to talk to you. I can only come twice a day, in the morning and the evening. In-between times she'll have to feed the child herself – she'll have enough milk for a couple of feeds, even if they are small ones. It's important that she does, though. Otherwise, she may reject the baby altogether and that would be bad. If she doesn't do it willingly then you must make her. That might not be easy, but you'll have to grit your teeth and do it. I've seen many women like her before and what you've got to remember is that it's not them who's talking – at times like this there's a devil in them and they can't help themselves.'

'But I needed a wet-nurse for my boy,' Gwen replied, 'and I was never like this.'

'Aye, but you remember how you felt when you had to do it? Well, for some it's much worse.'

After a few minutes Elanor fell asleep and Mrs Hollins put her back in her cot. She laced herself up again. Gwen watched her.

'You know, there's one thing Kate had partly right. We can't have you coming up to the house dressed as you are. I hope you do not mind my asking, but could I not prevail upon you to take another of my dresses?'

Gwen Hollins looked her up and down with a twinkle of mirth in her eye. She laughed quietly once more. 'And I reckoned it might have fitted me – four babies ago.'

She shook her head. 'No, don't you worry none on that account – on seven bob a week I can afford to get myself something, as long as it's not too fancy.'

Upstairs, Kate watched the woman go up the street into town. She had heard Elanor stop screaming practically as soon as she had left her. There were still tears in her eyes. She had been a mother for less than a week and already she had failed her child. There was a knock on the bedroom door; she did not answer. Presently, Gwen came in uninvited.

'So she has gone, has she?' Kate said without turning away from the window.

'Yes. She will be back this evening.'

'I cannot believe you brought a filthy woman like that into my house.'

'She is not filthy,' Gwen replied, 'she is just poor, that is all.'

There was a long silence. Gwen sat down on the corner of the bed. 'I used to know her when I was a child.'

Kate turned around. 'And I suppose I should take that as some kind of recommendation?' she asked tersely. 'You have some very strange friends.'

'She is a good woman, Kate. You should see her children; they are clean and well cared for, even if they have little enough to eat. . . .'

'Rather like my own child, in fact.'

'Don't torture yourself, Kate. I had to have a wet-nurse and she has done the same for many women. Why, even John had to have one.'

'And where is he now? We have seen neither hide nor hair of him since New Year.'

'That is unfair, Kate. He has written at least half a dozen times since then.'

'Oh yes, he writes. But what use is writing when he is not here? I have married a paper man.'

'How can you say that? He is out there risking his life fighting for us.'

'Fighting your war, not mine. This is your people fighting your own war. It is nothing to do with me.'

Gwen was on the point of walking out when she remembered the woman's words: it is not Kate talking, she said to herself. She felt drained, but still she turned back to her sister. 'Come on, Kate. Elanor is asleep now. Let us go downstairs.'

'I shall come down when I am good and ready. Now leave me alone, will you? I need some time to think.' She turned back to the window. Gwen closed the door quietly behind her and went downstairs.

Thirteen

John looked out over the city of Exeter, which was still holding out against them. The earth shook as yet another barrage of cannonfire rained destruction on the citizens. All around him the camp was a hive of activity. Fairfax had ordered the army to be ready to storm the city. Columns of horses rode past him at breakneck speed, missing him by inches, yet he remained unmoved – he did not even notice them. His mind was taken by the news he had received from his sister that morning. He took the letter out again and re-read it.

Ely, 5th March 1646

My dear John,

I have little time to write this as my coach awaits me. I have to return to London straightaway. Michael has been wounded and is at home. Though it grieves me to leave Kate to her own devices, when she has such mischief in her, my darling Michael has the greater need of me. Gwen Hollins, the wet-nurse I told you about, has been a tower of strength, coming out in all weathers for little Elanor and the child is thriving – you need not worry on that score.

My concern is for Kate; she is not better. Indeed, if anything her depression deepens with each passing day. I have had to force her to take up her duties for the child, which she does with very bad grace. I have no faith in her continuing after I am gone. I implore you, John, if you can get away, then please come home with all speed. I am sorry to burden you with this, but you need to know the urgency of the situation.

My love as always.

God Bless.

Gwen

As he put the letter back in his breast pocket, his fingers touched the other letter he had received that morning. It was from Kate, though she had not signed it. He did not take it out, for the message was as clear as it was painful. She had simply scrawled, *Come home – damn you* on the paper. He had been stunned by it – this was surely not his Kate. Somehow he would have to get home. There was nothing else for it but to go to the general.

John slowly took himself to the house where Fairfax had set up his headquarters. He had never spoken to Fairfax before, but he had heard that he was a good man and fair. He thought he had a better chance with him than with Cromwell, whose fanaticism for the cause brooked no other considerations.

He was admitted to the general's rooms without question. Fairfax was brooding over a map of the city. John knew what he was doing, it was something he had often done himself, looking for weaknesses in the city's defences. As John came to attention, he looked up and smiled. His eyes were tired, but there seemed to be a genuine warmth in them. John's hopes rose.

'What think you of this, Captain Barnard?' he asked, waving his hand at the map. John came forward, emboldened by the general's apparent interest.

'Exeter is a strong city and strongly defended. We might lose the lives of many men in storming it – and that would be a great tragedy with peace so near at hand.'

'My thoughts precisely,' he agreed. His deep, dark eyes looked at John sadly. 'Too much blood has been spilled already, I fear.' Then he smiled. 'So, Captain, you have a reputation as an astute soldier, what would you have me do?'

John was taken aback by this. He had never thought his actions had been so closely marked by the general. Still, he had been asked for his opinion, there was nothing else he could do:

'After Torrington, the last royalist army in the west was scattered. Exeter has no hope of relief. I would step up the bombardment of the walls for a couple of days and make a great show of arms. Then I would offer them terms for surrender. They have made a gallant defence through the winter. They must realize now that their cause is lost.'

Fairfax nodded. 'Again, we are of a mind. I will put this case to my General Council this evening. The hotheads would prefer a storm, but I can see no advantage to it. I fear it would be another Bridgewater, and I would rather not have that on my conscience when I meet my Maker.'

He sat down on a large leather-bound chair and indicated that John should do likewise.

'Now, Captain, what have you come to see me for?' He clasped his hands across his chest and smiled.

John watched his expression change as he related his tale. He showed him the letter from Gwen, though he kept Kate's letter hidden. Fairfax handed it back to him when he had read it. He was clearly upset by it.

'I heard of Michael's injury and it is very grave. Lady Gwendoline does right in returning to his side. I met her once. I thought her a cheery spirit. It vexes me to hear of her in such a dilemma. I am sorry to hear about your wife. So, you have come to ask permission to go back to her?'

John nodded. 'In all the four years I have fought this war, I have never asked for anything for myself. I have raised two companies of cavalry and I know that my needs must always come last. Now that the war is nearly over, I have come to ask this one thing for myself. I must go home to her.'

Fairfax was silent. He stared at the palms of his hands. John could see that they were trembling slightly. At last he spoke.

'The army does not remain intact out of a love of

me,' he said quietly, almost to himself. 'There are many conscripts that would desert at the drop of a hat, were it not for the discipline and example of officers such as yourself. If I were to let you go – what sort of example would that set?'

'I believe these circumstances to be exceptional, sir, or I would not come to you,' he replied.

'Would you be surprised to learn that they are not?' the general countered. He rubbed his eyes as in thought. 'Even for myself, there have been times when I was desperate to leave – my own family in Yorkshire has had a very hard time of it, these past years. There were times when I did not even know if they were alive or not.'

John stood up. 'Then I take it I do not have leave to go?'

Fairfax waved his hand for John to sit down again. 'Please, do not be so impetuous. Give me a moment to think, I beg you.'

John resumed his place; the general had not ordered him – he had asked him like one man to another.

'If I let you go, willy-nilly, then people will start to talk. I would be inundated with young officers with "exceptional circumstances". No, I could not have that.' He laughed at the prospect. 'Now, listen, this is my bargain. It rather neatly ties together our two conversations. It is my only offer and I hope you will see the reason in it. I shall offer terms to the city of Exeter – and you will take them. If they accept, that is to say, if you can convince them to surrender – then you can carry the news to Parliament. When you have delivered that news you may have leave to attend to your wife. I shall expect you back at midsummer. I believe that is fair. What do you say?'

John considered this for a moment: the general was offering the most humane solution to the problem that he could. He nodded. 'When might the barrage start?' he asked.

'If I can persuade the General Council tonight – then we may start tomorrow morning, the seventh of April.'

Gwen Hollins dragged herself through the mud of the flooded streets. The rain lashed down on her and her clothes were soaked. She felt the wet mud seep through the holes in her shoes. She put her hands under her arms to keep her fingers from freezing. It was not far now, she thought, at least the house would be warm – even if her welcome was not.

Finally, she reached the door. She knocked on it. Inside, she could hear the baby crying and Mrs Barnard screaming at her companion. Perhaps they had not heard her. She knocked louder. Eventually, the door was opened. She smiled at Mrs Barnard's companion, Ruth. She returned her smile and shook her head in resignation. Mrs Barnard was waiting for her with her arms crossed.

'So, you're here at last. You are late. Well, you can hear the baby. You had better get on with it.'

She stood, shivering on the doorstep. 'Might I have a few moments to warm myself before I start?' she asked, meekly.

'I pay you to feed my baby, not to enjoy the comforts of my house. Get on with it,' she said coldly.

Ruth closed the door behind her and Gwen came in. Mrs Barnard glowered at her. She pointed at her shoes.

'How dare you come to my house covered in mud. Get into the kitchen. In future you can come to the back door.'

Mrs Barnard brought the baby out to her. It was still screaming. She led her into the kitchen and indicated that Gwen Hollins should sit down on a stool by the door.

'Might I not sit by the stove, madam?'

'You may not,' she replied. 'You will sit where you are told.' She turned on her heel and left them. They heard her go up the stairs, then she called down to them, 'And when she has finished, she can go straightaway.'

Gwen tried to unlace her bodice, but her fingers were too cold and she was shivering too much. She looked up imploringly at Ruth.

'Can you help me with this?' she asked.

Ruth looked down on her and sighed. She glanced up

the stairs. 'Come on dear, she won't come down again while you're here. Come and sit by the stove. I'll clean up the mud afterwards.'

She helped her up – she was so cold and soaked to the skin. Her skirt hissed as it touched the stove. They both looked up for fear that they had been heard. Ruth helped her unlace her bodice. Immediately the baby started feeding, Ruth smiled.

'It's the only time we have any peace in the house,' she said.

As she fed the baby, Gwen pulled back its blanket. It was looking even thinner than she remembered it had the last time. She looked up. 'Your mistress still isn't feeding her, then?'

Ruth shook her head. 'It was all right when Lady Gwendoline was here – she made her do it. They shouted at each other, but the mistress did it in the end. Since she went, well, I've tried, but what can I do? I'm just a paid companion, and she keeps on reminding me of that. I swear, if it wasn't for the little one, I'd be gone from here.' She looked ruefully at the child.

'Well, I'm doing all I can – God knows my own little one is suffering for her, but what else can I do? If I try and give her too much she'll be sick and then what?'

Ruth took a plate from the stove. 'Here you are, it's not much. It's leftovers mostly – she won't let me do anything specially for you, but I make sure I do too much each time.'

She looked on as the woman ate ravenously. She knew that even though she was nursing two children she was still denying herself. It was not merely Elanor who was looking thin. Over these last few weeks she had watched Gwen Hollins as her cheeks hollowed and her bearing became bowed.

A piece of food caught in Gwen's throat as she bolted it down, she started to cough. Ruth patted her on the back – she could feel every bone of her spine. The food came up, but the coughing did not stop. It changed its quality and became a harsh racking bark. Her chest seemed to rattle as she tried to suppress it. Then she choked and held her hand up to her mouth. She looked up guiltily.

'What's in your hand, Gwen?' Ruth asked quietly. 'Show me.'

She shook her head. But Ruth did not need to see any more. The dark gouts of blood which oozed between her fingers told their tale. Gwen Hollins looked up at her fearfully.

'Don't tell, I beg of you. I need the money so bad – I can't have her turn me away, we'd all starve.' She stared up at Ruth imploringly.

'How long has it been?'

'Oh, a few days, a week maybe – well, maybe a bit more. But I'm all right, honest. I've had this before and there's nothing wrong with my milk.'

They were interrupted by a shout from upstairs. The mistress wanted to know why Gwen was still in the house. The baby was sleeping quietly, so she did herself up and handed the child to Ruth. She went to the back door.

'You won't tell, will you?' she whispered.

'Only if you promise to feed yourself properly,' Ruth replied. She grabbed a large loaf of bread and gave it to her. 'Here, take this. I made one extra, she'll never notice.' She shrugged. 'Even if she does – well, I'll cross that bridge if ever I come to it.' She opened the door for her. The wind drove the rain in. She watched from the window as the woman set off into the night.

Gwen Hollins did not return the next morning. By ten o'clock the child was screaming and blue in the face. Kate was frantic. She sent Ruth out to find her. She took a horse from the stable and rode it, as fast as she was able to, into town. When she got to the house, there were two women coming out, bearing a large bundle. They looked at her furtively and darted past. Inside, she could hear children crying. She recognized the signs. With a heavy heart, she pushed the door open and went in.

She was laid out on a bare pallet. Her wet undershift still clung to her body – at least they had left her with that. She had been rolled over to the side of the pallet when they had taken the bedding from under her. Ruth could not leave her like that. She went to straighten the body. The eldest boy stood up and tried to block her way.

'It's all right, I haven't come to hurt your mother,' she said, gently.

He looked down and touched his mother's hair. 'No one can hurt her now,' he replied, wiping a tear from his eye.

She rolled the body over. She noticed the bruising on the finger where they had wrenched her wedding band from her – they were very thorough. She took a comb from her bag and started to comb Gwen's hair. Her face was as white as marble. All the lines of pain and suffering were gone. She had been released. When she finished she went to go out and find someone to help her. The little girl came up to her, dressed only in her underclothes. Her cheeks were red and streaked with tears, though her eyes were empty, lifeless as her mother's.

'They took away my dress. The women came and they took away my dress.'

John rode like the wind. He had changed horses at Dorchester and Salisbury. He was hoping to get to Andover that night. He was exhausted, but still he forced himself on. He had taken the surrender of Exeter that morning. It had been no easy thing, even though Fairfax had offered generous terms. He had had to use all his powers of persuasion. He would have offered them the moon, if only he had been able – just to force them out so that he could escape. Then he had to wait for the garrison to leave and for the general's dispatch to be written. In fact the whole thing was over by ten o'clock, but it had seemed like ages to him. Still he pressed on through the waning light.

He reached Andover at midnight. He slept in the stable, fully clothed so that he could get away as soon as it was light. By dawn he was away again. With changes of horse at Reading and Brentford he was at Westminster by noon. He approached the gates at full tilt and only just managed to pull his horse up before he crashed into the crossed pikes of the guard.

'A message from General Fairfax,' he bellowed as the Captain of the Guard came up to him.

'You seem to make a habit of bringing messages. You should change your name to Mercury, John Barnard,' the captain laughed as he recognized him. 'Let him pass,' he ordered his men.

The Captain of the Guard escorted him to the same passageway where he and Kate had sat, nearly two years before.

'Are you going to try and lecture them again?' the captain enquired.

'It is not my business anymore,' he replied. 'We are soldiers. Deciding the peace is up to them.'

'Everybody is talking about peace, but I wonder whose idea of peace will prevail?' the captain mused. 'I will have a message sent to the Speaker that you have arrived.'

'Thank you, friend,' John called after him as he went. He settled himself down to wait.

It was long after sunset when a messenger came out to him and told him that the House would not be able to hear his dispatch until the next day. He was ordered to return at ten o'clock the next morning. It seemed that Parliament was no longer so keen to get news of the war. He went back to his horse and took himself back wearily to his sister's house in Chelsea. He was relieved to find that all the lights in the house were still burning. Dodington seemed surprised to see him – but not half as surprised as his sister was.

'John! God in heaven – what are you doing here? You should be in Ely now, not here.'

'And well I know it. I would have been on the road now, but I have to attend the House tomorrow morning.'

'Why, have you done something wrong?' she asked anxiously.

'No. The only way I could get away was to carry the

news of our taking of Exeter up here to London. And now they will not hear me. I have been at Westminster since noon.'

A man's voice called out from the parlour, 'Hey there! What's all that noise? Who is there?'

'It's John, dear,' Gwen cried.

'Well, bring him in!'

Gwen whispered, 'Please, do not keep him up too late. He needs his sleep – he has only been up and about these last two days.'

John nodded and they went in. Michael was lying on the couch. He held out his left hand to his brother. The right was swathed in bandages.

'John, you're looking . . . well to be frank, somewhat dishevelled – have you never heard of a razor?' he laughed.

'Well, at least you are looking better than I had hoped. Convalescence seems to suit you.'

Michael looked down at himself. 'Yes, I have never been so pampered in all my life. It is almost worth having a cannonball shatter beside me to enjoy this – though I would not wish to experience it again.'

'So, how are you?' John asked.

'I cannot complain. They managed to get most of it out after the battle – the rest had to be taken out when I returned home. That was uncommonly painful, I can tell you. But I am well enough now. My arm is a fearful sight, but the doctors say it will heal.' He patted his sling lovingly, then winced a little and smiled.

'Michael, can I use your writing table? I have to send a message off to Kate as quickly as possible.'

'Of course, please do.' He smiled again, then he became more serious. 'Gwen tells me that things are not faring too well for Katherine. I am sorry that I dragged Gwendoline away from her, but I had little choice in the matter. When I finally got home I was delirious. Gwen brought me back to the land of the living.'

'In all truth, Michael, I do not know how things are faring; the last news I had was from Gwen herself, and that was over a month ago when she wrote, so God knows what is happening now.'

John was made to wait another three days, kicking his heels in the corridors of power before he was finally admitted late on Friday evening. When he went in, there were less than a score of them in attendance. He read the dispatch and was dismissed without any further comment. The whole process had taken less than two minutes. Ordinarily, he would have been affronted by the offhand treatment he had received. Now he was just glad to be free to get home.

His horse was saddled and ready for him. He could not make very good time going through the streets of London: even though they were clear, the cobblestones were so wet and slippery that he had to go slowly for fear of laming his horse. He passed through the gates at Shoreditch just before eleven, and he eased the pace up to a steady canter. It was about seventy miles to Ely and most of the way was along old Roman roads. If he made good time, he might get there by mid-morning. He cursed the easy pace he had to adopt, but he was not carrying dispatches now, so he could not commandeer fresh horses. He had to go easy on this mount.

He was feeling quite pleased with himself. He had reached Cambridge just after sunrise and within the hour he would be back with his beloved Kate. He smiled at the prospect of seeing his baby daughter for the first time and spending two whole months with his loved ones. Even though the Great Ouse had been in flood and he had to take the ferry across, still it did not dampen his spirits. At the back of his mind, there was a nagging doubt, created by Kate's last letter, that everything was far from well. He would have to make up for lost time, he thought.

It was Kate who answered the door. Her face was pale and drawn and there seemed to be no life in her eyes. She was dressed in black. She glanced up at him and then looked down again.

'How appropriate,' she said in a dull, flat voice, 'you have come just in time.'

She turned and walked into the parlour. John followed her. On the table by the window there was an open box, fashioned of black polished wood. It was only when Kate went up to it and placed her hand tenderly inside that John realized that it was a coffin. Suddenly, his limbs felt very heavy. His stomach churned. He stood, unable to move, in the doorway. Kate did not take her eyes from it. She spoke in the same monotonous voice, 'Do you not want to see your daughter?'

Slowly, as though his body was resisting each step, he walked across the room. Sunlight streamed through the window, catching the white christening shawl that was her shroud. Her tiny face, perfect in every feature, was dulled by a grey cast. John tried to imagine her in life.

'She is very beautiful . . .' he said, half to himself. 'What colour were her eyes?'

Kate sighed. 'They were blue. Babies' eyes are always blue.' Still she did not look at him. 'Your father will be here soon. She is to be buried this morning.' There was a long silence. John could think of nothing to say. Finally, Kate spoke again, though it was merely a thought, made words, 'Why did you not come when she was yet alive . . . ?'

John could not think of any answer which did not seem futile now. He went to put his arms about her, but she flinched at his touch. He did not try again.

'When?' he asked.

'Tuesday night . . . the small hours of Wednesday morning. I woke at three to see if she was all right – and she was gone.'

'I am sorry.' It was all that he could think of; he was so empty.

Kate laughed, briefly and silently. She looked sidelong at him. 'Yes, I suppose you are . . . now.' Her eyes betrayed a bitter mockery.

There seemed to be nothing else to say. After a while,

John went and slumped down in the chair by the empty grate. His mind numbed, staring into empty space. Kate stayed by the tiny coffin.

The funeral was a simple affair. John bore the coffin. Carrying the child he had not held in life. The grave was so deep – it seemed to swallow her up. The rattle of the soil on the coffin shook John to the depths of his soul. Though it was a warm morning, he shivered.

When it was over, Kate took Ruth's arm and walked away without a word. John went to follow them, but his father stayed him.

'Walk with me, John. I would talk with you.'

They waited for the women to get ahead, then the old man spoke quietly. 'You must not blame her. She did everything she could to save the child, you know. . . .'

'Gwen told me that she had rejected her, that she had to be forced to feed her.'

'That is true, I cannot deny that. But when the wet-nurse died, Kate seemed to return to her senses. She took another woman in and she fed the baby herself, as much as she was able. Elanor was beginning to thrive once more.'

'Then how did she die?' John asked, alarmed at this news.

'The child died of consumption, we think. It happened very quickly and she was still too weak to resist it. Kate stayed with her all the time, but in the end it was all in vain. I am sorry, John.'

They walked along in silence for a while. John's father moved very slowly and the women were already a long way ahead.

'What do I do now?' John asked his father.

'I do not know. I will not hide it from you; Kate blames you for not being by her side when she needed you. I will not hold out any false hopes, my son. In all honesty, I think you have lost her. Why could you not have come sooner?'

John shook his head. 'The war, Father. The bloody war.'

* * *

When the others had gone, Kate and John were left alone. Kate busied herself gathering up some small things and putting them away. John watched her. Finally, she turned to him. Her face was tense and tight-lipped.

'Had you not better be getting back?' she said sarcastically.

'Back to what?' he asked, though he knew what she had meant.

'To your precious army. To the soldiers who needed you more than I did.'

'I have been given leave until midsummer.' The words rang hollow in his mouth.

'For what? It is too late now. If you could not be here when I needed you – then I certainly would not want you here now.'

'This is still my home,' he said quietly.

'Your home?' She screamed at him – the words beat into him like blows. 'How can you call this your home? You've not been here more than six weeks since we were married. This is not your home – go back to the army. Back to your killing – back where you belong!' She stood before him, white-knuckled and defiant.

'You are still my wife, Kate,' he growled as the anger rose within him.

'You might call me wife,' she said icily, 'but I am no wife to you, for you are no husband to me. Get back to your mistress.' She looked at him scornfully, 'I thought I had married a real man – you're not a real man at all. You are a killer . . . you follow death around and death follows you – even to this house – even to your own child. Get out!'

John closed his eyes and tried to master himself. He spoke quietly once more. 'I will not leave you like this, Kate. I am staying, no matter what you say.'

'To what end?' she taunted. 'Do not think you can come sneaking back into my bed once more. I have no need of you and I do not want you.'

'Then I will sleep down here by the fire.' He smiled

ironically. 'You fell in love with me once, when we were in such a place.'

'Do not delude yourself, John. I fell in love with the idea of a man – the reality turned out to be very different.' She turned and went into the kitchen, slamming the door behind her.

The rest of the day was filled with terse, bitter exchanges. Kate had left him and taken to her bed early. John made himself up a bed on the settle. It had been a long and draining day. Suddenly he felt very tired and very old. He remembered that he had not slept the night before. He laughed inwardly at his foolishness. He eased himself into his makeshift bed. There were so many things to think about – too many things. He stared up at the ceiling with his hands behind his head. His mind was a blank. Slowly but surely, the welcomc waves of sleep drifted over him.

He was woken in the night by the touch of an icy hand on his breast. He opened his eyes to see Kate standing above him, her face as white as her nightshift in the moonlight. She brandished a kitchen knife in her tightly clenched hand. Her eyes burned with hatred.

'I want you to go, John. I do not want you here,' she said with unconcealed malice. 'This is a warning. If you sleep here tomorrow night – you will not wake in the morning.' She turned and walked quickly away, still holding the knife above her.

The next morning John woke to the sound of Kate in the kitchen. For a moment the clatter of pots and plates sounded so familiar that he forgot himself. Then the events of the past day came crushing down on him once more. He dressed himself and went into the kitchen. Kate had prepared a breakfast for one.

He looked into the porridge pot – it had been scraped clean. Kate did not look up. The message was clear. He sat down on the opposite side of the table.

'Kate,' he said, placing his hands flat on the table, 'may I talk with you?'

Her eyes were fixed on her food. 'It depends on

what you have to say,' she replied, not giving him any encouragement.

He took a deep breath. 'If I were to say that I would go . . .'

Kate looked up. 'Then yes, we may talk.' Her tone was frank and candid – but hostile.

John carried on. 'But I have certain conditions.'

'If they mean that you will go, then I will listen to them.' She dabbed her mouth with her napkin and pushed back her seat. 'Well, get on with them.'

'I will go and stay with my father for the rest of my leave if you will do these two things for me. Firstly, I want Ruth to be here with you, and secondly, I must be allowed to come and see you every day and you will make an effort to talk with me.'

Kate frowned and sucked her teeth nonchalantly.

'That seems like three conditions to me – just because you come to my house does not necessarily mean that I should talk to you. Anyway, what if I do not agree to your "conditions"?'

'Then you will have to carry out your threat of last night.'

She shrugged, and proceeded to clear up the breakfast things. 'Very well, I agree. Ruth should have been here yesterday anyway – she only stayed away because she mistakenly thought we had things to discuss. And yes, you may come calling when you like – during the daytime; though I assure you it will avail you nothing. Is that all?'

John nodded his head sadly.

'Then would you oblige me by getting out of my house?' She started washing the dishes as though he was not there.

For John this was the most painful time of all. He was true to his word, every day he came to visit his wife. Most times she would receive him in the garden. She seemed very apprehensive about letting him into the house. At first, their conversations were very stilted. He found it difficult to think of things to say and Kate seemed disinclined to talk at all.

There were times when he dreaded these visits, despairing of ever seeing the woman he loved again. Kate had set a wall about her, never allowing herself to be at ease in his company, tensing her body if he came close to her, as though his proximity revolted her. She could be cruel, too. She was ever watchful for an opportunity to turn anything he said around to remind him of his inadequacies.

As the days wore on into weeks, though, they became accustomed to this strange ritual. They found it easier to talk, though Kate was always on her guard. There were a few times when her guard slipped and John caught a brief glimpse of the woman he knew and loved. These were the most painful times of all, for, as soon as she realized what she had done, the wall came down again as she redoubled her guard.

When midsummer finally came, it was with a sense of relief that he returned to his company. Perhaps Kate had been right, perhaps he was no more than a killer and the army was indeed his home. Their conversations had gradually chipped away at his confidence. He was aimless and rudderless now – the dangers of the war seemed more like a sanctuary to him.

Their parting had been cordial enough, she had asked him to keep safe – but there was no warmth in her valediction. She had even been prepared to shake his hand – she had been wearing gloves for the first time that day. He had wanted to take her in his arms and hold her tightly to him, to break down the wall between them, but he knew that if he tried, she would have held herself rigid in his arms, like a stone statue. He would have to content himself with her cordiality and hope that the next time they met things would be better.

As he rode away, he looked over his shoulder to see if she was still there, but she had gone inside and closed the door. He did not see the curtains part as she watched him from the window. No one saw the tears Kate cried as she watched him go.

Fourteen

Kate hardly noticed that the summer had passed. The winds blew chill once more and the green splendour of the trees was stripped bare. She held herself away from the watchful eyes of the outside world, becoming a prisoner within her own house and her own soul. The anger which she had felt, the anger which had driven her husband away, had receded and was replaced by a cold and hollow emptiness. Only her pain seemed undiminished, the pain which was always with her, gnawing and tearing at her heart, stifling her love of life.

She looked at herself and she looked around her. She hardly recognized herself in the mirror: she was thin and gaunt. She tried to move her hair around, to put some life into it, but it was no use, she finally left it hanging lank and limp.

She could tell that the people around her despised her. These were John's folk – they only suffered her for his sake. She saw their eyes as they looked down on her, felt their disgust: so she resolved to make things easier for them. Rather than allow them to shun her, she shunned them, avoided their company, safe within the walls of this house. This house which had become her cell. Winter closed in about her.

At Christmas John had called a few times, but he had seemed more shy and reserved than ever. She no longer hated him with the same intensity as before, but she could not bring herself to show any affection. The gulf between them grew deeper and wider. When he finally left, she did not cry. It was as though he had never even been there.

The only thing which kept her in her whole mind seemed to be her garden. She watched now as the early spring flowers broke their way through the cold, hard soil and a strange longing grew within her. She realized that this place was no longer home. She wished she could go home to Ireland, to Kilerin, but that was still impossible; but, at any rate, she knew that it was time for her to move on, to leave Ely and make a fresh start to her life. After some thought, she decided she would go to London.

She wrote to Mr MacAulay, asking him to find her a house where she might set herself up – or at least somewhere to make a start. She was surprised when her letter was answered, not by her lawyer, but by her sister-in-law.

At first she felt affronted by this intrusion into her affairs. But as she thought more about it, the idea grew more attractive. It would provide her with a firmer base in London – at least for the first few months. She knew, though, that she would have to be on her guard. Gwen would almost certainly attempt to drive her back into John's clutches.

At the end of May she was ready to leave. Her baggage had been sent ahead and she had hired a coach to take her to London in some style. She was alone again for the first time in years: there was no one to wave her off, she had told no one in Ely of her plans and she had sent Ruth ahead with her baggage.

She viewed this new adventure with some trepidation but, she reminded herself, she was a woman of means in her own right now. The thought, though it did little to encourage her that her course was the right one, at least allayed some of her fears. She tapped the coach wall and the driver whipped the horses forward.

She watched as the countryside unfolded before her. Even though it was not Ireland, she thought, it was still a very beautiful place. Now that it was at peace, there were more people in the fields and everything seemed to be returning to orderliness. She delighted in going through Cambridge, watching the townsfolk as they stared at her passing. Even though they said that money was not everything, still it had its compensations, she mused.

After the city, her view returned to mile after mile of rural idyll; some of the countryfolk waved to her as she passed, she waved back and smiled at them. She realized with a start that she was indeed smiling – she tried to remember the last time she had really, genuinely smiled, it was too long ago, but at least she was smiling now and that was what counted.

Although the war was over and England was supposed to be at peace, Kate noticed that there were still a great number of soldiers on the roads. As the coach approached the Great North Road, she was alarmed at the number of soldiers there were about. The coach ground to a halt. Their road was blocked. Kate tapped the roof.

'What is happening?' she demanded. A flap opened in front of her and the driver's face appeared.

'The road is barred, madam. There are soldiers checking all the comings and goings of the travellers,' he replied, then shut the flap as two cavalrymen approached. They opened the door and peered in.

'May we see your travel documents?' they asked in a civil tone.

Kate was alarmed. 'Travel documents?' she replied uncertainly. 'What travel documents?'

They glanced at one another suspiciously. 'All commerce must be accompanied by a warrant, signed by a commissioner.'

'But I have no such warrant – I did not know it was necessary.'

'Then I regret, madam, that you must come with us.' They ushered her out of the coach, which was directed to a compound off the main road. She was escorted to a small house, which was guarded by troopers.

Inside, there were a great number of people, all apparently waiting. The cavalrymen ordered a large fellow to vacate his seat and asked her to sit down. Then they left her. The man glowered at her, she felt embarrassed at this, but she did not move. Finally, a young lieutenant with a large sheaf of papers asked her to come with him. They went into a small room with a wooden table and two rather unsteady-looking chairs. He asked her to be seated. He sighed as he found himself a blank sheet of paper, then produced a writing set from beneath the sheaf.

'Now then,' he began, 'why is it that you are travelling without a warrant?'

'I had no idea that I would need such a thing, we did not need them when we were at war. . . .'

'Things have changed,' he interrupted. He glanced up at her. 'Irish?' he enquired. Any trace of civility had disappeared from his manner now. Kate felt the old anger rising in her once more.

'Anglo-Irish. My husband is an Englishman,' she retorted.

'What is his name?'

'Would you not prefer to know my name first?'

He shrugged, unconcerned. 'It makes little difference to me.'

'My name is Katherine Barnard. I was born Katherine Butler of Kilerin.'

'And your husband?' he continued, as though her identity was a matter of no interest to him.

'John Barnard of Ely,' she said quietly, mastering her wrath.

He looked up again, this time his eyes widened. 'Captain John Barnard?' he asked.

'Yes,' she said, weary that her own identity was still of secondary importance to that of her estranged husband. She looked on as the young man's manner became apologetic, even polite.

'Madam, you must excuse this delay. If you can show me some proof of your identity, then I shall have papers drawn up immediately.'

Kate took out the letter from Gwen and showed it

to him. 'I am going to stay with my sister-in-law, Lady Nevers, in Chelsea.'

In a matter of minutes they were back on the road again.

The driver talked to her through the peep-hole. 'They were saying in the village that the army is on the point of mutiny. They have the King as their prisoner at Newmarket. It seems that they haven't been paid for a while. Reckon they're going to march on London, they do,' he said, laughing at some joke of his own. Kate closed the hole. Events had certainly moved on since she had last been abroad.

Events were moving fast. A few miles away from where Kate had been detained, John was engaged in a fierce dispute with many of his fellow officers, a dispute which was more bitter than all the battles he had fought. On the heath at Kentford, near Newmarket, the army was falling out amongst themselves. They had won the war, they had the King and now it seemed they would fail at the final hurdle – they would lose the peace.

It seemed that every faction in the army had a different solution and they would hear no other opinion. The dispute had raged for days, yet still there was no sign of agreement.

He had been called to General Fairfax's side, for John's company was one of the few that maintained any semblance of order. When he had arrived at the general's quarters one of the first people he saw was Michael, his arm still in a sling after over a year, but otherwise whole and back in command of his own troops. He came across and greeted him warmly, though he seemed worried. He took John to one side of the room. His voice was hushed, but there was an urgency in it which made John listen intently.

'John, things are very bad here, and I hope you do not mind me asking you this, but how strong is your hold over your men? We need to know.'

He was taken aback by this, but he answered his brother candidly.

'We have had long and hard discussions – but my lads are no fools. We know that we must stand firm. Without discipline we will all go down. My men have faith in me, they will not mutiny. I can give you my word on that.'

Michael's expression did not change. 'I would have expected as much from you. Come with me, John.' He led him into the general's own room. Fairfax seemed to be waiting for them.

'Good morning, gentlemen,' he said, his dark eyes holding their attention. 'I shall not beat around the bush, Captain Barnard. Just over a year ago, you came to me for assistance and I was able to help you. Now the boot, I am afraid, is on the other foot. I must ask you to do something which will make you very unpopular with your fellow men.'

'You have only to command me, sir. You do not need to remind me of my debt to you.'

'Thank you for that. This afternoon I shall address the army as a whole. I have no idea how strong their bond of affection for me will be. I intend to summon all the agitators together and, if necessary, force them to sign an engagement to keep their discipline and allow us to negotiate on their behalf with Parliament. I shall make them swear to it. I may well need to resort to force of arms – or at least the threat of force. If we succeed, then the army will remain unified and there is hope for a lasting peace, but those who follow me will become marked men in the future. If we fail . . .' – he made a small futile gesture – 'then we shall have anarchy and all that we have fought for will have been in vain.' He looked down at his hands. 'I will not delude you. If you do this for me then you will have my protection for as long as I command the army, or as long as I have any influence left. But I can see that events are moving away from me. The future belongs in their hands.' He pointed out of the window to where the army was assembling. 'The Henry Iretons and suchlike.' He laughed briefly. 'When this is all over, I hope to retire quietly back to Yorkshire, if I am allowed. I would like to see some real hills again – it is too flat round here for my liking.' He smiled at them.

John realized his meaning: that after he had relinquished command of the army then his support would be of little or no value at all. Still, Fairfax was right. If the army disintegrated or, worse, turned on the country, then they would have played into the King's hands. Either way, John's choices did not appear good. He cleared his throat to give him time to think: still his thoughts turned to Kate. At least she might gain some satisfaction from his downfall. At all costs, though, Michael should be kept from this.

'I will take your commission, sir, but as you can see, if this came to sword-play then my brother is in no fit state for a fight. I would ask that his command be made over to me for the duration.'

Michael protested, but Fairfax saw John's wisdom in this and agreed to it. They called the companies together immediately. John was one of only eleven commanders remaining. With less than a thousand men, Fairfax would face the whole army.

They lined up around the perimeter of the field – Fairfax would not allow any man to stand between him and his troops. The men cheered as he climbed onto the podium. He waved his hands for them to be quiet and then he began. He spoke of all the things they had shared, the hardships as well as the victories. He reminded them of the blood that had been shed and the friends that they had lost over the years. Thus far the men were with him. Then he turned to events at hand. They fell silent. As he continued there were murmurs among the crowd. He appealed to their reason and to their comradeship. John sensed the atmosphere becoming more tense. His horse smelled it too and started stamping and snorting as though they were about to charge.

Suddenly, Ireton held up his hand and announced his support for the general. He strode forward, followed by the other leaders of the agitators. The moment had passed. John felt relief sweep over him and he loosened the chin strap of his helmet. He smiled grimly as he noticed a little man rushing back and forth along the line of mounted troopers, writing down the names of all those who stood for Fairfax. He looked up and down the line. At least, he considered, he was in good company.

Although Kate had not really thought about what sort of reception she would receive from her sister, she was deeply moved by the warmth of Gwen's greeting. She had welcomed her into the house as though the events of the last year had never happened. That first day they had just sat and talked until late into the night.

At first it was Gwen who did most of the talking, then after a while, Kate began to regain her confidence. They avoided talking about those things that divided them over the first few days. It was only after a week that Kate felt able to discuss those things which troubled her.

It was late at night, they were both tired and they were getting ready to go to bed. Gwen had been talking about her plans for when Michael left the army, which they hoped would be soon. She looked keenly at her sister.

'What are your plans for the future, Kate?' she asked.

Kate raised an eyebrow in surprise, but she did not smile. 'And do they involve John, I suppose you are thinking?'

'I did not ask that,' Gwen replied, still looking keenly at her.

'I would like to go home to Ireland. I do not ever want to go back to Ely. There is nothing there for me.'

'But you cannot go back to Ireland yet,' Gwen observed.

'No, not yet. Well, since Mr MacAulay must have spoken to you in the first place, I suppose you already know that I am looking for a house in London.'

Gwen nodded. 'Then why not stay here with me?'

Kate fell silent while she considered this. She spoke quietly, reflectively. 'Because I must be my own woman for a while . . . because I have been under an obligation to you for nearly three years now . . . and if I stay here long enough I am bound to encounter John again. . . .'

'So your plans do not involve John.' Gwen's eyes were very sad as she said this, Kate thought she would cry.

'No. They do not include him, Gwen. I am sorry, but even the thought of him leaves me cold. I cannot seem to find it in me to love him any more. I suppose you might think that a tragedy, but I can only think of it as a release. I was as bound to the army as he was – only for me it was worse, much worse. I was alone in a place which was not my own. A tiny cage of a place – I have always hated cages – where I only came to life for a few brief weeks in a whole year. Then, when . . . Elanor died, it seemed to take something else with it. The part of me that . . . I don't know, Gwen – I think it took away my capacity to love.'

'And that was so great a part of you. You will never be the same until you rediscover it.'

'Then I will have to live on in spite of it, for I cannot ever see it returning. I have become so embittered I cannot even remember how it feels to love. Can you forgive me for that?'

'You do not need my forgiveness. And truly there is nothing to forgive. I only regret what you have done to yourself. You have made another cage for yourself, only this one will be harder to escape from, for the bars are wrought in your own mind.'

'Then I shall be content that they are well wrought. Good night, sister.'

That summer, Kate used Gwen quite shamelessly to gain herself an entrée into London society. She accompanied her to each and every gathering, always seeking out the racier elements there. She was looking for excitement above all else – something which had been sadly lacking from her life in Ely, excitement which would help fill the void within her, and help her forget the misery of the past year.

She fell in with a group of young Irishwomen who, like herself, had been sent over to England when the troubles had started at home. Chief among these was Mary Ormond, a first cousin to the Earl of Ormond: a wild, strong colleen of a girl with a passion for horseriding and fast living. Her Royalist connections gave her a certain notoriety.

As time went on, Kate no longer needed to rely on Gwen for introductions – she had her own circle of friends. She could see that they were not altogether respectable, but respectability was just what Kate was trying to escape from.

Living at Chelsea was becoming increasingly difficult. Gwen disapproved of her sister's new lifestyle, but thus far she had said nothing. Matters came to a head one evening, as Kate was getting herself ready to go out. Ruth was just buttoning the long sleeves on Kate's gown, when there was a knock on the bedroom door. Gwen stood in the doorway. She would not come in.

'You are going out again, I see. May I ask what tonight's entertainment will be?'

Kate looked at her in the mirror. She smiled. 'Why, I believe we are going to Clerkenwell to see a droll.'

'You know that theatrical productions are banned. They are the lowest form of entertainment and they attract the lowest kind of people.'

'Perhaps that is why I go to them. . . .'

'Do not undervalue yourself, Katherine. You are head and shoulders above these folk you go about with.'

'Am I really? It is strange – you know, I feel perfectly on a level with them. We enjoy the same wit and the same pastimes. They are women of the same quality as myself – they are not slatterns or drudges, I assure you.' Kate stood up and walked toward her sister. 'Yet you do not approve of them, do you?'

'No, I do not – they will do you no good. I have seen what has happened to their acolytes. They drop them – in the end.'

'Or I might drop them in the end, mightn't I? What would you have me do instead – weaving, or perhaps some embroidery? Pretty ways of filling the time while we wait – for what?' She opened her hands and then clapped them together, all the time looking keenly at her sister. 'Nothing. I have nothing to wait for – so had I not better occupy my time with more enjoyable, if less edifying, pursuits?'

'Kate, my dear Kate,' Gwen said, shaking her head, 'you have people here who love you – I love you, Michael . . .'

'And where is he? The war has been over for nearly a year and still he is with his precious army. He was nearly killed, yet still he returns to them.'

'He is doing what he knows is right.'

'Doing what is right? They are holding the country to ransom. Why, only yesterday they marched to Hounslow Heath, hovering like vultures on the edge of the city, waiting to strike.'

'They want fair treatment for their men.'

'So, the army stands now for its own self-interests.'

'Kate, I have not come to talk to you about politics, I have come to talk about you.'

'I have no need of counsel, Gwen. I know what I am doing.'

Gwen looked at her with doubt in her eyes. 'Do you, Kate? Do you really?' She turned and walked away.

Kate heard Mary's carriage draw up outside. She dashed down the stairs to join her friends. She was surprised to find only Mary herself.

'Where are the others?' Kate asked as the footman helped her into the carriage.

Mary's eye twinkled mischievously. 'Well, I might tell you that they had been detained and they would meet us later, but I would be lying.' She placed her hand on Kate's. 'Truth to tell, I have some need of your assistance this evening. There is a certain gentleman I am . . . well, one might say that I have an interest in him . . .'

'Yes,' Kate interrupted, 'but why do you need my help?'

'Well, you see he has a friend. I do not know him, but it seems that he is up from the country and he is accompanying him to the Red Bull this evening.'

'And you would like me to distract this other man so that your beau is not distracted from you. . . .'

'You have my plan in a nutshell,' Mary agreed gleefully. 'Of course there would be no impropriety – we have our reputations to consider.'

They both laughed as the carriage drew away into the night.

Since Parliament had outlawed theatres, small secret venues had sprung up around the city. All types of people, from the highest to the basest, frequented them. They provided the clandestine trysting places where men and women took their discreet pleasures, away from the disapproving eyes of London society. The Red Bull was just such a place: it had been closed down on a number of occasions, but each time it secretly re-opened. The demand for worldly delights, and the prices people were prepared to pay for them, meant that the risk of fine or imprisonment was one its owners were prepared to take.

When Kate and Mary arrived, the place was already heaving. The air was thick with tobacco smoke and warm from bodies packed closely together. Mary looked around, trying to find her companion for the night. Her hand went up as she saw him. A man waved to her from across the room. He was sitting in one of the booths on a platform by the stage. They fought their way through the multitude of people to get to him. As they reached the booth, he held out his hand to help them up on to the platform. He was a bright-faced young man who smiled as he introduced himself simply as Peter Mastermain.

Mary laughed. 'That is not his real name, Katherine. I fear he's on the run from the Roundheads.' She laughed as she allowed him to kiss her hand.

He seemed to be embarrassed by this. 'You must not construe anything from what Mary says. I am not really that important – a minor player in this tragedy, though it would be safer for me to be somewhere other than England for the while.' He smiled as he took Kate's offered hand and kissed it.

Mary began the introduction. 'Peter' – she giggled at this – 'May I introduce . . .'

'Mistress Katherine Barnard.' A deep, dry, man's voice completed the introduction from behind her.

Kate shuddered at the sound of it.

'Thomas!' the young man cried. 'I was beginning to despair of your coming.'

Kate felt him walk around her. He held out his hand to the other man.

'Peter – you should know that I would not have deserted you, my friend.'

He took off his wide-brimmed hat and hung it on the post beside him. He shook back his mane of grey hair. His eyes settled on Kate.

'This is very strange company for you, Katherine. I heard that you were back in London – I wondered if our paths might cross once again.'

Kate felt a mingled thrill of disgust and pleasure as he took her hand and kissed it, allowing his finger to pass along hers as he released her, though his piercing pale eyes still held her in their thrall.

He was distracted by his companion.

'Thomas, allow me to introduce Mistress Mary Ormond. Mary, this is Thomas, Lord Fitzmaurice.'

He took her hand and held it between both of his before he kissed it gracefully.

'I know your cousin well. I can understand why he fights to defend your land if such flowers grow therein.' He smiled and bowed deeply.

Mary turned to Kate, reproaching her. 'I am disappointed in you, Kate – keeping such a charming gentleman from me.'

The droll was about to begin. Fitzmaurice called for a large flagon of wine to be brought over, then sat down opposite Kate; his brooding eyes were upon her again as if he were considering her. He raised an eyebrow.

'So, our roundhead friend did not prove to your liking after all . . .' He allowed his words to trail off in a low growl, then smiled, questioningly.

'What gives you that impression?' she replied, defiantly.

He took a draught of wine and encouraged her to do the same. 'Why else would you have ventured forth from your cosy little nest in East Anglia – where you could drink of the milk of Puritan kindness? And why do you shun the company of the good Lady Nevers to come to such a place as this?'

Kate thought he knew full well her reasons already. There was little that passed him by. Nevertheless, she thought it better to keep up the pretence.

'John is still with the army and I am at my leisure. I can go where I please.'

The other man choked at the word 'army'. Fitzmaurice smiled indulgently.

'Do not worry, Peter. Though this lady is the wife of one of our enemies, she will not betray us.'

'What gives you that impression?' Kate taunted him.

'Because you and your . . . husband have barely spoken in a year, because you have thrown him out of your house . . . because you remain married in name only.'

'And how do you know these things?' she said, alarmed, but not altogether surprised.

'Oh, come now Kate. You have hardly been discreet since you came up to London: and I have many friends who keep my interests at heart.'

'I can think of no interest you might still have in me.'

'That remains to be seen.' He took another draught of wine and turned his attention to the play.

They had been there barely an hour when Fitzmaurice's attention was distracted from the stage. He glanced over to the entrance, where a scuffle had broken out. Kate looked across. Above the crowds she could see the helmets of troopers, making their way across the room toward them. Fitzmaurice tapped his companion on the shoulder.

'I pray you do not look around – we have company. I fear we shall not see the conclusion of this little performance. Ladies, we should be less conspicuous if you would accompany us.'

He led them out through a back door, behind the

stage. Outside, they walked around the building to where Mary's carriage was waiting, out of sight, down a back street. He ordered the driver to take them to his house in Westminster.

'I hope you will not mind the delay, but we cannot risk the city gates at night, they are closely guarded.'

As the carriage took them through the dark streets, the men talked together in hushed tones, sometimes glancing up at Kate and Mary. They were challenged by the night watch as they crossed Holborn, but they reached Westminster without any further event. Fitzmaurice climbed down from the carriage.

'You may come in, if you like, ladies, but I am afraid you may only tarry a few minutes – we shall be very busy this night.' He helped the young man down. Mary was on the point of accepting, when Kate interrupted her.

'I am sure you have much to do, Lord Fitzmaurice. We shall not detain you.'

'As you wish, Katherine.' He bowed and swept off his hat as the carriage took the ladies into the night. Mary was incredulous.

'Why in heaven's name did you decline his offer? Lord Fitzmaurice seems like a most courteous and exciting man. Are you trying to keep him to yourself?'

Kate shook her head ruefully. 'Fitzmaurice is, as you say, a most courteous and exciting man – but I would rather not be party to the sort of excitement he has on offer. Believe me, Mary, he is not the sort of man you should have anything to do with. . . .'

'Then he sounds like exactly the sort of man I would like to have something to do with,' she laughed.

'Yes, Mary. I am sure you would,' Kate agreed.

The next morning Kate stayed in bed late. She did not want to face Gwen after the previous night. She thought that it was about time she moved into her own house.

She resolved to see Mr MacAulay that afternoon to see what progress he was making on that front. As she was considering this, Ruth came in.

'You have a letter, Mistress Kate. It is not from Master John: perhaps you have a mystery admirer.' She handed her the letter, then proceeded to open the curtains.

'Oh no, Ruth, please do not . . . oh, never mind.' It was too late, the room was flooded with brilliant sunlight.

'You cannot read your letter in the dark,' Ruth quipped as she left her.

She looked at it; the hand was unfamiliar. The seal broke easily and she opened it. Her heart beat faster as she recognized the signature. It was from Fitzmaurice.

My dear Cousin,
I cannot express my surprise at my seeing you once again, nor my admiration at the manner in which you conducted yourself last night, adequately with written words. Meet me at the west front of the abbey at three o'clock – you have nothing to fear from me, I assure you.

Thomas.

She was stunned by the effrontery of the man. She knew that she should not see him, with the same certainty that she knew that she would. She could still feel the thrill she had felt at his touch: it was a sensation she had not felt in such a long time. It had been so long. . . .

Fifteen

Kate arrived at Westminster Abbey at a quarter past three. She looked around but there was no sign of him. She was about to leave when a figure detached itself from the shadows. It was Fitzmaurice.

'Forgive me, Katherine. I was watching you. You are even more beautiful in the sunlight.'

'You should be careful that you do not stretch the bounds of your flattery too far, Lord Fitzmaurice. I am not beautiful now, and I doubt that I ever was.'

'You do yourself no justice, Katherine – besides, it is for me to say if you are beautiful or not, and I judge that you are. And please call me Thomas, as you used to. I have not changed from the man you went riding with.'

'You changed before, remember?'

He looked at her remorsefully. 'I was a different man then. I was driven mad with grief after the death of Antonia. I think you can perhaps understand better now how grief can make a prisoner of a person's soul. You do me no service to remind me of those times.'

'I can hardly forget them. I will never forget how you treated me.'

'I do not think you have come here to reproach me, and I did not ask you to come so that we could resurrect painful memories.' He took her by the arm and they walked across the square to Whitehall. It was a hot, early August afternoon and they walked slowly and aimlessly. Fitzmaurice's conversation was charming and effortless; Kate remembered just how charming and amusing he could be.

As they reached the top of Whitehall, they found their way blocked by a cordon of troopers. After a few moments they heard the dull roll of drums in the distance, coming up the Strand. Fitzmaurice sneered as the parade came into view.

'It seems that we are about to be reminded who the actual masters of the country are.'

Ahead of the parade came a number of rough folk, carrying flags, which they handed out to the waiting crowd. When they were offered one, Fitzmaurice declined.

'Let us wait and see. When the soldier-boys have passed, there will be a similar group gathering back their tawdry pennants.'

'You have little love for the Parliamentarians, then?' Kate whispered.

He shook his head and frowned. 'They have the upper hand at the moment, so publicly I espouse their cause. Privately, well, you have seen an example of my more private work.'

'That young man?' she asked.

He nodded as the parade passed them. There were thousands of them, cavalry and infantry. The roll of their drums was deafening. Fitzmaurice took her arm again and led her away to a side street and down toward the river.

They were alone again and could speak openly.

'Were you helping that young man escape last night?' Kate asked.

'What young man? I saw no young man,' he joked. 'You met someone called Peter Mastermain last night. Peter Mastermain does not exist, so you must have been mistaken, Katherine.'

'Do not play with me, Thomas. What are you doing?'

He looked out on to the river. 'You will have noticed that my house backs on to the Thames . . . well, the young man you met is now on a boat bound for France. From there he will join the Prince of Wales. After that, who knows? But at least he will be safe.'

'But surely, is it not dangerous?'

'Yes, I suppose it could be – if I were unwary, but I am very careful.'

'Then why do you do it? Do they pay you?'

He laughed out loud. 'My, my, Katherine. Obviously you still hold me in very low esteem. No, I have enough money of my own, you should know that.'

'Then, I repeat, why do you do it?' she persisted.

His eyes narrowed as he looked at her, as though he wondered if she could be trusted.

'I do it for influence. Clearly, at the moment the King's star is on the wane, but it will rise again. That parade just now, for example – that was not for our benefit. Parliament and the army do not altogether see eye to eye at the moment. They do not know what to do with the King, and they are deeply at odds about what to do now that they have victory in the field. Their time will pass and the King will come back into his own once more. It may take years, but in the end the monarchy will prevail. In the meantime, I keep the dogs at Westminster sweet with occasional loans of money – they think I am one of their closest allies. But when the King returns, he will remember those who aided his cause during these troubled times. The men I save will become powerful in the new order, they will remember their friends.'

'So, whichever way things turn out, you will not lose,' Kate observed.

'Men like me never lose, Katherine. You should know that by now.'

They walked together along the streets until sunset. It seemed that Kate had the lion's share of the conversation. Fitzmaurice listened avidly to all she had to say. She found herself saying things that she had kept from the world for so long. He seemed to understand her grief and her bitterness. He related the tale of his own grief at his loss and it seemed to be so close to her own experiences. In talking, in sharing her sadness with another she found that she was not unique. By his very presence and his demeanour, it became clear to Kate that her own troubles would, one day, come to an end. Still, it was strange to find solace in this man, who had haunted her nightmares for so many years.

After sunset, his mood changed. He became merry. He took her to a small tavern near the Fleet. They laughed and joked. He teased her and she found herself returning his jibes and pleasantries. He was a man of great wit and charm. Kate remembered just how good a companion he had been. Indeed, she recalled just how attractive she had found him when they first met.

The evening passed too quickly. It was after midnight when they left the tavern, though the air was still warm. The sky was clear and the stars seemed to burn with a fierce clarity. They walked back to his own house. When they reached the steps, he took her hands in his.

'You may come in if you like, Kate. Though I will make no assurances this evening about your safety.'

Kate smiled as she looked into his eyes. It was never easy to tell what he was thinking from looking at them. Not like John's – he could never keep a secret. 'Honest John.' She laughed inwardly at the thought. Thomas was such a different man. He stood only a little taller than herself; she did not have to look up to him. He had none of John's stiff reserve, he was a man of the moment, living by his impulses. She could still sense the fierce cruelty that lay hidden beneath his charming veneer, and she wondered how long the charm would last when she submitted to it.

'No, I will not join you, tonight. Not because I am married, nor for any reason to do with my husband. Tonight I shall go home for my own sake. I hope you can understand, Thomas.'

He smiled and nodded his head slightly. 'I will call out my coachman – the streets are not safe and it is a long walk to Chelsea.'

He went to go up the steps, then he turned. He put his hands up to her face. His touch was very gentle, but assured. Slowly, his hand moved around to the back of her neck and his fingers rested on her nape, burying themselves in her hair. He was not smiling any more. Kate felt a cold chill as she wondered what he would do next. He held her with his hand and his eyes for a long while like a cat considering when to devour the mouse he had trapped. Then he smiled and his hand dropped. His voice was soft and low.

'I hope you do not mind. Your beauty inspires me to take liberties which I should not. Goodnight, Katherine. I shall see you very soon.'

Soon after, Kate moved into a house in Leicester Fields. Life in Chelsea was becoming very difficult for her. She needed the freedom of her own establishment and the new houses in Leicester Fields offered the double advantage of convenience and anonymity. Over the winter she held some quite lavish parties, attended by some of the younger blood of the pro-monarchy group. Fitzmaurice was always in evidence and was always the last to leave, often staying until the small hours of the morning. From time to time he would remind her of his offer, but still Kate refused him; gently, politely – even humorously, but always firmly. She sometimes amazed herself at her refusal, for he was most certainly a very attractive man and she felt more and more attracted to him, but still something made her hold back.

She was thinking about just that matter one morning in late January. After all, why did she not sleep with him? There was nothing to be lost by it. Half of London already thought they were lovers. On the other hand, she thought, there was little to be gained from it either. She was happy with their relationship the way it was and he obviously enjoyed the chase. Everything would change after he had finally run his quarry to ground. She wondered how she might be affected by it: she was happy with herself the way she was, an independent woman, no longer the possession of some man, doing as she pleased and when she pleased to do so. She relaxed back into her armchair by the fire and sipped her chocolate. She sighed deeply with satisfaction: if this was how life was going to be in the future, then she could be content with it.

Her reverie was disturbed by a sharp knock on the front door. It was unfamiliar, she wondered who it was.

Gemma would attend to it. Such a sensible girl, not at all like Ruth – whose disapproving looks had bothered her so much that she had been forced to let her go.

Presently, there was a knock on the parlour door. Gemma came in and seemed perplexed.

'What is the matter?' Kate asked.

'There is a woman at the door. She says that she is your sister-in-law. Shall I let her in?'

There was no need for Kate to answer, for Gwen appeared behind the maid.

'Good morning, Kate,' she said, coldly. 'I am pleased to see you looking so well.'

Kate gestured to the maid to leave them. 'Please sit down, Gwen. I have not seen you for so long.'

'Not since you moved here, in fact.'

'No, that is true, now that you come to mention it. Still, it is a pleasure to see you here now. Do you like my place?' she asked, her hand describing the room around her.

'The house looks well enough, it is what goes on here that bothers me.'

'I see,' Kate replied, 'and just what do you think actually does go on here?'

Gwen shook her head. 'God only knows, but if the half of what is rumoured is true, then I am surprised that you have not been arrested for running a bawdy-house.'

Kate laughed. 'Then I would love to know what people are saying, for no impropriety has gone on here, I can assure you.'

Gwen's defences deemed to drop. 'My dear Kate. I fear I have gone awry from the outset – that idiot girl's attitude riled me. Can we start afresh?'

'By all means. Please sit down. Would you like some chocolate?'

Gwen declined the offer. 'Thank you, but no. Your maid looks like the sort of girl that would spit in it before she gave it to me.' She laughed sardonically. 'Kate, I had to come and I am deeply sorry if what I have to say offends you, but nevertheless, it has to be said.'

Kate braced herself for an onslaught of moral indignation, but it never came. Gwen sat forward, her manner was confidential and cordial, but above all her love and concern revealed themselves in her words.

'They say that you and Fitzmaurice are lovers – that you are no better than his whore.'

'We are friends, Gwen. No more and no less,' she snapped. 'I would like to know the source of these rumours. Tell me. If you love me then you will tell me, Gwen.'

'I heard it from Jane . . .'

'I might have guessed. She hated me from the very first.'

'. . . who heard it from Fitzmaurice himself – from his own lips, and there were others present to witness it. He was drunk, but he was insistent. He says that he has you at his beck and call.'

The blood seemed to drain from her. She slumped back in her chair.

'How can he say such a thing, when it is so manifestly untrue?'

'I cannot say, but all of London believes him. After all, they have no reason to believe otherwise.'

'I do not understand. We are friends . . . or at least I thought we were friends.'

'You forget how plausible he can be – I think he believes his own lies some of the time.'

'But why should he do such a thing?'

'Out of malice, perhaps? At a stroke he is revenged on all of us: you are ruined, John is made out to be a cuckold, and our whole family is disgraced.'

'Just with a few words of a lie.'

'Aided and abetted by your own unwariness and people's willingness to believe the worst of others.'

'All these months . . . all the things he said . . . and I believed him, every word. He used his own grief as a lure to trap me. . . .'

'He told you what you wanted to hear. He manipulates people to his own ends. He is wholly evil.'

'What can I do?' Kate asked, entirely at a loss.

'To him – nothing. For yourself? Well, that is up to you. As you kept reminding me, you are your own woman now. Though, if you want my advice, for what it is worth, you will forsake this reckless lifestyle. If you would only consider it, I would strongly suggest that you make some moves to reconcile yourself with John.'

'Does he know, do you think John knows about this?'

'I cannot see how he can have avoided it. His regiment spent most of the winter here in London.'

'And he did not come to see me? Did he not know I was here?'

'He knew you were here, but he did not come. He said it was out of respect for your wishes and your privacy, but I know when he is lying. When he lost you – he believes that he has lost you – then the spirit drained from him. I will say no more, for you will only think I am trying to blackmail you, but it would be best if you saw him when he returns.'

'If he will see me. What will he say?'

Gwen left not long after, promising to come and see her again soon. Alone again, Kate's rage began to boil. Her mind was filled with the thought of Fitzmaurice and his lies. She would confront him, she decided. It might not do her any good, but at least she would feel better. She seethed at the thought of him.

It did not take her very long to get to Whitehall and her anger was unabated. Fitzmaurice's servant saw her coming and admitted her directly. She waited in the lounge for him, watching the clock. The servant returned.

'The master is indisposed at the moment, he asks if you will wait for him and if you would like something to drink?'

'Tell your master if he is not down here in five minutes I shall drag him down here myself. Go!' Kate raged.

He rushed out of the room, Kate could hear him clattering up the stairs. After four minutes, she heard softer footfalls coming down. Fitzmaurice entered the room. He was still in his nightshirt. His eyes, like two glass beads, fixed on her. He smiled a broad, satisfied smile, though his eyes remained unchanged, still they encompassed her.

'I see you have found a whore of flesh and blood to replace the one in your mind,' Kate taunted.

'I see that the news has finally reached you. It took its time. Was it your loving sister – the whiter-than-white Lady Nevers?'

'How could you say such a thing, you had no reason . . .'

'On the contrary, I had ample reasons: you denied me, then you marked me and then you escaped into the loving bosom of the sickly-sweet Barnards. You thought I would rest easy? It was a long campaign, but I can see that it has been worthwhile . . . now. I only wish I could have been present when your husband heard the news – make no mistake, I am very thorough in my revenge. I had my man relate every detail of his reaction back to me. I do not need to have you now – it is more deliciously ironic that the world thinks you a whore, even though both you and I know that your virtue remains intact.'

He laughed, though still his eyes stared at her, unwavering in their concentration. Kate was about to speak, when the door opened behind him. It was Mary. She wore only a man's shirt, but Kate hardly noticed this. Kate looked, appalled, at her face. It was swollen down one side from the temple to the jawbone and discoloured by a long, black bruise. Fitzmaurice smiled as she entered. He pulled her forward, then held her chin so that Kate had a full view of her disfigurement.

'It seems that you were right, Katherine, I do have a whore of flesh . . . and blood.'

Mary stared sidelong at him, her eyes wide with terror. He raised his hand, as if to strike her. She cowered away, but he had her firmly held in his hand and she could not escape. He laughed and let her fall. He returned his attention to Kate. His eyes glittered with malice.

'I would ask you to join us but, of course, you are a married woman, I was forgetting.' He turned back to

Mary. 'You can take her with you if you wish. I have nearly finished with her.'

Mary shook her head. 'No, Kate,' she said, her speech slurred. 'I cannot go out in the daylight like this. I am all right, honestly.' She shuddered as she spoke.

Fitzmaurice put his fingers to his lips, as though he was thinking. 'Perhaps I made a mistake at your friend's party: I should have said that Mary was the whore I had at my beck and call . . . but, then, you Irish girls, I can never tell you apart.' He looked down at Mary, his head to one side. 'Of course, Mary is my creature. . . .'

Kate pushed past him and made for the door. He called after her, 'I have taught her some delightful tricks. I would love to show you them.'

Kate slammed the front door as she flew out of the house.

His voice became quiet. 'But I'm afraid they might offend your delicate sensibilities.' He smiled as he looked down on the woman cowering before him.

Kate ran down the road to find help. She found two soldiers and demanded that they come with her. But, by the time they arrived at Fitzmaurice's house, he had anticipated them. Mary was dressed and her face powdered, though the bruising was still apparent. When the soldiers asked if Mary wished to register a complaint, she declined. Kate tried to persuade her, but she was adamant. Eventually they took her back to Kate's house and out of his reach; she still would not press any charges. She was afraid of him, she confessed, but was more afraid of the scandal. Kate sighed. Fitzmaurice had caused so much misery and yet he could walk away from his mischief a free man.

Kate was at a loss. Her reputation was in ruins: she knew that there was no point in trying to publicly deny Fitzmaurice's allegations, for that would only lend greater credibility to them. Her whole London adventure was a shambles. She could not return to Gwen's – she did not want her to be further tainted by the disgrace. By the same token, she knew that any hope she might have held, lingering at the back of her mind, of reconciliation with John would now be hopeless. There was nothing else for it; she would have to brazen it out here in London until such time as she could return to Kilerin. Just the mention of its name set off a deep-felt longing in Kate's heart. She had had enough of this place: as soon as it was humanly possible, she would go home.

Sixteen

John sat brooding in his saddle as the rain lashed down on him. His face was grim and sombre as he ordered his company forward. Their horses' hooves clattered on the cobblestones. He watched as the crowd in front of him recoiled at their advance, then their ranks hardened as they prepared to meet the charge. He drew his sabre and heard the slither of steel behind him as his men followed his lead. The pace quickened. He pointed his sword towards the mob and cried out the charge. The crowd set up a menacing chant as they brandished sticks and clubs at the approaching Ironsides.

With a sickening crunch they rode into them, over them and through them. He heard the cries of pain behind him. He had ordered his men to use their sabres only at need, but many folk had been ridden down in their onslaught. He held up his hand for the men to turn about, ready to charge again, but as he came back to the front of his men, he saw that the crowd was broken: men and women dragged away the dead and wounded. A child's screams resonated in his belly. He thought he would vomit.

He rode along the line, checking his men's swords for blood, ready to admonish any man who had used his sword. There were none. No one spoke; they were all aware of what they had done, their faces were as grim as his own. He led them back towards the crowd at the walk. As they passed the remains of the crowd, they screamed at them, shaking their fists and slinging mud at them. The troopers did nothing, but rode on through with heavy hearts.

When they had passed, Jack came riding up to the front. They rode together in silence for a while and then he finally spoke his thoughts.

'John, I think not that the men will take any more of this. We joined up to fight for the liberation of folk, not to kill them. That's two days in a row we've had to do that – and for my own part I'd not want to do it again.'

John kept his eyes fixed on the road ahead. 'What will you do Jack, are you going to desert? We have lost a quarter of our men already. If you go, I reckon half of those left will follow your lead.' He laughed, a bitter hollow laugh. 'You know, Jack, it is ironic to think that six months ago those same folk were cheering us as we marched into London – now look at them.'

'True enough, I fear we've lost some of our popularity since then. Cheer up, John. I'll not be deserting, you know that. Something will turn up soon. After all, the King's escaped to Carisbrooke and he's bound to be hatching some nonsense for us to deal with.'

John turned to him, his face devoid of emotion.

'Well he had better do something soon, or you might just wake up one morning and find me gone.'

They rode on through the streets, barely noticing the looks of fear and hatred on the faces of the passing Londoners. Jack leaned across in his saddle and spoke in a low gruff voice, 'If ever you feel like getting out, lad – don't forget to wake me before you go. I'd rather be a deserter by your side than carry on without you.'

John glanced across and laughed to himself. 'Then let us hope that Charles does something soon. I would not want you by my side if I have to face a firing squad.'

They did not have long to wait. After an interminable prayer meeting, lasting three days, the most of which time Jack and John spent in the tavern, they were sent as part of Cromwell's command to South Wales, where the garrisons were in mutiny. John did not relish the thought of fighting against men who had fought by his side only two years before, but war was war, and he had come to think that it was his business, his calling even. Kate had probably been right when she said he was fit for nothing else. At least it kept him from thinking about her all the time, of how they had been – and what they had become.

When they reached Pembroke, they found that the old medieval castle was held against them and they prepared for a siege. The news from around the country was not good: all of Kent was ablaze with rebellion and Fairfax had gone down from London to suppress it; there was a mutiny in the navy; and there was the rumour of a Scottish army mustering on the northern borders, ready to invade. Meanwhile, the siege dragged on.

John had never been in Wales before. The countryside was uncommonly beautiful, but the Welsh themselves deeply resented the presence of yet another invading army from England. The thing that surprised him most was that they had their own language – he had heard about it before, but he had not believed it. He and Jack had taken up quarters in the town itself, at a safe distance from the cannons in the castle, and they both made a determined attempt to learn some of this strange, rich tongue. Wherever they had been on the continent, they had done the same: but Welsh defeated them utterly. Still, they made many friends there through their vain attempts at it. They often made laughing-stocks of themselves, but they enjoyed it nevertheless. John was reminded of the times he had spent in the Rhineland, surrounded by people whom he could not understand. The experience was a tonic to him. Jack watched as his friend started to genuinely laugh again – he had needed so badly to laugh, to forget all his troubles. It was like seeing the old John return again.

The siege took two months, but by mid-July they were on the road again, this time heading north to face the invading Scottish army. The weather was awful and they knew that the force that they would face was much larger than their own, but this could not dampen their spirits. The New Model was on the march again to face a real foe. Their ranks had been thinned by desertions but there was no talk of desertion now – they were going to fight a proper battle and they had never been defeated. Cromwell drove them on through a series of forced marches, through Otley and Skipton and up into the Pennines, up to the roof of the country and then down into Lancashire. They were tired, dog tired, but ready to fight. John looked around at his men; there was a change in them, their spirits were higher and their eyes brighter than he had seen them for nearly two years. He felt a surge of pride welling up within him.

The next day, in the midst of a summer squall, they finally caught up with the Scots. They were drawn up across a terrain of enclosed fields, their pennants flying, silently waiting for the English to come on.

'This is pretty bad country for cavalry,' Jack observed, apprehensively. He pointed out the difficulties of the land. 'Just look over there at those hedgerows – we'll never get through that lot – and if we ever do, we'd be trapped and unable to move.'

'Aye,' John was forced to agree, 'it is far from the best of situations, but at least it is better than kicking our heels and breaking up riots in London.'

'Ah, well. You're probably right there.' Jack laughed and rode back to rejoin his troop as the trumpeters sounded the advance.

It was a quick and bloody battle. The Scots were underfed and ill-equipped to fight a modern army, but they had the advantage of numbers and they fought with a desperate bravery. Slowly, they were driven back to the river. Then the news went out that their general, Lord Hamilton, had deserted them, crossing the river in a cockle-boat, and they broke. The pursuit turned into a rout as Hamilton tried to rally his forces near Preston. They followed them into the night. From time to time there were fierce exchanges as they encountered pockets of resistance. On they followed them through the next morning, crushing a rearguard at Winwick. They finally surrendered at Warrington, their general having deserted them yet again. John's company were dispatched south in pursuit of Sir Marmaduke Langdale.

Langdale and his men had left the field before the surrender and had a good start on John's company. There was no time to lose, they set off straightway. They did not see them at all that day, nor the next, though the rumour of their passing was rife wherever they had been. They had looted many villages along the way. They were heading south and east; John could not fathom out the reason for it – they were making straight for Fairfax's own army.

They caught up with a contingent of them near Matlock. The cavaliers sued for mercy. John merely disarmed them and carried on. He could not afford to waste time. The pursuit continued through the Peaks and ended just outside Nottingham. The two forces were roughly equal in size, but the Royalists had no more stomach for fight. They surrendered without conditions. The Royalists were consigned to the Nottingham garrison, whilst John escorted Langdale himself down to London.

John felt in awe of his illustrious prisoner. Sir Marmaduke Langdale, commander of the Northern Horse – nicknamed 'The Ghost' by his own men at the very outset of the war. He was one of the King's most devoted supporters and one of the most charismatic leaders of men on either side. He had offered John his sword on the condition that his men would be well cared for. John had declined.

'I will give you my assurance of your men's safety in return for your parole that you will not escape, sir. You may keep your sword and surrender it to General Lord Fairfax, who is the only man who is fit to take it.'

Langdale seemed surprised at this. 'Well, young man. That is a very sweet and fitting sentiment, and I am sure that Tom Fairfax will be only too glad to accept my sword. I have been pricking his side with it for long enough.' He smiled. 'But now it is over and I am very tired. So, old Ferdinando Fairfax is dead and Tom is Lord Fairfax now. A pity, I liked Ferdinando – he could be a merry man when the mood took him. I should have liked to have paid my respects to him before he went, but this little matter unfortunately prevented me. Come, young man, we shall talk as we go – there is much I would like to learn about this Brave New World that we have fought over for so long.'

They rode at their leisure, taking many days to reach London, stopping often along the way. They were given free quarter wherever they went, more because of Sir Marmaduke's celebrity than for any love of the Parliamentarians. He attracted great cheering crowds wherever he went. As they neared their journey's end, he gave John a heavy purse, full of silver coins.

'I would be grateful if you would disburse these funds for the good people of Derbyshire whose villages we were obliged to take victuals from. It was an act of desperation and it has weighed heavily on my conscience.'

'Might you not need these funds to defray the cost of your imprisonment?'

Sir Marmaduke laughed quietly, then sighed. 'I do not imagine I shall be a prisoner very long, my dear Captain.'

In November, John was summoned to a Council of Officers at St Albans. There was only one item on the agenda: the conduct of, and the fate of the King. Though Lord Fairfax had summoned the council, the main protagonist was, inevitably, Henry Ireton. Cromwell was still in the north, many said that he was keeping away deliberately. . . .

Fairfax himself was in the chair and Ireton was the first to speak: he denounced the King for his duplicity in pretending to negotiate with Parliament and the army, at the same time as he was conniving with the Scots and the French to send armies against England.

'From the very start, he has listened to our pleas at the same time as he has been writing our death warrants. He has played us off against each other: Parliament against the army, the army against the country. Dangling the hope of settlement before us, keeping us in confusion, while he hatches his plots against us, with foreign powers.'

Ireton carried on in this vein for many hours, and after that his supporters took up the cudgels, and so the debate ran on. After the second day, John grew alarmed that this was no debate, but a justification to depose the King by spreading the blame across the whole officer corps. That night, he went to see Fairfax.

Fairfax was sitting by the fire, reading a book. He looked up as John entered.

'Ah, John Barnard, I was wondering if you might come to see me tonight.'

'What made you think that I might come, my Lord General?'

'We are alone, and "my Lord General" is over-formal. Please, be seated and call me Thomas – or even Tom, if you like.' Fairfax put his book aside as John sat down. For a long while he said nothing, but studied his hands, as John had so often seen him do. At length, he broke the silence.

'You have come to me tonight because you are dismayed by the course of events of the last two days. Am I right?'

John nodded. 'I simply cannot believe they realize the conclusion of their actions.'

'Oh, they know full well the course they are taking. I can assure you of that.'

'But surely the majority of the officers are against it?'

'Indeed; but which of them will be the first to stand against them? When Henry Ireton speaks his lips may move – but you know that the thoughts behind them are Master Cromwell's own. You had the courage to stand against them before, do you have the courage now?'

'Will you not speak yourself?' John asked.

'I cannot speak,' the general said, staring into the fire.

'May I ask you why?'

'I will speak after the debate, but not before. If I do, then my men will be swayed in whatever direction I take and that would defeat the purpose of the council.'

He looked into John's eyes. 'Before, you opposed them as one of a group and under my protection. This time you will stand alone – and my ability to protect you is nearly at its end. I ask you again, do you have the courage to speak?'

The next morning the council reconvened. Henry Ireton started with a very erudite speech on the history and evils of monarchy, which was greeted with tumultuous applause from his supporters, many of whom stood up to be heard next. Fairfax's eyes fell on John, waiting for him to stand. John's limbs felt heavy, willing him not to stand, but now other eyes were turning toward him. Almost against his will, he felt himself rise.

'The Council recognizes Captain Barnard of the Eastern Association.'

Fairfax nodded to him as he struggled to find the right words to start.

'Gentlemen . . . my fellow officers – my friends.' He held on to the railing in front of him as he realized that there was no going back from this point.

'I have sat here these last two days, listening to General Ireton and his friends making their eloquent – and sometimes less than eloquent – case in favour of the abolition of the monarchy. To turn England into a republic – the Commonwealth of England, as they call it. And, in all honesty, I have found it difficult to contain myself.

'Charles has proved himself to be a liar and a tyrant – unworthy to have the stewardship of a fish-stall, let alone the rule of a great nation such as this.'

There were nods and murmurs of approbation at this, which encouraged John to continue.

'Yet we knew these things at the outset, when we embarked on this war – but we did not take up arms for this. If, when I was raising my first company, I told my people that they would be fighting to create a republic – then I could not have called a single man to my standard. And yet they came. They came to fight for the restoration of their rights under Magna Carta – rights which were granted, albeit unwillingly, by a monarch constrained by his people. Have we fallen so low that we cannot constrain Charles to restore those rights, that the only recourse we have left to us is the abolition of the monarchy and the murder of our own King?'

John was interrupted by boos and shouts of 'not true!' from Ireton's supporters. Ireton himself glowered at him.

'Hear me out! Hear me out, I say!' Slowly, the shouting died down, and John continued, 'Murder, I said, and murder I meant. We all know Charles – he will never relinquish his throne while he yet lives. He believes that it has been granted him by God Himself. Do you think that we can merely say to him that he is King no more? What shall we do with him then, shall we retire him to a country retreat? His supporters will flock to him in droves. Shall we make a lifelong prisoner of him? But still his family are free: they will soon enlist the help of foreign monarchs, for even though they might hate each other, they will hate us more. While we prevail their own thrones will not be safe – mark you, they will come for us, like the Crusades of old. Finally, for the same reasons, we cannot banish him over the sea, for while he yet breathes, he will return again and again to these shores and we shall never have peace.

'Charles is a man alone: we have stripped him of his armies, his property and his power. All that he has left is his posterity. While he lives, he is still King of England and the only way we can strip him of that is to strip him of his very life. And I, for one, will not be party to that. Gentlemen, thank you for hearing me out.' With that, he resumed his seat.

After that, there was silence for a moment, then other men stood up to be heard, not Ireton's supporters, but men who held more moderate views. The debate proper had started. John looked across at Ireton, who stared at him with unmitigated hatred. Ireton nodded his head as he stared and John knew that his fate was sealed.

Moderation won the day that day. But within a few weeks,

Ireton had staged a purge of Parliament, throwing out all the moderate members. The King was ordered to be put on trial for his life. In the midst of all the confusion, the arrest of one relatively insignificant cavalry captain went practically unnoticed. . . .

Seventeen

For the first time in her life, Kate spent Christmas Day alone. Gwen had invited her to spend the day with her, but Kate had declined for fear of encountering John – she felt she could never face him again. Gemma had left her a few weeks before and she had not bothered to replace her yet. The house was empty, her footsteps echoed on the floor as she wandered about the place, trying to find things to occupy her time, on this day which was no different to any other.

She was about to go out for a walk, the streets would be empty and there would be little likelihood of encountering anybody, when there was an urgent knocking at the door. When she opened it, there was a little urchin boy eagerly waiting for her, skipping from foot to foot to keep himself warm. Before she could say anything, he gave a little formal bow and went into a short speech, which Kate felt sure he had been rehearsing.

'Good morning, my lady. May I offer you all the best of the season – even though I shouldn't,' he admitted, shyly. 'I have come with a message from a gentleman. He said you would pay me well when you received it.' He handed her a sheet of paper, rough stuff and unsealed. Kate looked at it dubiously, wondering if this was some new trick of Fitzmaurice's. Her hand began trembling as she recognized the writing. It was from John.

25th December, 1648.

My Dearest Kate,

Merry Christmas! I hope that this little letter will

not disrupt any festivities. I would have come myself, but I fear I am somewhat indisposed at the moment. Still, this forbidden festival has provided me with an unexpected opportunity.

I regret to say that I am being detained at the Fleet. My cell is not too uncomfortable, for it is the condemned cell. I fear I may not write too much – this is the only paper my gaoler could find. The boy will bring you to me. You must come with him now and bring some money with you – at least a pound – for his father. Come quickly, I beg you to come, or in all honesty, I shall not see in the New Year.

Know now that I have never stopped loving you. The wretch Fitzmaurice sent me a vile message. I was dismayed by it at first, but when I thought of you, I realized it could not be true.

Come now – if you still bear any love for me, come now!

Your loving husband,

John.

When she had finished, she looked blankly at the little boy. He smiled at her, the same look of eager anticipation was in his eyes.

'My lady, the gentleman said that if you did not come with me, you will pay me anyway.'

Kate nodded and returned his stare with the same eagerness. 'Wait here a moment. I shall be with you in but a twinkling.'

Her mind was filled with the vision of John in some prison cell, alone and in danger, but even so, she was practically beside herself with joy. She would see her beloved John. All the fears and reservations which she had built around her were gone. In his moment of need he had called on her for help. She would do everything in her power to save him and she would never forsake him again.

The streets were indeed empty and Kate was glad of it, as the young boy led her to a small concealed entrance by the watergate of the Fleet. Inside, the air was dank and musty. A foul stench issued up from a stairwell which led down below the water level. The boy grabbed her arm.

'Fear not, my lady. Your gentleman is not down there – that's where we keep our naughty prisoners.'

At the sound of his voice, a number of moans and cries for water came up. The boy smiled wickedly.

'They are never satisfied, some people. Why, they have water a'plenty down there – it's just that they can't drink any of it.' He led her on up a stone staircase.

The stairs led them up to the sunlit levels of the Fleet. Kate realized that they were going up to a tower. At the top of the stairs they were met by a short, burly, bearded man. He smiled, showing a row of uneven and broken teeth.

'You came quick, my lady. The captain was right to have faith in you.' He held out his hand for payment. Kate went to her purse and took out some coins.

'Here is ten shillings. I will give you another ten shillings and something for the boy – when you have allowed me a good long time with my husband.'

The gaoler's eyes widened as he stared at the two crown pieces. 'Well, for a pound, you can have all the time you like, my lady. I only wish it was Christmas every day.' He opened the cell door.

John was standing in the middle of the room, waiting for her.

'I heard you outside. I could not have dreamed that you would come so quickly. I am . . . unprepared . . .' he said meekly, holding out his hands, hopelessly. His voice was dry and weak and his hair was wild and dusty. He had not shaved for a number of days, but to Kate he was wonderful to behold. For what seemed like a very long time, they just looked at one another. At length, John spoke again.

'I am that happy to see you . . . and I am so very encouraged that you came so quickly.' His voice trembled. 'Might I venture to ask . . . if I may hold you?'

Kate sighed with relief. She smiled and held out her

arms to him. 'Oh, John. After all the trouble I have caused you – it should be me who does the asking.'

Their hands touched. They were both very cold, but it was not from the cold that they were trembling.

Kate pulled him to her and they embraced. She freed her arms and put her hands up to his face, running her fingers through the stubble on his cheeks.

'I do not like you looking so rough and grizzled. It makes you look rather disreputable.' They both laughed at the silliness of the comment. John put his own hand up to his chin, rubbing the stubble.

'I could ask the gaoler for some soap and a razor, but I have very little money and all of that I need for my food. The money is running out fast – though I expect to run out of time before I run out of money,' he added, grimly. This reminder of John's predicament brought Kate sharply back to her senses and her manner became at once more urgent.

'John, why are you here? Surely Parliament can have few more loyal supporters than you?'

John sighed and indicated that they should sit down at the rude table by the tiny barred window.

'Aye, Kate, I was loyal – indeed I am still loyal to the cause. But the cause has changed and I am afraid I was a little too outspoken in support of the cause we had fought for.'

'You were ever outspoken, my dear. But surely men may speak openly in this new order?'

John nodded. 'It rather depends on what you say – and more importantly, who hears what you say. I fear I have annoyed some very important people, Kate.'

'But you cannot be put in prison for that?'

'No,' John admitted. 'But those people may construe charges which may well cost me my life.'

Kate shook her head and looked at him, perplexed. 'I do not understand. . . .'

'I am held on three counts, two of which are punishable by death, and the third would result in my transportation to the Indies.'

Kate looked at him aghast. 'What have you done?'

He sighed. 'I am accused of deserting the scene of the battle; of aiding and abetting deserters; and finally, of accepting bribes from Royalist criminals. You must admit, they are three very serious crimes.'

'There cannot be any substance in them, though.' Kate looked at him, waiting for him to deny them out of hand. 'Is there any substance in their claims?'

John looked up. 'Well, on the surface, yes. There is a case to be made. I left the scene of the battle at Langport – though I was accompanied by Lieutenant-General Cromwell. I did take money from Sir Marmaduke Langdale, but it was for the relief of some villages in Derbyshire that he had looted. On the least serious charge, that of aiding deserters – well, I fear I am guilty. Though I persuaded most of them to return to their regiments, there were still some that I let go. It seems that a spy was planted in my own company and was reporting to General Ireton. It appears that I was right, after I made my little speech to Parliament I was indeed a marked man.'

'But when your case comes to court. . . .'

'I do not know if it will come to that. I have been allowed no defence. In fact, I have been allowed no contact with the outside world until today. I was only allowed to write to you because today is Christmas and Dickon is on guard here alone – and he was open to a bribe.'

'Then why did you not write to Michael and Gwen – they would be better placed to help you, whereas I . . . well, you know how helpless I am.'

'If I am going to die' – he looked earnestly at her – 'and I may well die, then you are the only one I wanted to be with at the end. I can sleep easier, knowing that at last we are together again.'

Kate took his hands in hers across the table and held them tight.

'Do not talk nonsense, John. I am going to get you out of this, believe me. I shall not rest until you are free.'

John smiled at her. 'I hoped you would say that, Kate. But we will have to work quickly, I rather think that Ireton has me pencilled into his calendar of events for the New Year.'

There was no time to waste. In spite of his jests, it was clear to Kate that John was in terrible and immediate danger. If she did not act quickly then there was every possibility that hers would be the last friendly face he would ever see. She would brook no further pleasantries from him, but insisted that he go through every minute detail of the charges he was facing.

By the time he had finished, the light was failing. She had questioned him and cross-questioned him on anything and everything she thought might help his case. He got up from the table and knocked on the door for the gaoler. Kate could hear the key turning in the door. She knew that she would have to go. She took John in her arms and kissed him, long and tenderly on the mouth. She squeezed him tightly, then held him at arms' length.

'I shall get you out of here, I swear it . . . oh, God, John. You are everything to me. I shall not ever forsake you.'

John nodded. Tears stood in his eyes. 'My dearest Kate. These years we have been apart and all the misery we have suffered . . . I would suffer them again if I knew that they would lead to this moment.'

They pledged their love to one another and parted. Watching the door close on John was one of the cruellest moments of all, but Kate knew what she had to do. As the gaoler led her back downstairs, she went to her purse.

'Here, as I promised, is ten shillings and a shilling for the boy's trouble. See that he gets it. Here is another ten – if you will ensure that my husband gets all that he requires, and there will be another ten when I hear that you have kept to this bargain.'

'He shall want for nothing – save only his liberty, and that is beyond my gift, my lady,' he replied.

As they spoke, they passed the subterranean stairwell. The cries went up once more. Kate looked at the gaoler.

'And, since it is Christmas, and you have been well paid, I would consider it a favour to me if you would give those poor wretches some fresh water.'

'I will attend to it, my lady.' He touched his cap as he let her out into the clean evening air. Kate shuddered at the feel of it, but she did not tarry. She had much work to do.

The lights were burning in the windows as she reached her sister-in-law's house. She hoped to God that they were all at home: she would have need of all their services. Dodington came to the door. He seemed surprised to see her.

'We did not expect to see you, Mistress Katherine. The family is still at table.'

'So much the better, Dodington,' she said sharply, but not harshly. 'I want to talk to all of them. Go fetch Lady Gwendoline. I will wait here in the hall.'

Gwen seemed as surprised as her servant to see her, but she smiled and welcomed her with open arms. Kate kissed her, but then came straight to her business.

'Gwen, is Michael here, and your father too?' she asked.

'Why, yes, of course. It is Christmas.'

'Good. Two lawyers and both of them influential – exactly what I need.'

'My God, Kate!' Gwen exclaimed. 'What have you done now?'

'Me?' She smiled briefly. 'Nothing. I have come to see them about John.'

'He is not here – we were expecting him, but he did not come.'

'I know that, Gwen. I have come from him myself. Come, we have no time to lose. I will explain to you all together.'

Gwen led her uncertainly into the dining-room. There were only four of them at table. There was an empty place where John would have sat. Mr Barnard was on the point of raising his glass to his lips when he saw Kate come in. At first there was a look of surprise on his face, but it quickly turned to a smile as he rose to greet her.

'Katherine, my dear. It is the sun and moon to me to see you here at Christmas. My only regret is that John is not here to welcome you back.'

'I have been with John today, though in much less salubrious circumstances than these, I fear. He is a prisoner at the Fleet.'

The news hit the family like a thunderclap. Mr Barnard was unable to speak. Michael stood up, his face alarmed. Even little Stephen seemed to grasp the gravity of Kate's tidings. Michael was the first to speak.

'But that is impossible. His company has been dispatched to Wales. . . .'

'But he is not with them. As I have said, I have been with him at the Fleet. Today. He is to be hanged.'

She sat down at John's place and poured herself a glass of wine, then explained her whole tale to them. They did not say a word until she had finished. The two lawyers nodded and glanced at each other meaningfully. Michael took the lead.

'This is an outrage. John is worth a hundred of his detractors. I shall have a writ of habeas corpus drawn up first thing in the morning. Our main problem will be that his case should be heard – we shall make sure that his case is heard – but it will be heard by a court martial. We could petition for the case to be heard in open court, but that would take time and we do not want John languishing in the Fleet for any longer than he has to.' He raised an eyebrow, as though even the thought of it disgusted him.

'I left ten shillings with the gaoler for his upkeep and promised him more if John was well cared for,' Kate reassured him.

'You did well, Kate – especially as you promised him more on that condition. They are a crowd of cut-throats there, but they understand the power of money. I would not want to dwell on the fate of those poor souls who are detained there without it.'

Kate shuddered. She knew full well what their fate was. . . .

They stayed up late that night, drawing up their plans. Michael would handle all the legal formalities – he was able to practise in London, even though he was still in uniform. He was due to resign his commission, but now he would remain in the army so that he could defend a brother officer. Mr Barnard would use his influence with the remaining members of Parliament, many of whom Mr Barnard referred to mysteriously as 'his clients'. He would also go to the Tower and speak with Sir Marmaduke Langdale. It would fall to Kate and Gwen to go to Wales and take a summons to Jack Wyatt, then to go on to Derbyshire to take statements from the villagers there. Finally, and Michael stressed that this last task might well prove to be impossible, they were to seek out any of the deserters whom John had persuaded to return to their regiments. They were constrained by time – they would have to be back in two weeks at the latest. Kate felt sorry that she would not be able to see John at the Fleet, but she had sworn that she would do everything in her power to ensure his release, and that was what she would do.

By the next afternoon, she and Gwen were on the road west to Wales. Michael had furnished them with a summons for Jack and a letter of introduction to any notaries they might have need of there or in Derbyshire. They had to go on horseback – the roads were far too bad to take a coach, but they were both good horsewomen and they were travelling fast and light. By nightfall, they were at Oxford and by the next evening they were with Jack and the company, at Chepstow. The old sergeant looked at the summons as though he was about to tear it up.

'You didn't need to bring this along with you,' he muttered grimly. 'You should know by now that I would come to John's aid – even if it were to the end of the world.'

Gwen pointed out that it was not for his benefit, but to show his commanding officer and get him released from duty. His face brightened.

'Ah, yes, I can see the reasoning in that: it's so that I don't have to desert. I never was much of a one for the law – and that was my undoing when I was a lad.'

He took them straightway to his commanding officer. As he went, he related to them the story he had been told about John's disappearance. They had been told that John had been assigned to other duties with the London garrison.

'I thought it was a bit strange at the time, what with him goin' off and not sayin' goodbye and all – but how was I to know? After all, orders is orders.'

The new commander, a Captain Poynter, seemed ill-disposed to talk to them. He was a radical, and no doubt an appointee of General Ireton's. At first he challenged the authority of the summons, but they were ready for him. Kate was unrelenting.

'Captain Poynter, if you refuse to surrender Sergeant Wyatt to our charge, then we are empowered to have a summons made out in your own name to have you brought before a court of law for obstructing the course of justice.'

'But, ladies, Sergeant Wyatt is on active service,' he countered.

'And you will notice that the sergeant is called before a court martial,' Kate replied. 'Obstructing the course of justice, however, is a criminal offence and you would be tried before a civilian assize. If you do not release him now, we shall have the appropriate documents drawn up first thing in the morning.'

At length, Jack was released into their keeping. As they walked back to his quarters, Jack was full of praise for the way Kate had handled herself.

'You know, Kate, you even had me going in there – I didn't know you were so up on the law.'

Kate and Gwen both laughed. 'We are not,' Gwen admitted. 'But we were well rehearsed by Michael before we left. In all honesty, there was a great deal of bluff in our case.'

'There certainly was,' Kate continued. 'In point of

fact we have not any powers at all. It is just as well that your new captain was not a lawyer like John. But we had better leave tonight, before he discovers his error.'

Within the hour, they had left Chepstow and were heading north to Derbyshire.

Kate's spirits were at a low ebb as she surveyed the landscape before them. She had never been this far north before, nor in such high country. The wind tore at her cloak and fingers of cold crept in through every chink in her clothing. The high mountains overhung her and daunted her. She screwed up her eyes, dazzled by the whiteness of the snow all about them.

Jack looked up doubtfully at the sky. Although it was clear at the moment, there were dark clouds lowering on the horizon to the east. He pulled up his horse, for Gwen was lagging far behind again. While they waited, he took stock of the situation.

'It looks like we're goin' to be ridin' into that bit of weather before too long. We ought to make Matlock in two or three hours at this rate, but that means that we'll be right in the thick of it long before we get there. One thing we can't do, though, is keep on stopping like this or we'll never make it.'

'What shall we do about Gwen, then?' she asked, anxiously.

'I'll have to tether her horse to my own. I'll drag them along if needs be. You'll have to follow up behind and make sure she doesn't fall off – but just you mind not to fall back yourself.'

Kate nodded. She knew that she would not fall behind. She was carrying much too valuable a cargo. She put her hand behind her and touched the pannier, just to make sure that it was still there. At all costs she must not let it fall and lose it, for it contained the depositions they had taken from all the villages they had called at and each one helped to prove John's innocence.

At each place they had called, they had found the villagers only too keen to speak up in John's defence, for the money had been delivered faithfully and, they assured her, they would surely have starved through the winter without it. Strangely enough, they were also full of praise for Sir Marmaduke, who had caused them all this misery in the first place. They called him a 'great gentleman' and would not hear a word against him.

In the end, they had been forced to restrict themselves to three or four depositions at each place. If they had not, then they would have been there all year. They were also forced to restrain the villagers themselves from coming south with them, to speak up in John's defence. They had discussed it amongst themselves, but Gwen had held out against it. She pointed out that a prosecutor would twist the words of these simple folk if they ever came to court, whereas these statements, duly notarized, were unequivocal and far more eloquent than any testimony. Besides, Jack had said, if they had taken half the population of Derbyshire down with them, they would never get back to London in time. They were good, honest folk and their intentions were honourable, but they knew in their hearts that they would be needed there to help their families to weather out the bitter winter.

And the winter was bitter indeed. Gwen finally caught up with them. She smiled defiantly and there was a fire in her eyes – Kate knew that they would all make it down from this high country, no matter what. Jack tied her horse's reins to his saddle and they laboured on into the approaching storm.

In London, Michael was having less luck. So far, he had been unable to see John and the army council were blocking him at every stage. It was beginning to look as though Ireton would get what he wanted after all and John would swing at the gibbet before January was out. His only success had been in getting a stay of execution granted, but still there was no sign of the case coming to trial.

Mr Barnard had been to see Sir Marmaduke and had managed to take a statement from him, which corroborated John's own story, but there was precious little chance that he would be able to appear in court. In fact, Mr Barnard observed grimly, there was every likelihood that by the time John's case came to trial, Sir Marmaduke Langdale might already be dead.

They stared at one another across the table, which was strewn with papers, neither of them willing to speak the thought which was present in both their minds.

Michael looked down at the documents before him, he picked one up and started to read it, then cast it aside with frustration.

'We have tried everything, Father, and all we have achieved is a prolonging of John's agony. There is nothing else we can do.'

'Within the law . . .' Mr Barnard muttered, darkly. 'We have tried everything within the law, and they have made the law their harlot. How can we hope to achieve anything when, in less than two weeks' time, the King himself comes to trial for treason? No, Michael. Thus far the law has failed us – now we must try other methods. We have other weapons in our armoury, which I have disdained to use until now. Michael, I want you to arrange to have a pamphlet printed. It is time to remind some of our friends in Parliament that they have not led altogether blameless lives.'

'You would do that? You might find yourself swinging next to John.'

'And what of it?' There was a bitter irony in his words. 'You and I are men of the law – my own life has been dedicated to but two things: my children and the pursuit of justice – and now both are threatened. If they both go down into the darkness, then I would rather go down with them than live on in a world without them.' He poured himself a large cup of wine, and drank from it. He smiled. 'Michael, I want you to take a pen and paper and write all that I say. Do not omit a single word.'

Michael did as he was told, though he could scarcely believe the words he was writing. The old man dictated a litany of dark deeds and indiscretions he would have considered unthinkable of any man in public office. He wrote until he thought his hand would seize, yet still his father-in-law continued. When he had finished, Mr Barnard took another long draught of wine.

'There, it is done,' he said, simply. 'I want you to take this to a discreet publisher – one who handles legal documents would be best – and have the first copy back to me by tomorrow night.'

Michael stared down at what he had written. 'But is all this true? And if it is, can you substantiate all these allegations?'

Mr Barnard nodded slowly and deliberately. 'Everything you have written is true – all too true, I am afraid. As to proofs, I have documents to support nearly all of them – and those that I have not? Well, the "gentlemen" in question will surely believe that I have indeed the proofs that I would need to make such allegations.'

Michael shook his head in amazement. 'If all this is true – then what sort of people are they, these men we have entrusted the rule of our country to?'

'They are politicians, no more and no less. Men who seek after power as an end in itself. They climb over the backs of better men than they to achieve their ends. Remember, Michael, if honesty, integrity and ability were the principal criteria by which men were allocated power, then men like you and I would be running the country. Well, you and John at any rate.'

He drained his cup and left Michael alone with his thoughts.

Michael did as he had been bidden and the next night he handed the first dozen copies to Mr Barnard. He looked at the cover and smiled at the title.

'*Parliament's Cabinet Open'd* – a fitting title; you have a gift for satire, Michael,' he remarked drily.

'Since *The King's Cabinet Open'd* will form the substance of Charles' trial, I thought it rather appropriate.'

'I shall take this up to my bed, have some supper brought up to me. By the way, which printers did you use?'

'Wilmscott's in The Temple. A legal firm, as you requested.'

'Good,' Mr Barnard replied, 'then Parliament will be forewarned of my coming.'

The next morning, Mr Barnard set out to the Houses of Parliament like a soldier about to do battle. Michael could do nothing but stay at home and work on his defence, should John's case ever come to court. He did not have long to wait, for just after midday there was a commotion in the entrance hall – Gwen and Kate had returned from the north. He rushed out to greet them. Their cloaks were muddy and travel-stained and they were tired, but they were in high spirits. Jack followed them in. They were laughing and joking among themselves. Gwen rushed into her husband's arms.

'Oh, Michael! We have had such an adventure – I never want to travel anywhere by coach again!' she exclaimed, enthused.

Kate was unimpressed by this. 'For my own part, I would be much happier if I never saw the back of a horse again.' She stretched as though every inch of her body ached.

They did not wait to get changed, but followed Michael directly into the dining-room, where all his papers were still strewn across the table. To this Kate added the pile of depositions from the Derbyshire villagers.

'Well, Michael. What news do you have for us? How is John?'

He bade them all sit down before he spoke. 'John is alive, I can tell you that much. We managed to get a stay of execution. But beyond that I can tell you nothing. I have not seen him.'

'What?' Kate cried, shocked at this news. 'But you are his defence – how can they deny you access to him?'

'That is the thing, Kate. We still do not know if there will be any defence. At every turn, we have been confronted by a stone wall of silence.'

They listened, horrified as Michael related the whole tale of his efforts to get John's case to court. Finally, he told them about Mr Barnard's last-ditch efforts to save his son. When he had finished, Jack whistled appreciatively.

'Why, he's a craftier old beggar than ever I gave him credit for – I'll have to watch myself if he ever finds out about me and the widow. . . .'

For the rest of the day they busied themselves sorting out the statements and going over Jack's testimony, though in fact, they were merely filling the time while they waited for Mr Barnard to return. They all knew that if he failed today then all their efforts were in vain. At nine o'clock, they heard the sound of slow, weary footsteps on the gravel outside. The door opened and Mr Barnard came in. They met him in the hall, silent, waiting for him to speak. He slowly took off his cloak.

'Well, I have made many enemies this day, of men I had counted as my friends. Though, if they had denied me, I would have counted them as friends no more.' He sighed deeply. 'John's case will be heard in the High Court – I thought I might as well be hung for a sheep as a lamb, so I pressed them on that too. We go to court on the twentieth of January – the same day as the King.'

The courtroom was packed full. Kate looked around at the faces of the gathered crowd. The vast majority of them were John's supporters – Kate had never realized before just how popular a man John was. When he was ushered into the defendant's box, he stood tall and erect, dressed all in puritan black – Michael had insisted on this and had bought this garb especially. She thought he looked every inch the man she had always admired, an English gentleman in the real sense of the word. He looked across the courtroom at her and smiled.

They all rose as the judge entered. Mr Barnard leaned back from the defence bench and whispered to her, 'This is better than I could have imagined. Judge Downing is one of those who refused to sit in judgment on the King. He is a good man. It will be a fair trial.'

Kate looked at him: a very sour-looking man with a long face and pebble spectacles resting on his nose. He did not look anything like Kate's impression of a 'good man' – still she thought, appearances can be deceptive. She hoped to God that they were in this case.

He took some time to arrange his papers about him and to adjust his spectacles, then he called the court to order. There was a hushed silence as they waited for him to speak.

'Good morning, ladies and gentlemen. We are here today, on this sorry day for the law, to hear a rather unusual case – one which should, by right, be heard by the courts martial. I have read the appropriate papers and I consider that, given the nature of the arrest and detainment of the accused, the High Court is the only court which remains competent to make any sort of disinterested judgment in this case.'

Kate noticed Michael and Mr Barnard smiling at each other. From this she surmised that things were already going well. The prosecution opened the proceedings and after introducing their case, they called only one witness, a blond-haired young man called Nathan Prynne. As he came to the witness stand, Jack leaned across to Kate.

'Here, he was in my troop – I thought he had deserted when we were in London!'

He was about to stand up and denounce him, but Kate held him down. Michael looked over his shoulder to see what all the noise was about and Jack leaned forward and whispered his story to him. He nodded and smiled, then turned his attention back to the witness, who had just begun to testify. He said that he had witnessed all three of the crimes which John stood accused of. Within a few minutes it was time for Michael to start his cross-examination. He rose to his feet.

'My Lord.' He bowed to the judge, who inclined his head to him. 'Am I to take it that the prosecution's case rests solely on the testimony of this one solitary witness? Are there no other supporting affidavits?'

The judge rummaged around among his papers and shook his head. 'This appears to be the substance of the case.'

Michael smiled. 'Then if it please your lordship, I shall proceed with the cross-examination.'

Michael fairly ripped into the young man, destroying his evidence at every juncture. Kate almost felt sorry for the boy. She had never before seen such a display of verbal and intellectual aggression in her life. The boy was shaking when it seemed that Michael would finally allow him to stand down. Michael made to sit, then, as if he had suddenly remembered something, he glanced up again at him.

'Nathan Prynne – your company is at the moment in . . .' – he looked down at his notes – 'Chepstow, I believe?'

'I believe so. I do not know for sure.'

'You do not know for sure? Why is that?'

'I am no longer with my company . . . I was released from service.'

'Released by whom? I have your troop commander and your company commander here in court. They are prepared to testify that, not only did they not release you, but that they never received orders for your release. I think that, since you are testifying against my client on two counts of desertion, the court would be pleaed to know the nature of your supposed release from service.'

The prosecutor protested, but the judge silenced him.

'Answer the question, Mr Prynne.'

The boy was cornered. He licked his lips and looked to the prosecutor for support. The judge grew impatient. 'The witness will answer the question or I shall hold you in contempt.'

'I was released under the special order of General Ireton.'

Michael feigned surprise. 'By special order from General Ireton? And what, may I ask, was the extraordinary service you performed to be accorded such treatment?' Michael demanded.

Again, the witness was silent.

'Mr Prynne,' the judge growled, 'I have already warned

you about the dangers of not responding to a question put to you under oath. I direct you to answer.'

The prosecutor rose to his feet. 'The witness is unable to answer that question as his service is a matter of state secrecy.'

The judge glowered at him. 'I find it very hard to believe that the affairs of this uncouth fellow could ever be construed as a matter of state secrecy.'

'Nonetheless, my lord, such is indeed the case.' He bowed and resumed his seat.

'It is no matter, my lord,' Michael interrupted. 'For I have issued a summons for General Ireton to attend the court.'

The prosecutor rose again. 'I regret that General Ireton will be unable to respond to the summons. He is detained by important matters of State.'

'So, he is too busy to attend my court? And we all know why that is. Very well, I shall hear the case for the defence.'

Michael rose to his feet once more. 'My lord, since the case for the prosecution rests entirely on the testimony of a discredited witness, I would move for dismissal. You have signed statements from a number of witnesses, attesting to my client's innocence.'

There was silence as the judge sifted through the documents before him. He glanced up. 'I see here that you have called Lieutenant-General Cromwell as a witness for the defence?'

The prosecutor rose again. 'I regret that Lieutenant-General Cromwell will be unable to respond to the summons. . . .'

'I know, I know – important matters of State . . . very well, I am prepared to throw out the indictments on the charges of desertion of the field and bribery but on the count of aiding and abetting deserters, I note that no defence has been raised. Would you care to explain that?'

Michael rose to his feet. 'May it please your lordship, no defence was raised on the grounds that appropriate witnesses have been impossible to find at such short notice, and that we felt that there was no case to answer.'

'I shall be the judge of that, sir. And there is a witness to this charge. The court calls John Barnard to the stand.'

John strode across the courtroom. He paused and bowed to the judge as he passed him, then took his place on the witness stand.

'Captain Barnard,' the judge began. 'Whilst you have been cleared of the two more serious charges, you still stand accused of aiding and abetting deserters. What do you have to say in your defence?'

'My lord, these events took place during the campaign in the west in 1646. Desertion was rife among the infantry and General Fairfax had issued orders that all deserters were to be shot. We were under orders to take any that we found back to their own regiments for summary execution. We caught many of them – raw conscripts, mostly, unwillingly pressed into service. I was able to persuade most of them to return willingly to their own regiments and some I placed with other regiments as though they were new recruits. However, there were three men who could not remain. They claimed to have families who had need of them, and I had no reason to disbelieve them, so I let them go . . .'

'That's a lie!' The cry rang out around the courtroom. Jack was on his feet.

'He's lying, your honour – it was me who let them go!'

John smiled. 'That is my sergeant-at-arms, my lord. Forgive him: he is trying to bear my guilt on his own shoulders.'

The judge nodded, indulgently. 'His loyalty is commendable, Captain Barnard, but if he makes another outburst like that I shall have him placed under restraint. Captain Barnard, am I to understand that, in spite of your express orders from General Fairfax, you admit that you allowed deserters to go free?'

'I fear it is true, my lord. Although I have been a

soldier nearly all my adult life – I have never been a wanton killer.'

The words tore at Kate's heart as she remembered the accusation she had levelled at him before. And now his innocence of that crime would condemn him. She was struck dumb as the judge summed up.

'John Barnard, by your own admission, you are guilty of the charge of aiding and abetting deserters. Under Natural Law you would be considered a great gentleman, but you are subject to military law – which is necessarily severe. It gives me no pleasure whatsoever in passing the minimum sentence allowable under the regime.' He paused, as though the very words pained him. 'John Barnard, I sentence you to a period of ten years' penal servitude on the island of Antigua.'

The rap of the gavel shook Kate to the very depths of her soul. She overheard Michael whispering to Mr Barnard. 'Ten years in the Indies, that is a death sentence in itself – my God, what have we done?'

Kate looked on in stunned silence as they took John away.

Eighteen

'Ten years, damn it! Ten long years!' Kate railed at them. 'And I heard you in court – you do not think he will survive it. All we have done is to substitute a quick, merciful death for a slow, lingering one – you call that justice? Surely we can appeal – we must appeal!'

Michael and Mr Barnard sat in gloomy silence, dismayed. Michael looked up as he realized what Kate was saying.

'Appeal? We could only appeal against the sentence and as Judge Downing gave the lightest sentence permissible, there is no point to an appeal. John is guilty by his own admission – there is nothing else we can do.'

'There must be something else we can do,' she replied. 'For heaven's sake – a ship might come and take him away at any time!'

No one replied to Kate's protests. There seemed nothing else to be said.

At length, Mr Barnard stirred. He rose and went over to the fire, staring into the flames. He spoke almost to himself. 'Of course, in the old days, we could have appealed for a pardon to the House of Lords or the King. . . .'

Michael laughed bitterly at this. 'But the Lords has been abolished and the King is on trial for his own life. I fear we shall find little help from those quarters.'

The gloomy silence returned. If anything, they seemed to be even more despondent than before. Kate looked around at their faces, they seemed to be utterly defeated.

Even Jack had nothing to say for himself. Her mind, though, was still racing – there must be something they could do. Finally, the germ of an idea came to her.

'You say that the King could have granted John a pardon, but since he is on trial for his own life, then that course is no longer open to us. But the power to grant a pardon must still be vested in somebody or in some group.'

'Aye,' Michael replied, 'it lies in the hands of the very people who tried to have John hanged.'

'Then that is where I must go next.'

'You might as well appeal to the Devil,' Michael said, scornfully.

'If needs be, then I would even do that – but in the meantime, who do you suggest? Should I go to General Ireton?'

Michael's mood changed as he realized that Kate was actually serious. His eyes and his thoughts focused on her.

'No. Ireton's name was on all the indictments. He was determined that John should hang – he would not lift a finger to help him now.'

'Then who?' Kate replied, sharply.

'It is hard to see who will come out on top after all this, but the man most likely to take the reins of government would be Oliver Cromwell.'

'Then I must seek out Oliver Cromwell. Where do I start?'

It seemed strange to Kate that a man who had waited so long in the snow to wish her well on her wedding day, now proved so difficult to get to. She began to realize that obstacles were being put in her way: for the first week he was indisposed while he attended the trial of the King, but the King had been dead for nearly two weeks now and still Cromwell would not see her. Every day she went to the Commons and waited, and each evening she returned to Chelsea with nothing to show for her pains. Yet she would return the next day, unabashed, patiently waiting to be seen. The guards were kind to her, bringing her food and drink and making sure she was warm, but still her lonely vigil produced no reaction in the corridors of power.

Then one day her luck changed. Evening was drawing in and Kate was thinking about going home, when one of the guards came running down the corridor.

'He's coming this way, Mistress Kate!' he cried. 'Now is your chance – it is now or never!'

Kate steeled herself. She could hear many voices, all talking loudly. In the distance she could see a crowd of men coming towards her. She could not see Cromwell, though. They were almost upon her now and still she could not see him. She stood, stock still, blocking their way and she did not move. They started to walk around her and she began to panic. Then she saw him, right in the midst of the crowd, his head down, reading a document, whilst all the others tried to attract his attention. She pushed herself forward.

'General Cromwell! General Cromwell!' she cried.

He looked up, alarmed at the sound of a woman's voice. Though he saw her, he did not speak. She carried on regardless.

'General, I am Kate Barnard – do you remember me? We met after my wedding in Ely. I must talk to you. It is about my husband. . . .'

Cromwell did not seem to recognize her. The crowd swept past her and she ran behind, still calling out, 'General Cromwell, you must listen to me!'

They were out in the courtyard now and Cromwell was mounting his horse. He was about to ride away, then he suddenly looked down at Kate. His face was stern.

'Come back tomorrow,' he said simply, and rode away. The crowd dispersed and Kate was left alone in the courtyard. What was she to do now?

The guard returned to her side, he was smiling. 'You did well there, Mistress Kate – much better than all the others; they're professional petitioners, but you were the one who got his attention and we all heard you. He said that he would see you tomorrow and we'll make sure that you're taken to him. I hope you can argue a good case – because old Noll Cromwell is a hard man.'

The guard returned to his business and Kate was left alone again.

The guards were waiting for her when Kate arrived the next morning. They escorted her straight to Cromwell's first secretary. He was writing at his desk and did not appear to notice them. The captain of the guard drew himself to attention, loudly clattering his sword hilt on his breastplate. 'Mistress Katherine Barnard here to see the general.'

The secretary slowly looked up at them and scowled. 'The general is indisposed. He cannot see anybody without an appointment, you should know that, Captain.' He resumed his writing.

'The general told her personally to come and see him today . . .'

'The general may tell whom he pleases whatever he pleases, but I have no record of it and she does not have an appointment, so she cannot see him, do you understand?'

Kate sighed deeply. 'Then when can I see him?' she asked, wearily.

The secretary did not look up, but spoke while he was writing. 'You may make an appointment with my secretary, who will ascertain if your petition merits my attention, whereupon he will make an appointment with me and I will make the final decision as to whether or not you may see the general.'

'And how long might that take?'

'As you can see, I am a very busy man – I could not possibly see you before the end of March at the earliest.'

'The end of March?' Kate cried.

'Precisely. Good day,' he said coldly.

The rage boiled within her. She had waited so long and come so close that she would not be turned away.

'By the end of March my husband will be on a ship bound for Antigua and I may never see him again!' she shouted at the top of her voice. 'If you think I have waited all this time – only to be fobbed off by a pen-pushing lackey like you, then you are sorely mistaken!'

Still the secretary remained unmoved and continued writing. He had been shouted at by more formidable characters than this. He looked up at Kate and smiled. There was a note of triumph in his voice. 'I take it from your accent that you are an Irish . . .'

At this Kate's anger boiled over. 'I could be a Turkish Moor for all it mattered!' she screamed. 'Cromwell said that he would see me today and I am going to see him now!' She stormed past him toward the doors on the far side of the room.

The secretary nodded to the guard. 'Restrain her and take her away!' he snapped.

Before she reached the doors, Kate felt her arms firmly held and dragged behind her back.

'Let me go! Let me go, damn you!' she cried in pain and anguish. But it was to no avail. Slowly but surely she watched the door recede from her as she was dragged away. Kate's eyes widened as suddenly the doors opened and Cromwell appeared.

'What in God's name is going on?' he demanded.

The secretary was apologetic. 'I am sorry to have disturbed you, General, but this Irish claimed to have been granted an audience with you. Naturally, I . . .'

'This "Irish", as you put it, is the heiress to one of the largest estates in that land. She could buy and sell you a hundred times over and still not notice the expense. And she is here at my express invitation. Release her.'

Kate felt the grip on her arms loosen, and she heard the mumbled apologies of the guards behind her. She nodded her head in acknowledgement, but she did not turn around. Cromwell stood aside and held his hand out toward the door.

'Please, Mistress Barnard, come in.'

Inside his chambers, Cromwell indicated that Kate

should be seated opposite his desk. He sat down at his own chair. He did not waste time on pleasantries.

'Mistress Barnard, your reason for being here and my reason for inviting you are entirely different matters. I think we had better start with yours.'

'I am sure you know full well why I am here, General Cromwell,' Kate replied.

'Ah yes, young John – I had great hopes for him, you know. Well, he had a fair trial – a remarkably fair trial if I might say so, and he was found guilty by his own admission . . . without recourse to duress, even. His sentence is the lightest that could possibly have been imposed.'

'Yet it is still likely to be a death sentence,' Kate interrupted him.

'Not necessarily so. I am sure that there are many men who have served their time and returned to their loved ones.'

'Not a one, to date,' Kate replied.

'Then let us hope that your husband will be the first. What would you have me do, Mistress Barnard – pardon him?'

'That is exactly what I would have you do, General Cromwell. John is a good man, an honest man who fought long and hard for what he believed in . . .'

'There have been many good, honest men who have fought for what they believed in – and yet they still swing at the gibbet. They believed in the wrong things, they believed in Charles Stuart. Even he was a good and honourable man – at the end.'

'I still ask that you pardon him. As you said, you had high hopes for him. Might he not still fulfil these hopes? He has not changed since then, you know,' she implored.

Cromwell dismissed this idea with a wave of his hand. 'Your husband might not have changed, but the world has changed around him. He believed that we could come to an accord with Charles Stuart – and that was his downfall. No, at loose in England he would be a token of the weakness of our new order.'

'But I could take him with me to Ireland – we would be out of your way there.'

Cromwell's eyes glittered. 'That brings me to my own reason for seeing you. I think we should turn to that now, for time is pressing. As you know, we are about to embark on a campaign to liberate that unfortunate island. For too long the people there have suffered under the papist yoke.'

'I know that only too well,' she replied. 'But what do you want me to do about that – I am powerless.'

He looked down at his papers. 'Kilerin is a large estate I see – and you have considerable assets here in England. You are a wealthy woman, Mistress Barnard, and should Kilerin be restored, you would be a very wealthy woman indeed.'

'I am aware of that – but what is it to you?' Kate was put on her guard.

'Simply that I am looking for "investors" in my Irish campaign. You would stand to do well from our success and so I would expect you to be one of our more generous investors.'

'And, if I make a – as you say "generous investment" then might John be freed?'

'That is not negotiable at the moment. The two matters are not linked. But, if you agree, in principle, to making . . . let us say a considerable contribution, then I am prepared to revoke your husband's transportation order. He would still be at the Fleet – and I would allow you to visit him straightaway, if you will agree to my proposal now.'

'And if I refuse?'

Cromwell smiled indulgently. 'Then, when Ireland is liberated, Kilerin will be made over to another investor and, as the wife of a traitor, all your assets here in England will be sequestrated. To put it bluntly, you will be beggared and your husband will embark on a very long sojourn in the Indies. Of course, I would far rather that you contributed willingly.'

'It seems that I have little choice,' Kate remarked icily.

'Of course you have a choice – it is just that one

of your choices is not particularly attractive.' He smiled.

'Very well – but if I agree, then I have your word that John will not be transported?'

'I have the order on my desk before me. And I shall send you forthwith, under escort, to see him.'

In the end, Kate agreed. She signed a guarantee to the sum of £10,000 and Cromwell signed the revocation order. She was on the point of leaving when Cromwell called her back.

'Mistress Barnard, you might consider what other services you might perform to ensure your husband's release. You were quite right in your initial supposition. It is within my power to grant him a pardon. My secretary will admit you at five o'clock tomorrow evening – without all the trouble you were subjected to this morning. Good day, Mistress Barnard.'

When she arrived at the Fleet, she was admitted straightaway, and without question. The very name Cromwell seemed to open any door. To her surprise she was not taken up to the tower, but led along the ground floor. At the end of a long corridor, the gaoler heaved open a heavy wooden door. At once, a dreadful stench issued from within. The gaoler took a torch from the wall and led her into the lightless, airless room. Kate had to cover her nose.

He took her along a line of wretched, filthy men, each one chained to the wall, each one surrounded by pools of unspeakable filth. As they passed, the gaoler held the torch up to the prisoner's face. The men shrunk away and shielded their eyes from the blinding light. The gaoler seemed unable to find John. He called out, 'Barnard! Where is Barnard?'

A voice replied from the far end of the cell. 'Over here.'

They followed the sound and presently they came to John. He was still wearing the same black suit as he had worn at his trial, but it was covered in grime. His beard had grown and his hair was straggly and unkempt. He shielded his eyes from the light.

'You have a visitor, Barnard,' the gaoler said gruffly, then he turned to Kate. 'Ten minutes – that is all.' He handed her the torch and left them.

'John, oh my God, John. I never realized. I thought . . . if ever I see that Dickon again, I will have him horsewhipped!'

'Kate, is that you?' He blinked as he became used to the light. 'No, you must not do that. It is not his fault I am here. Without Dickon's help I would be rotting downstairs. He feeds me regularly too. I have enough to share with my fellows.' He indicated the two men on either side of the recess. 'And, as you can see, we are slopped out regularly too. He had done all that he could. I would beg that, if you can, just get him some more money.'

Kate leaned over him and would have kissed him, but he held her back.

'No, do not come near. I am not feeling altogether well.' At this one of the others laughed grimly. 'And God only knows what I have got, so please, do not come near. Just give me the torch and let me look at you.'

She did as she was bidden. John's chains rattled as he raised his arm to take it. For a while he just looked at her. Kate could see the tears in his eyes.

'Oh, my darling Kate. You are a vision of loveliness. I suppose this will be the last time I see you. I am sorry that you have had to suffer this place, but it is a great gesture and I am so very glad to see you. I suppose my time has come. Do you know when I sail?'

'That is why I am here, John. You are not to be transported. I went to see Cromwell.'

'You did what? Why did you go to him of all people?'

'To see if he would grant you a pardon.'

'A pardon – from Cromwell? All three men laughed at this. 'Oh, I am sorry to laugh, Kate. But you see, it was Cromwell who put us all here. Ireton may have signed the warrants, but it was Cromwell who guided his hand.'

'Nevertheless, he needs money for his Irish campaign.

He has dangled the promise of a pardon in return for money,' Kate lied – she did not want him to know the truth she suspected. John's face became serious as he considered this.

'You must be very careful of him, Kate. He is a crafty old trickster at the best of times. But if you can pay my way out of here . . . well.' He glanced across at his fellow prisoners. 'Much as I enjoy your company, gentlemen, I am sure you could understand my reasons for leaving you.'

The other two laughed and joked at this. Kate was relieved that at least John was in good company, to keep his spirits up.

The rest of their brief time was taken up by the men's demands for news from the outside world. They were saddened to hear that the King had been executed. Kate did not have any good news to relate. At length, the cell door opened and the gaoler returned. He snatched the torch from John's hand and led Kate away before she could even say goodbye. He was rough and brutal, but Kate was still careful to leave him a substantial tip – with the promise of more money when she came again.

Once again, she was out of the noisome stench of the Fleet. Her mind, though, was as clear as the air about her. She had made up her mind the moment she saw the conditions John was being held in. She would do whatever Cromwell wanted of her to ensure her husband's release.

The secretary was very deferential as he admitted Kate to Cromwell's private chambers. The general was standing by the fire, solemnly reading a document. As Kate entered, his face brightened. Somehow, Kate got the impression that he had been standing like that, waiting – so that he might cut a more impressive figure.

'Mistress Barnard. Come in – may I offer you some port wine? It is very good.'

Kate accepted, and he indicated that she should sit down on the *chaise longue*. He handed her a large glass of ruby-red wine, then resumed his place beside the roaring fire. There was a long silence between them. Neither of them seemed willing to speak first. At last it was the general who spoke.

'Have you considered what service you might perform to secure your husband's release?' he asked, cordially.

'I am prepared to perform whatever service the general requires of me.'

'Good.' He smiled. 'And have you any idea what that service might entail?'

Kate's heart beat faster, but she maintained a composed appearance. 'I assume that it might entail the granting of sexual favours. If that is what you require, then I will assent to it – providing John is released into my care once more.' She did not take her eyes from him.

Cromwell laughed quietly to himself and stared down into his wine glass, swirling the liquid around in it. He glanced up at her.

'You would do that – to secure your husband's release?'

She nodded, still staring at him.

'Then you misjudge me. You are a very beautiful woman and if I were only a slightly lesser man, then I might take advantage of your offer. But I am not. Your offer does credit to your loyalty to your husband, but I do not imagine he would be thankful for his liberty if he knew that had been its price. No, the service I require of you is altogether different, and one which you might take some delight in. At any rate, you might find it more agreeable than bedding a crusty old soldier like me.' He smiled with genuine affection.

Kate's curiosity was aroused. She had come to this place prepared for the worst and in a minute Cromwell had turned her expectations on their heads. She was intrigued by this man.

'What do you want, Master Cromwell?'

He looked keenly at her. 'I want names, Mistress Barnard – or, more appropriately, a name. I will trade your husband's freedom in return for this name, my only condition being that your husband resumes his command and joins me on our Irish adventure.'

'What sort of name do you want? I know many people.

I am not trying to be obstructive, but if you would be a little more specific. . . .'

'Of course. I want you to denounce someone – I believe you might be privy to certain of his activities. I will make it easier for you: he is a traitor, a man whose considerable estates, when confiscated, will go a long way towards defraying the costs of the Irish campaign – I might not even have to call on your investment, Mistress Barnard. He is, I believe, well known to you. You may wish to go through your list of friends, or, better still, why not run through the alphabet – but I would suggest you begin at the letter F. . . .'

Kate's face brightened as she realized where the general's riddles led. 'Fitzmaurice!' she exclaimed with delight.

'Exactly,' he concurred. 'Do you have the necessary evidence to at least denounce him as a Royalist traitor?'

Kate nodded. 'Oh yes, General Cromwell,' she said softly, 'I have all the evidence you need. . . .' She raised her glass and Cromwell refilled it. Cromwell proposed a toast to the Irish campaign, but Kate insisted that it be changed to 'absent friends'.

That night, Kate and the general went to the Fleet with a company of his Life Guards. John was released immediately. Kate pleaded with Cromwell for the release of his two companions. Cromwell acceded to this request on the condition that they both sign up for service in Ireland – under John's command – and without pay. As they left the cell, John whispered to Kate, 'I know not if I want your answer to this, but have you been getting Cromwell drunk?'

When they got back to Chelsea it was late at night and the house was in darkness. They wondered for a moment whether they should sneak in quietly and not wake Gwen. They looked at each other and, as if by common assent, they decided to rouse the whole house.

'After all,' John said, 'we should celebrate the return of the prodigal son.'

They hammered on the door and hollered up at the

windows above. One by one, tiny lights appeared at the windows as candles were lit. They watched gleefully as a candelabrum was carried down the hall stairs. The locks on the door were unfastened one by one and the door opened a little way. Michael peered out.

'What in heaven's name is . . .' His eyes widened and he gawped in amazement.

'John! My God!' He threw the door open and shouted upstairs, 'Wake up everybody – John is home!'

'So far, so good,' John whispered to Kate as they all went in.

'Michael, we have some guests – may I introduce Joos Van Oosterhuis, a Dutch gunner and . . .'

Michael rubbed his eyes. 'This other gentleman I know already. Martin, I thought you were dead!' He clasped the man's hand firmly in his. He looked questioningly at Kate. 'How did you manage to . . . well – how?'

Kate laughed and took from her pocket a large sheet of paper with a great seal on it. She waved it at him.

'See, Michael – a full pardon from Cromwell!'

'Yes, but how . . .' He was interrupted as the others came downstairs.

'I will tell you all in a minute, when we are all together,' she confided.

Gwen was last to come down. She was still half-asleep and, as ever, she was in a foul mood. At first, she did not recognize John in the candlelight.

'Michael! Why in heaven's name have you let these people in – are these beggar friends of yours Kate? This is hardly the time for . . .'

'It is time for a celebration, sister,' John said, smiling.

Gwen was dumbfounded. All she could manage was a feeble, high-pitched 'John?' as she followed them into the dining-room. They lit all the candles and Dodington brought in some wine.

It was the first time Kate had seen John in bright light. His beard had concealed the fact that his cheeks had become hollow and his eyes were slightly sunken. He looked for all the world like a scarecrow, but he was home and that was what mattered. John introduced the two strangers to the company.

'Jack, these two gentlemen will be joining us – as common troopers and without pay I fear.'

'I'm right glad to have 'em, sir. But I'll find it a mite bit difficult giving orders to Captain Rowse here.'

'Simple Trooper Rowse,' he corrected him, 'and I shall be happy with that. Anything to be out of that place. Joos and I have been there for over a year.'

'They have been released into my charge as volunteers for Ireland,' John added. 'And since I have been placed under Kate's charge – then we are all under her command.'

Everybody's attention was turned to Kate, who had stood to one side away from the merrymaking. It looked to the others as though she was modestly avoiding their attention – though in fact, the after-effects of Cromwell's strong port wine were beginning to take their toll. Her head throbbed, but still she allowed herself to be dragged into their midst to answer their questions. She related the whole story of her efforts to secure John's release. When she finally got to the part about Fitzmaurice and the deal she had struck with Cromwell, they all fell silent. Michael nodded his head as he considered this.

'If you succeed, Kate, then your victory will be complete – though running that particular fox to ground might not be an easy task. Be very careful.'

A few minutes later, John excused himself, saying that he wanted to splash a little water on his face, just to refresh himself – he would be back down in a few minutes, he said, as he took his leave. After half an hour he had still not returned and Kate went upstairs to see if anything was amiss. When she got to the bedroom, John was slumped on the floor, the basin of water upset over him. Kate ran across the room to help him. He was unconscious.

Kate looked down at John's face as the doctor examined him. It was grey and pallid. His pillow was soaked in bitter dark sweat. His lips moved as though he was speaking in his delirium. Kate bent over him to catch what he was saying, but the doctor pulled her back.

'He has a fever, madam – do not go near him and, above all, do not breathe any air from him.'

'Do you know what it is, Doctor?' she asked anxiously.

'I have examined his throat, his groin and the pits of his arms. They are swollen, as one might have expected of one in a fever, but they are not, I think, buboes of plague – and that we should be grateful for. I am hoping that it is some relatively trivial ailment which has been exacerbated by his poor diet and unsanitary conditions, but only time will tell. Normally, I would bleed him, but I consider that he is too weak for that. He will need careful nurturing. And I suggest that his two companions are kept in quarantine for at least the next week.'

He packed away his instruments and left Kate alone with her husband. Presently, Gwen came to join her.

'Oh, Kate. Things never seem to go easily for you two. But, I swear, all will be well for you in the end.' She placed her arm around her shoulder and together they looked on as John fought the sickness within.

At midday, Kate was forced to leave her husband's side. A coach arrived for her to take her back to the Palace of Westminster. She had to fulfil her side of the bargain and start the process of testimony against Fitzmaurice.

Cromwell listened intently and in silence, as Kate dictated the whole story of her dealings with Fitzmaurice to his clerk. When she had finished, he looked up at her.

'A most unfortunate and, if I might say so, very foolhardy way for a married woman – or indeed any woman of virtue – to conduct herself,' he observed.

Kate nodded in agreement. 'I cannot make any excuse for my actions, except to say that – even though he might deny it – Fitzmaurice and I never indulged in any impropriety. I can assure you of that.'

Cromwell turned this over in his mind. 'That is as may be, Mistress Barnard. But we shall have to word your testimony extremely carefully to make sure you are not implicated. You say that on four separate occasions, you went back to Fitzmaurice's house and on each occasion you were accompanied by a gentleman, whom you knew to be a royalist fugitive, travelling under an assumed name?'

Kate nodded and Cromwell sighed. 'Then you knowingly gave assistance to them, since you did not report these events to the authorities.' He rubbed his brow. 'It will avail you little if, having engineered your husband's release, you then take his place in the Fleet. If you were to be placed on the witness stand you would be bound to implicate yourself. No, this will never do. I cannot accept this evidence. Do you have nothing else on him?'

'What about the affair of Mary Ormond?' Kate suggested hopefully.

'No. That is no good either. Mistress Ormond will not file a complaint – and assault is hardly a treasonable offence. I need something that will enable me to confiscate his lands and assets.' He looked at her sombrely. 'If you remember, the bargain was your husband's freedom for Fitzmaurice. If we do not get him, then your husband returns to the Fleet.'

'I would never allow that!' she cried.

'It is not really a question of what you will or will not allow, is it?' He considered the problem. 'What we must do is catch him red-handed. We can try him on one count and your evidence becomes purely circumstantial. You say that he brings these men back to his house in Westminster and then they are spirited away, by boat, from the water gate at the back. Very well, we can snare the royalist as he tries to escape down the Thames, but we shall have to have some evidence to link him with Fitzmaurice – that will be your role.'

'But how can I possibly win my way back into his confidence? He knows that I hate him.'

'And you hated him before – yet you still went to him, is that not true?'

Kate was forced to agree to this, but still the plan seemed implausible. 'Will he not know that John has been released – he would surely suspect something?'

'Not necessarily. Your husband's name is still on the manifest of the brig *Star of Corinth*, which sails tomorrow. Did you realize that, had you not intervened, John would have been on it? No? A strange circumstance.'

Kate listened carefully as Cromwell outlined his plan.

The next morning, Kate was standing by the dock at Blackfriars as the *Star of Corinth* sailed with the tide. She was crying, partly for effect and partly for the poor souls who had been driven and beaten into the ship's hold. From there, she had her carriage take her to her house at Leicester Fields. When she went in, the house smelled cold and musty. No one had been there since Christmas. She detested being there; it reminded her of all the foolish things she had done and the vain and empty people whose company she had so eagerly courted. She went into the parlour and sat down at her bureau.

The note she wrote was carefully worded. When she had finished, she sealed it and took it to her coachman, instructing him to deliver it to Mistress Mary Ormond. Then she went upstairs to her wardrobe and selected a dress for that evening: a sombre colour, but revealing, was the disguise she sought. When she had found the one which fitted her mood, she laid it out and waited for nightfall.

As her coach drew up opposite Mary's house in the Strand, she was about to send her man in to announce her, when she saw Mary herself come running out, her cloak billowing in the cold night air. Kate opened the door for her and helped her in. Mary was quite breathless.

'Kate, my dear, it has been so long. I thought you had forgotten me.'

'I would never forget you, Mary dear, but since our last meeting was so . . . well, so difficult, I was shy of making any approach. I was waiting for you to contact me.'

'Yes, but I hear that you have been very busy in the interim, Kate. It all sounds so exciting – you must tell me all about it.'

'Yes, it was exciting at the time,' Kate remarked enigmatically, 'but in the end, I failed. John's ship sailed this morning. I do not expect to see him again.'

'So, you have come out to drown your sorrows – I can commend that course of action. Where shall we go?'

'I thought The Red Bull at Clerkenwell.'

'An excellent choice!' Mary exclaimed. 'We might even run into Thomas,' she said, wistfully. Kate knew then that Cromwell had been right – in spite of all his mistreatment of her, Mary was still seeing Fitzmaurice.

Kate nearly misgave as they reached The Red Bull. She had to master herself to go in. Once inside, the air was hot and fetid with the breath and smell of many bodies. They were shown to a table on the platform by the stage, near the one where they had met Fitzmaurice before. In the absence of any conversation, Kate was forced to listen to the play. It was a ridiculous nonsense of *double entendre*, but she pretended to enjoy it nonetheless.

As the evening wore on, they were approached by a couple of young men, foppishly dressed, with very affected manners, who tried to engage them in conversation. The evening was drawing to a close and Kate was beginning to despair of Fitzmaurice's coming, when she saw his mane of grey hair in the crowd. He was making his way toward them. Her heart sank as she saw that he was alone.

'Good evening, Katherine. This is indeed an unexpected pleasure,' he purred. He peeled off his tight leather gloves, finger by finger and threw them casually on the table. The young men left at once. 'I was sorry to hear about your husband, denounced by his own people – they say that a pack of hounds will turn on their own in the end. And all the ministrations of the worthy Barnards could not help him. A pity.'

He smiled at her, gloated over her, feeding on those parts that she had allowed to be naked.

'And so now you have come here for distraction, returning to the fold.' His hand drifted on to her shoulder. She winced at his touch, his icy fingers, like leeches, crept about her flesh. She pulled herself away from him.

'Not now, Thomas. Not tonight – I feel as though I am in mourning.'

'And so you should, Katherine. Your man will never return from the Indies alive. He was a walking corpse from the moment he admitted his guilt. A very noble, but very foolhardy gesture, I thought.'

'You were there?' Kate remarked, alarmed.

'I would not have missed it for the world. I remained discreetly at the back of the court – it would not do to be seen in the company of criminals.'

After about half an hour of this, Kate could take no more. She announced that she was leaving. Mary seemed dismayed at this, but Fitzmaurice reassured her that she could come home in his own coach. He turned to Kate.

'I am sorry that you feel you have to leave. They say that three is a crowd, but I find that three is a number I take great pleasure in. I might be here tomorrow night. I hope Mary can persuade you to join us.'

'Oh, yes Kate. Please come,' Mary added, with feigned enthusiasm. 'We could have such a merry time together.'

'I might come,' Kate said, disdainfully. 'But I pray you, do not think to include me in any of your games.' With that parting riposte, Kate left them.

'Do not be so sure of that, Katherine!' he called after her, confidently.

She went back to her lonely house in Leicester Fields. Immediately, she washed the shoulder where he had touched it. She felt dirty already. Her heart ached to go to Chelsea to see John, or at least get some word of how he was, but she knew that she could not. Cromwell's instructions on this had been explicit: if Fitzmaurice had even an inkling that she was having anything to do with Gwen or her family, he might become suspicious and all their efforts would be in vain.

She returned to The Red Bull the next night, and the next, and the one after that. She endured his pawings and his maulings, though they made her flesh creep. She even laughed at his jokes and his lewd suggestions, which sickened her. And at the end of each night, she declined his offer to come into his house. Finally, on the fifth night, Fitzmaurice arrived with a companion. He introduced himself as 'John Barnard'. Mary giggled at this and the others laughed aloud; Fitzmaurice loudest of all.

'I thought that, since your erstwhile husband would have no further use for the name, we might as well borrow it.' His eyes fixed keenly on her for her reaction.

'That is a cruel joke, Thomas . . . but I suppose it is worthy of you,' Kate replied, disdainfully. The others laughed even louder.

Kate seethed with a cold white rage within, but on the surface, she maintained her composure, content at last that she would be revenged on him.

The evening passed much as the others had done; Fitzmaurice's hands were all over her, but tonight her determination gave her the strength to suffer him.

As they had done before when they had a fugitive in their company, they took Kate's coach back to Westminster. Fitzmaurice was not so eager that Kate and Mary should join them in his house that night, and they parted.

When they had gone in, the coach turned about and started back toward the Strand, to take Mary home, but after they had gone a little way and out of sight of Fitzmaurice's house, Kate ordered the coachman to turn about again. She put her head out of the window.

'The Palace of Westminster – with all speed – go like the wind!' she cried.

The coachman turned his team about and they set off, wheels and hooves clattering on the cobblestones, at a great pace. Inside the coach, Mary looked at Kate with horror.

'What are you doing? Where are we going?' she demanded hysterically.

'We are going to see someone,' Kate snapped.

'Why? Who are we going to see?'

Kate wished that she had been able to get rid of Mary before, but there was no time for that.

'I can't tell you right now – you will have to trust me.'

'Trust you!' she cried as she realized what Kate was doing. 'You are going to betray him!'

She flew at Kate in a fit of wild rage. Her hands were about her throat. 'I'll kill you first!' she screamed through gritted teeth.

Kate began to panic as Mary's hands gripped tighter and tighter about her throat, shaking her head up and down, banging against the back of the coach. Mary was a big girl and stronger than Kate. She tried to release her grip, but she could not. Kate summoned up her strength and clenched her fist. With a great shriek she brought it across, punching Mary full in the face. Her grip loosened, more from shock than from the strength of the blow. At the same moment, the coach went over a rut in the road and Mary was thrown to the floor. Straightaway, Kate dived on top of her, pinning her arms with her knees. Mary struggled, but Kate had wedged herself between the seats and could not be moved. Mary kicked at her desperately, but to no avail.

'How far to go?' Kate cried out to the coachman.

'Not far now – we're nearly there,' he replied as Kate felt the horses slowly come to a halt. Mary was still struggling and kicking as Kate looked out of the window. They were back at Fitzmaurice's. . . .

'What in God's name are we doing here?' she shouted. 'Take me to Parliament at once!'

The peep-hole opened and an unfamiliar face appeared. It was not her coachman.

'I am sorry, madam, but I could not do that,' he said impassively.

In her surprise, Kate relaxed her hold on Mary and she broke free. She struggled out of the coach and ran up the steps. She battered on Fitzmaurice's door.

'Thomas! Thomas! It's a trap! Save yourself!'

Kate looked in horror as Fitzmaurice appeared at the door. He stared across at Kate in the coach. There was nothing else for her to do. Kate leapt from the coach and started to run in the direction of the Palace of

Westminster. The coachman lazily whipped his horses into action and set off after her.

Kate ran as fast as she could, her heart beating fast in her breast. But she could feel the coach bearing down on her. The clatter of the horses' hooves grew louder and louder. She screamed for help. At the last moment, as she felt the horses nearly on her, she swerved to her left, down a side street.

The coach had passed, but she heard it pull up just beyond. The cobblestones were wet and greasy and Kate slithered and slipped as she ran on. She stopped suddenly at the sound of water lapping against stone. She realized with dismay that the road was a dead end. She stopped herself just before she went over into the river. She heard footsteps behind her.

'So, you thought you could ensnare me, Katherine.' Kate turned around at the sound of Fitzmaurice's voice, her heart pounding, though she could see nothing.

'And I so nearly did,' she replied, her strength returning to her as she realized all was lost.

'Yes . . .' he said slowly, approaching all the time, his footsteps growing nearer, but still she was blind in the darkness. 'A very simple plan. It would have been effective too – had I not taken precautions. You have proved to be quite an embarrassment over the years. I should have had you and then killed you while I had the chance.' He was right in front of her. In the darkness, she could only see the light glitter in his eyes, but she could feel his breath on her face. . . . 'I could have you now, Katherine,' he hissed, 'nothing would give me greater pleasure than to feel you squirm beneath me on the cold, wet stone.'

Kate felt the spittle on her face, smelled the stale wine on his lips. 'I would never let you – you know that,' she retorted scornfully.

'I shall never know the pleasure of taking your body, for time is pressing. I shall have to be content with taking your life.'

'If you move – you die!' The cry came from the water

behind her. At the far end of the street came the sound of many men coming towards them. Kate saw the gleam of his teeth as Fitzmaurice smiled at her.

'It seems that I shall have to forego even that pleasure – for the moment.'

He pushed her roughly on the chest and Kate felt herself toppling over, then falling. Water filled her mouth and nose as she struggled to get back to the surface. At last she broke free of its smothering hold and she could breathe again. Shots rang out around her and she heard the splash and hiss as bullets hit the water.

'For God's sake – you're supposed to save me, not shoot me!' she cried as she went under again. She felt herself being dragged along by the scruff of the neck and then up into a boat, coughing and choking, spluttering out the water from her lungs.

'My God, Kate, you look even worse than when I first met you.'

Kate looked up in surprise. 'John – my God. What are you doing here? I thought you were at death's door.'

'Not quite – but I can vouch for the fact that I was very sick for a while. I went to see Cromwell yesterday and he explained everything. I insisted on being here. We have been in these boats, just downriver from Fitzmaurice's these last two nights. Jack was not very happy about bobbling along all last night to no avail, but it was his boat that caught the cavalier, and tonight he netted Fitzmaurice himself.'

He pointed to one of the other boats, where Fitzmaurice was being dragged aboard with a gaff. There were torches everywhere.

'Why did you not light your torches before? I could see nothing in the dark.'

'Then he would have seen us as we rowed towards him.'

'Oh, John. Are you safe to kiss now?'

'As safe as I shall ever be. . . .'

He could not finish his sentence, as Kate threw her arms around his neck and kissed him, long and hard.

When she had finished with him, she looked up into his eyes, longingly.

'John, my darling, do you know, you could make me the happiest woman in the world?'

'How is that? I would do anything . . .' he replied, lovingly.

'Take me home, put me in a hot bath, and then in a warm bed – with you next to me.'

'Your wish is my command,' he replied before she took him in her arms and kissed him again.

'John?' Kate said, looking up at him and dripping over him. 'Revenge is sweet, is it not?'

'That remains to be seen, Kate.'

Nineteen

The men had gone up to town, leaving Kate and Gwen alone in the house with young Stephen. The boy had grown tired of playing with his mother and his aunt and was quietly reading a book by the fire. Kate had already done a circuit of the house, looking for things to do, but in the end she could find nothing of sufficient importance to distract her from the tapestry she had been avoiding. She had done very well thus far: it was supposed to have been finished nearly two years ago, yet it was still no more than a band, four inches wide, between the runners. She supposed she would finish it one day, but she could not imagine she would have the leisure to do so. She surprised herself today, however, the concentration necessary to construct the piece distracted her from the thoughts that were uppermost in her mind.

Her work was interrupted by Dodington. He announced that there was a gentleman to see her. Kate looked across at her sister in surprise; visitors seldom called in the morning. She asked who he was, this gentleman. Dodington replied that the young man had declined to give his name, but he did indeed seem to be a gentleman. In the end, they were swayed by Dodington's description and they allowed him to be sent in.

He was a tall, serious-looking young man, about their own age. He took off his hat and made a low bow as he entered, but he declined to give his hat and cloak to the manservant.

'Forgive me, ladies, if I do not introduce myself. My

identity is unimportant, I shall not detain you long.'

Gwen's brow furrowed, and Kate turned from her tapestry to face the young man. There was something about him, an urgency in his voice, and his refusal to declare himself immediately put the ladies on their guard.

'Since you do not even have the goodness to name yourself,' Kate replied, 'you had better state your business quickly and begone.'

The coldness of his reception clearly upset the young man.

'I pray you, forgive my need for secrecy. I mean you no harm.'

'I am pleased to hear it, yet the very fact of it disturbs my sister and I.'

He bowed again. Kate wondered at the way he conducted himself; his manners were too precise and there was a studied gentleness about him – this man, it seemed, was a cavalier.

'Mistress Barnard, if you will permit me. I would speak with you with regard to a certain gentleman, at present imprisoned unjustly. I believe you may be able to help his cause.'

'If the gentleman is indeed imprisoned unjustly, then I should be happy to help him.'

The young cavalier seemed to relax at this. 'I have been sent here by the friends of my Lord Fitzmaurice. He is a great and noble gentleman, who has done great service to the cause, yet now he languishes in prison, awaiting trial for his life.'

'Young man,' Kate replied, acidly, 'if you have come seeking assistance for that man – then you have come to the wrong place. Do you not realize that it is by my testimony he is imprisoned?'

'Even so, good lady. It is for that reason I have come to see you today. We should esteem it a great favour, and you would earn the undying favour of His Majesty, King Charles the Second, if you would renounce your testimony.'

'Sir, it seems that you have come on a forlorn quest. I presume you know that your friend "the great and noble Lord Fitzmaurice", tried to kill me on the night of his arrest.'

'A gentleman must needs do many things he might disdain to do when he is entrapped by roundhead scum,' he replied. His manner, though still charming, became aggressive.

'If those who trapped him were, as you call them, "roundhead scum", then you are indeed in the company of the same, for the officer who made the arrest was none other than my own husband.'

'Madam, I shall not bandy words with you. We will not suffer Lord Fitzmaurice to be tried, and we shall go to any length to ensure his safety. I would encourage you to reconsider your decision.' All trace of charm was fast disappearing from him.

'And I repeat, sir, that yours is a vain quest. It is clear to me that you are not acquainted with Fitzmaurice. The world will be a far better place when he is gone. It does your cause no good at all to be associated with such men. I think you had better go.'

'If that is your last word, madam?'

'It is,' Kate replied, firmly.

'Then I must warn you that things may not go so well for you. There are still many thousands of the King's devoted subjects hereabouts. We shall make sure that you do not testify. Good day.'

He turned on his heel and left, without further courtesies.

Kate seethed with anger. 'My God! Is there no end to the power of the man? Even from a prison cell he still seeks to dictate to me! Why, if . . .'

She was cut short by the sound of breaking glass in the hall. They rushed out to see what was amiss. The light above the door was smashed. On the floor was a large lump of brick, with a note wrapped around it. It had come unravelled and Kate could clearly see the message written on it. There was only one word: *Reconsider*, in a hastily penned scrawl. Outside they heard a horse being ridden away at speed.

Gwen stared at it. 'Well, Kate, what are we to do now?' she asked drily.

'I cannot go back on my testimony, for that would mean John going back to prison. Besides, do you think my life would be safe if Fitzmaurice were free? No. We must go on. But in the meantime I see no reason why we should not seek protection for ourselves. Get the coach ready, and bring Stephen with us – we are going to see Cromwell.'

Kate checked the coachman's face before she got in – a precaution she had become accustomed to over the last few days. They set off, but they had gone no more than a few hundred yards when they saw a crowd of rough-looking men, blocking the road ahead of them, carrying cudgels. Kate cried out to the coachman, 'Whip the horses – we must ride through them!'

The coachman obeyed, but they had not got much above a canter before the crowd was upon them. There was a smash of glass and they were showered with tiny fragments. Stephen cried out in pain as a sliver embedded itself in his hand. They could hear a tussle above them and then they saw one of the ruffians fall down past the window. They did not look back. There was a clattering of many stones as they hit the back of the coach. Still they rode on. After they had put a good distance between themselves and the men, the peephole opened. The coachman looked in and grinned.

'That was a merry little scrap, my lady. One of 'em tried to get the reins, but I did for him. I think he broke his neck when he fell. On to Parliament?' he asked.

Gwen nodded, still cradling Stephen in her arms.

'On to Parliament, and do not stop for anything,' Kate cried. 'And, thank you.'

'Part of my job, madam, to see you safe wherever you go. I'll go armed next time.' He laughed and closed the peep-hole.

They had to wait awhile in the secretary's room, but

they were soon admitted to Cromwell's chambers. Kate explained what had happened. Cromwell's face was grim.

'So, this is how the royalists conduct themselves now, frightening women and children. Very well, I shall place a troop of horse at your disposal, under your husband's command. I hope their presence will not inconvenience you. The trial is in less than a week. After Fitzmaurice swings I am sure they will lose interest.'

'And if they do not?' Gwen replied anxiously.

'I am sure they will, Lady Nevers. Revenge is an expensive luxury in this day and age. If they cannot dissuade your sister, then they will go away. In the interim, however, the presence of armed cavalrymen should be enough to keep them at bay.'

They returned to Chelsea under heavy escort. The cavalrymen rode before them and behind them and there were two on either side of the coach. Still they did not feel entirely safe. On the road out to Chelsea there was no sign of the crowd, although Kate felt sure she recognized the faces of some of the men who lurked in the shadows. When they got back, the house was in turmoil: great clods of mud had been hurled at the walls and more of the windows had been broken. Dodington was beside himself with worry. He seemed overjoyed to see them. The cavalry took up positions around the perimeter wall and the main gate. Half a dozen of them went out the back to patrol the riverside. They waited for the others to come home.

Just before sunset there was the sound of horses being ridden at speed. A challenge went up from the gate and the horses ground sharply to a halt. Kate went outside to see what was happening. It was John and the others. He dismounted quickly.

'John, what has happened?' she asked.

'We were set upon on the road. About twenty of them.' He looked over his shoulder at the dark alley beyond. 'We had to cut our way through. We killed a couple of them before they ran off, but Father has taken a nasty knock.'

Old Mr Barnard was reeling in the saddle as they helped him down.

'What is the world coming to?' he said ruefully. 'This would never have happened in the old Queen's time.' He shook his head as he allowed himself to be led away. John looked down at Kate.

'I take it this is Fitzmaurice's doing?'

'A cavalier came this morning; he warned me that if I did not withdraw my testimony, things would go badly for us – this all began just after he left.'

'I see.' He nodded. 'Who is in charge here?'

'Well, in truth, you are, John,' Kate admitted.

'Good. Very good. Then, with your leave, I will go and attend to our defence.'

The night passed without further incident, though none of them were able to sleep. At John's request, they all stayed together in the large bedroom at the back, next to the stairs. They tended to Mr Barnard, who was nursing a large bump on the side of the head, and Stephen, who had a gash across his hand. Michael and Jack joined the guard outside. As the sun rose, Kate opened the curtains and looked out. It was a beautiful, cold February morning. All seemed well, until she glanced down at the lawn. There below her, written in large letters, seeping pink into the frost, was the word *Traitor*. She ran downstairs and into the garden. She scuffed at the word with her shoe but, underneath the crust of frost, the blood was still wet and it splattered over her foot.

John came running up to her. 'Oh, my God!' he exclaimed as he looked down at the word. He called for some buckets of water to wash the blood into the grass. For a moment Kate was angry, then her anger subsided as she realized that all this was happening as a result of her own actions.

'What do you think they will do next?' she sighed.

'I do not know,' John replied, 'but next time we shall be ready for them, I promise you.'

The next night they started just after midnight, throwing stones and hurling firebrands over the walls into the gardens. There was a great shouting and commotion beyond the gate, but when John and his men sallied forth, they melted back into the darkness, only to return half an hour later and resume their attack. So it went on through the night. Inside the house, everyone was at the end of their wits. They stared across at each other, but no one spoke. They waited for the sunrise.

The third night was greeted by an uncanny silence. John and his men patrolled the perimeter; Kate and the others inside waited anxiously for the onslaught. But it never came. At sunrise, Kate went out into the garden. The air was clear and fresh and the birds were singing. She walked across the lawn, avoiding the scorchmarks on the grass, and finally came to where her husband was standing guard. He smiled as she approached.

'Well, John, do you think they have given up?' she asked with relief in her voice.

He stretched and yawned. 'It seems like it. We shall have to wait and see. Perhaps they are trying to lull us into a false sense of security – but we'll be ready for them if they come back.'

He took her in his arms and they stood quietly together, listening to the sounds of the morning.

At ten o'clock a rider arrived at the gates and they learned the reason for the silence of the night: Fitzmaurice had escaped from the prison. Even now, he was thought to be safely aboard a ship bound for France. Kate felt her heart sink; she knew that she would never be safe while Fitzmaurice yet lived.

Twenty

The events of the previous month were practically forgotten. Kate was totally engrossed in her packing, for when John departed to rejoin his company, this time Kate was going with him.

'Well, only as far as Wales and then Bristol,' she confided to Gwen, who was helping her. 'Then I will be back here – if you can stand to have me, that is. Things will not be safe in Ireland for quite a time yet, but when they are, I will join him over there. We have decided to start a new life at Kilerin. But that is all a long time away – John thinks they will not sail until August at least. So, can you suffer me coming back to stay with you then? Will you?'

'Of course,' Gwen said, whilst she supervised the servants packing. 'Life would be too quiet without you. Still, I shall be glad of the next few months' peace – if only to recover my wits,' she laughed.

The next morning, Kate was back on the road with Jack and John. It was a bitterly cold March day and still the frost had not thawed, but the sun was shining and Kate felt a thrill within her. She was with her two favourite men in the whole world and they had a long, leisurely ride ahead of them. It could take a week to get to Chepstow, for all they cared. She turned to Jack.

'Do you know, the last time I was on this road, it was in the midst of winter and we were coming to fetch you back to London.'

'Aye,' he agreed, 'but we took a very roundabout

route to get there, didn't we? There was a time when I thought we'd never make it, up in those mountains.'

'Ah, but it was all worth it, was it not?' John added. 'After all, where would you be without the dubious delights of my company?'

They laughed at his jest, making light of all that had gone before. Kate looked at the two men riding on either side of her. Even though she had no idea where she would lay her head that night, she felt she was home at last.

They stopped the night in High Wycombe. After dinner, Jack went out into the town in search of 'some amusement', as he put it. Kate and John were left together.

'In truth, John. He is quite incorrigible – you would have thought at his age he would have learned how to conduct himself.' She giggled with embarrassment as she considered what sorts of amusement the old sergeant was looking for.

'Ah, well,' John replied. 'He is making the most of his last months in uniform. He says that this Irish campaign is going to be his last. He is going to settle down with his widow, or so he says.'

'It will be strange for him, I imagine.'

'It will be strange for all of us, Kate. Do you know, I have spent the last twelve years of my life – well, with the exception of the last couple of months – in uniform. It will be hard for me to become accustomed to the life of an Irish gentleman. . . .'

'Ah, but there will be a great deal of work to do. I do not even know if Kilerin will still be standing. And then you will have to win the hearts and minds of the people – they will love you for your fairness, but they will resent you for what you are. They are a proud race, my people, but their pride is all they have.' There were tears in her eyes as she thought of them.

'You know, Kate, I swear your accent gets stronger every time you talk about home. In fact, since we decided we would go and live there, you have become more Irish with each passing day.' He smiled as he rebuked her.

'And why not?' Kate snapped, with mock chagrin. 'Why, Ireland is the very best place in the world – in fact it is far too good for the likes of you, now that I think of it.'

'Ah, well,' he said, glumly, 'I suppose I shall have to return to my dusty old law books when the war is over. I shall return to London and develop a stoop and a crusty face – I might even grow a few cobwebs.'

'Oh, no you will not, John Barnard,' she said, pulling him towards her, so that their lips almost met. 'When you get to Ireland, you will see how beautiful it is. And then when I come to join you, you will never want to leave, ever.'

She kissed him with such pleasure and excitement that, even though their bottle of wine was only half drunk, they left it and went upstairs to bed.

Kate found life at Chepstow very different from the army life she had known before. They were a peacetime garrison now, and many of the men had married, or had brought their wives and families up to join them. Kate found herself in the unusual position of being the mother of the company, mediating in disputes, finding accommodation for families and always pestering the colonel about the matter of the men's pay – which was always in arrears. She was ably assisted in this by Ruth, who had come to join Tomikin that winter, when Kate had dismissed her. She bore her no grudge, though, but she was unable to enter Kate's service again – due to the large bulge she bore before her.

'There'll soon be three of us and I'll have my hands full, I'll be bound. So, begging your pardon, Mistress Kate, you'll have to make do with me just as a friend, if you'll have me.'

Ruth was a good friend, and useful to know. She had already found out all the best places to buy things and she had the measure of the colonel.

'He's a good enough man in his own way, but he's too apt to make excuses for the shortcomings we have to suffer – he needs constant reminding – so that's what I do. It will do him good to have another voice badgering him, perhaps he'll get something done at last.'

That July, Kate and John were able to take a few days away from the business of preparing for the Irish campaign. They went up into the mountains. It was the first time they had been alone together since their honeymoon. It felt strange to have John to herself, for the first time in years. He was a man who gave so much of himself to others – he had so little time for himself.

They rode through villages with names they could not even start to pronounce and whose people they could not understand. This seemed to add to their feelings of separateness from the rest of the world, bringing them ever closer together. They rode side by side along deep mountain valleys, shaded from the light, and then out into brilliant sunshine. They rode at their leisure for hours on end through this most beautiful countryside. The mountains held no fear for Kate – it was hard for her to equate these majestic scenes with the cold, white, hard terrain she had had to endure in the winter.

In the late afternoon, they would make for the nearest village and find a place to stay for the night. They always found the folk hospitable, even if they could understand little of their tongue. After dinner, they would go out and walk under the stars, which seemed to be much brighter in the clear upland air, talking about everything that came to their minds. Kate discovered that John had a deep and passionate love of the stars, a thing she had never known before.

'You know,' he said, looking up, 'when I was a boy, I used to lie on my back in the garden at night, just gazing up at the stars. My father used to worry about me – thought I would become a lunatic, but it kept me out of mischief, so in the end, he let me carry on. I learned all the constellations; Orion, the hunter, which I have always thought of as my own. Whenever I glance up into the night sky, if I catch sight of him first, I treat that as a lucky omen.'

'I never thought you, of all people, would believe in omens – you are usually so logical and rational, and . . .'

'Boring?' he suggested.

'Well, sometimes you can be a little dry – and your sense of humour often eludes me altogether . . . but boring? No, I would never say that. Serious – you are a very serious sort of fellow.' Kate nodded as she found the right word to describe him.

John laughed at this. 'Yes, I imagine I am probably a little too serious for my own good – it has brought me into quite a deal of trouble over the years, has it not?'

Kate was forced to agree with this. 'But, if you were a more frivolous man, then I would not have fallen in love with you.'

'I always thought it very unusual that you fell in love with me at all. I would have thought a dashing young cavalier would have been more to your liking. A romantic hero.'

'So would I – before I met you. But men use romance to conceal their lack of character. Romance is naught but a veneer, a polish which all too quickly dulls. I am content with my dour-faced roundhead.'

Their time together passed so quickly. As soon as they returned to Chepstow, they were flung into preparations for the Irish campaign; John arranging supplies and transport for the men and horses, and Kate making sure that the families would be well cared for when their menfolk left. They only seemed to see each other at night – and then they were too tired to talk for long. At the end of July the long column of riders issued from Chepstow, making their way back up the Severn to Gloucester and down to Bristol, where they would embark for Ireland. Kate rode at the head of the column with John, whilst Ruth was in the baggage-train, too large to ride.

Kate looked back at the long line of troopers. 'You know, John, this is the first time I have ridden with your men without being in uniform.'

'I was just thinking that myself. You made a very

bonny cornet, though, but not as bonny as you look today.' He grinned at her.

'Maybe I will take out my uniform again, one day, and . . .'

'Not while you are in my company, young lady – I have enough trouble keeping myself from you while you are decorously dressed in skirts. I would not be responsible for my actions if you were clad in riding breeches.' He glanced mischievously at her.

'Why John! How dare you?' she cried, alarmed. Then her manner became very prim and proper. 'I shall keep that in mind . . .' she said, straightening her shoulders and pretending to ignore him.

Three days later, they were on the quayside at Bristol. John was supervising the embarkation of his men and horses. The horses had to be lifted on great slings, high up into the air and swung over into the holds of specially prepared ships. It was a slow process, the horses whinnied and kicked as the slings were placed under them, then when they were let down they were more often than not in a state of panic, their hooves clattering wildly about in the ships, so that it seemed that they would kick their way out. Finally, they were all in, and it only remained to wait for the tide.

It would be a long voyage, skirting around the Welsh coast and then striking west for Dublin. With a favourable wind, they reckoned on about six days.

Along the quayside there were many emotional scenes as troopers took leave of their wives and loved ones. In the distance, Kate noticed Ruth and young Tomikin; she was resting her head on his breast with her arm around his neck. They did not speak and Kate turned away – it was their own private moment and there should be no onlookers. She respected their privacy.

Still there was no sign of John. He was still on the ship, making sure everything was in order.

The sailors were shouting to each other and Kate realized that they would soon set sail; she began to panic as the men began to climb the rigging and unfurl the sails. She looked anxiously for John. Finally, she spotted him, running across the deck toward the gangplank. He smiled and waved to her. With a single bound, he was across the gangplank and in her arms.

'Forgive me for taking so long, Kate – it is chaos down there.'

'It would have been chaos up here if you had tried to sail without saying goodbye. You would have had another passenger on board if I had not been able to kiss you goodbye.' She took his face in her hands and kissed him on the lips. She wanted the kiss to last forever, but there was shouting from the ship – they were about to leave.

'Keep yourself safe, John,' she whispered. 'Do not go getting yourself shot.'

He shook his head and smiled, in the way that had become so familiar to her.

'There is precious little chance of that. I am far more likely to be kicked to death by the damned horses or die of seasickness – I never was a very good sailor.'

'Stop playing the fool for once John! Promise me that you will come back to me.'

'I promise you. The next time we meet, we shall be together in Kilerin.' He placed his hands on both their hearts, staring intently at her with tears in his eyes. 'I promise,' he whispered.

The shouting grew more anxious and Kate heard the gangplank grating on the quayside.

'But now I must go.' He flashed a smile at her and jumped on to the gangplank as it was pulled aboard. The ship started to pull away.

The fast-flowing estuary soon had the little ship in its grasp, dragging it far into the distance. Kate stood by the quayside until it had finally disappeared from sight. She had thought she was alone, but when she looked around her, there were many women, just like herself, who had waited to catch the last glimpse of their men. Among them was Ruth. She caught her eye and smiled. Ruth was fighting back her tears as she slowly walked toward her.

'Well Ruth,' Kate said softly, 'what are you going to do now?'

She shrugged her shoulders. 'My sister lives here. I expect I'll keep on coming back here until Tomikin returns – though I expect there'll be two of us by then. What about yourself, Mistress Kate?'

She smiled weakly. 'There seems to be little for me to do. I imagine I shall have to make my way back to Chelsea and wait for John.'

'Still,' Ruth remarked cheerfully, 'this is the last time we'll have to wave them off. When they come home this time, it'll be for ever.'

Twenty-one

The long lonely ride back to Chelsea gave Kate ample time to think: her time in England was fast coming to an end. Soon, she would be able to return to Kilerin, to pick up the pieces of her shattered life there. But at least she would not be alone. John would be by her side – he had promised her that he would be there and he had never let her down before. She smiled as she thought about the first time they had met and how he had protected her from that moment on. Still, at least she had been able to return the compliment – without her, he would have been languishing as a slave labourer in Antigua instead of leading his men on their final adventure, a free man.

She took stock of the last five years of her life – five years! It seemed strange to think it was so long and yet it had gone by in but a twinkling. So much had happened in so little time. She supposed that she must have changed somewhat, though inside she still thought of herself as the same scared little girl who sailed across the sea. And soon she would be returning home.

Back at Chelsea, Kate soon settled down to the waiting life of a soldier's woman, like tens of thousands of others around the country. Gwen and Michael were, as ever, the best of companions. Michael had left the army and returned to the law. He carried his damaged arm in an elegant black silk sling and all the time he wore a black leather glove, though his hand was unharmed. He said it lent a certain dignity to his manner, and he used it to good effect, gaining sympathy from compassionate jurors – he was gaining himself quite a name as a defence barrister.

Kate still went with Gwen into town and they made the most of the unusually late summer, playing on the grass with young Stephen and his friends. Still, the time seemed to Kate to have an unreal, dreamlike quality: all the while she was thinking about another time when she and John would be reunited and could start their new life together.

The best times for Kate were when she received letters home from John; he wrote frequently, though his letters often came in the wrong order, which frustrated her. Most of the time he would write about the country and the people – things which he knew Kate would want to hear about. He also wrote about his reactions to it all. It was clear to Kate that he was developing a love for her country, and this made Kate all the more eager to cross the sea and be with him. She even went to see Mr MacAulay to see if she could arrange a passage to Ireland, but he advised against it, reminding her that it was still a wild place and the rebellion was far from over. Cromwell, he said, may yet fail, like so many English adventurers before him. Kate was not sure, but she thought she detected a slightly hopeful note in his voice.

One letter she received from John gave her cause for great sadness. It was written from Drogheda – which was the nearest town to Kilerin. The town, John wrote, had been sacked and Cromwell had ordered thousands killed. She was moved to tears, not merely for the thought of the streets where she had gone so many times as a child, which were now, as John put it, *strewn with bodies – six deep in places*, but also for the thought of what that vision was doing to John himself. Still she waited, long into October.

It was a bright day with a stiff breeze and the leaves were coming off the trees in earnest. Kate and Gwen and some of the servants were busy sweeping them up into piles, whilst Stephen and his little friends picked up great armfuls of them and carried them off to the bonfire, dropping most of them along the way. Kate stood up, straightening her back and pushing away a lock of hair that had fallen over her face. She looked up. One of the house girls was running across the lawn to them.

'They're coming! They're coming up the lane. They're home!' she cried.

Kate's eyes widened as she realized what the girl was talking about. Already she could hear the sound of horses at the front of the house. Her heart beat faster.

She felt rooted to the spot. She could hear the sound of heavy-booted men dismounting and walking around the house. Still, she could not move. Something was wrong, but she could not remember what it was. . . .

They were in sight now. Kate heaved a sigh of relief as she saw that it was Jack, with a couple of other men from John's company. She ran across the lawn to greet him.

'Jack! My dear Jack – it is so good to see you!' She took him in her arms and spun him around. 'Does this mean it is all over?' She smiled at him.

He held her tenderly and patted her on the shoulder, but all the time his eyes were downcast. He would not look her in the eye.

'No, Kate dear,' he sighed, 'it isn't over. We've been . . . relieved.'

'I am not surprised after Drogheda – that must have been terrible for you.'

'Aye. That was – pretty bad . . .' he said haltingly. Still he did not look at her.

Kate realized that something was indeed wrong.

'Jack, something is amiss – is it John? Has something happened to John?' she demanded urgently, pulling at his sleeve.

He nodded and looked up at her. For the first time, Kate realized that there were tears streaming down his cheeks.

'I would have given all the world not to have to bring this news to you, but I wouldn't have it come from another.' He put his hand to his breast and pulled out a letter. 'This is the last thing he wrote . . . before he died.'

Kate took it and stared at it, blankly. She shook her head in disbelief. 'But it is not even in his own hand. . . .'

'No,' he said simply. 'He was too weak to write.'

Kate wanted him to say that it was all a cruel joke – that at any time John would come out from behind the house, but in her heart of hearts, she knew that it was not so. With numbed fingers, she opened the letter. As she read it, she felt her whole world come crashing down about her, all her hopes and dreams reduced to nothing, for though the writing was another's, the words were so very clearly his own.

My dearest Kate,

I have so little time. I hope I am spared long enough to say all the things I need so much to say – but of course I will not be, for to say all those things would take a long lifetime, and mine is ebbing away.

I love you. That is the most important thing of all. I love you so very much and I have always loved you from the first time I saw you, all covered in mud. You were beautiful then, but not as beautiful as the vision of you I have before my eyes now. I close them and I can see you, but if I close them, they may not open again, and I could not finish this. I will close them again soon.

You would laugh at me – a raw recruit's mistake. Jack cursed me, though his eyes were full of tears. I found I could not bring myself to kill another man. I stayed my hand and that was my downfall. I hope you can forgive me.

But I will not be breaking my promise to you. When you come home I will be waiting for you. Kilerin is not far, my lads will carry me there when I am gone.

Do not be angry Kate, and do not grieve for me. My life was dark before I met you and now I must return to the darkness. By your light, I was allowed a glimpse of happiness. You brought peace to my troubled soul when I thought I was lost.

I could not suffer you to be unhappy, Kate. You will find another to take my place and he will give you children to take the place of the little one we lost. I hope so much that your life will be long and happy.

I ask only one thing of you, that in all those happy years before you, you might find a quiet moment, when you are alone and unobserved, to remember that – for a brief while – you were once a captain's lady.